DREAMS OF THE DEADLY

MASSACRED DREAMS DUET ONE

ADELAIDE FORREST

Created with Vellum

CONTENT & TRIGGER WARNINGS

The Massacred Dreams is a dark mafia romance duet dealing with topics that some readers may find offensive or triggering.

Please keep in mind that the following list WILL contain specifics about the entire series and may spoil certain plot elements. Please avoid the next page if you don't have any triggers and don't wish to know the specifics.

The following scenarios are all present in the Massacred Dreams duet. This list may be added to as book two is finished.

- Situations involving questionable consent
- Stalking
- A slight age gap, with both characters being of legal age at the time a physical relationship forms.
- Forced/Intentional pregnancy
- Forced Marriage
- Graphic violence, torture, and murder
- References to childhood abuse (not committed by the H).
- Somnophilia

PART I

BEFORE

Note from Adelaide:

If you've already read the prologue novella, Dreams of the Vengeful, you can skip to Part II, chapter 18, to continue the story from there.

1

CALIX

Twenty years prior

The air inside the Karras home turned suffocating as soon as I scrawled my signature on the line, on the contract that bound me to a future no boy would choose for himself. Just like my father, Origen Karras had built his empire on lies and suffering, on business arrangements, and on the arrogance of a figurehead who sat behind a desk, striving to unite the six families for his own selfish greed.

Anyone could see it if they merely looked hard enough, seeing past the proper veneer of the image he tried to present. Glimpsing the monster residing beneath his skin.

I stumbled out the back door of the house, my lungs heaving with the ridiculousness of it all. The arranged marriage that loomed on the distant horizon, to a tiny slip of a girl I'd only seen in passing, sent me spiraling out of the stuffy estate and seeking fresh air.

The girl was five years old, far too young to already have which monster would share her bed when she was old enough to breed contemplated, yet that was precisely what a group of grown men had chosen to do on a sunny spring afternoon.

At thirteen, I'd already lost my virginity and appreciated what girls my own age could do with their changing bodies. The thought of that with a girl less than half my age made my skin crawl.

I leaned against the railing at the edge of the elaborate wood deck, my eyes catching on the bright green blades of grass that had only sprouted from the frozen ground weeks prior. As my gaze dragged up to the expanse of yard at the back of the estate, my focus narrowed on the form of a young girl twirling between the beds of narcissus that her mother must have been fond of to have so much growing on the property.

She looked at me, a smile on her heart-shaped face as she spun, completely oblivious to the contract that had been signed only moments before. The ink of my name probably hadn't even dried on the page yet, as our fathers and her brother toasted to the agreement.

To cementing the alliance between our families despite her mother's obvious desire to stall it. But there was no stopping tradition and there would be nothing to save little Thalia from becoming mine after she became a woman.

As a kindness to her mother, they'd agreed Thalia didn't need to know until she was old enough to understand. She could have her childhood and enjoy the promise of freedom when she would come of age.

Even if it was a lie.

My legs guided me toward her, closing the distance between us even though I knew I should stay away. To get close to her and never tell her the truth of what was to come felt like a cruelty she didn't deserve, and nothing of the five-year-old girl would last until our marriage. She'd be a new person by the time she became mine.

Our lives dictated that.

She continued spinning until dizziness overtook her, falling to her back in the grass and staining her yellow sundress. My mother would have disapproved greatly, because young ladies should always present themselves properly, not be stained with grass after rolling in the dirt.

She stared up at the sky, sun sparkling off the unique amber of her eyes, completely oblivious to my approach. "Shouldn't you be inside?" I asked, stuffing my hands into the pockets of the suit pants my father made me wear.

Already a man in his mind, ready to take the city by storm, I was no longer a boy.

She startled, pressing a hand to her chest as she flung herself up to sitting, and that distinctive stare landed on mine. Fixating on something on my face, she squinted as she tilted her head to the side. "Why?" She rolled her eyes and shrugged, dropping back to the grass, as if she couldn't be bothered to concern herself with what the adults might be doing inside.

Despite my better instincts, I moved closer and risked my mother's wrath to sit on the ground next to her. Kicking my legs out in front of me and feeling strangely awkward, I picked at the blades of grass beneath my hands. "That's a good question," I admitted and huffed a laugh.

"Being inside is so boring. Out here, I don't have to be so quiet." Her face pinched, not quite pretty enough to be adorable. Her eyes were too big for her face, her lips puffy, and her ears had an odd sort of point at the top like she was something straight from a fantasy book. Her face was intriguing, her features bright as she turned a smile my way, but between her odd face and undersized frame, no one would ever call Thalia Karras pretty.

Perhaps that would change by the time we married.

I swallowed back the despair that tried to settle over me, knowing the future waiting for us wasn't one either of us would have chosen for ourselves, yet trapped by the forces working to drive us together.

"What do you like to do?" I asked, thinking maybe I could send her gifts. Get to know her a little, bit by bit, without ever truly being a part of her life. Just enough so it wouldn't seem so agonizingly painful when the contract came due and her life became mine.

"Draw, but Daddy doesn’t like it. I like to draw flowers, but the colors are always wrong, and—" She cut off suddenly as if she’d realized she'd said something she shouldn't. With a swallow, she sat up, curling her arms around herself protectively.

"You're five. Flowers can be any color you want," I said, in an attempt to comfort whatever nervousness had settled over her.

"Can they be black and white?" she asked, her eyes turning hopeful as she pinned me with that wide-eyed stare.

"Wouldn't you rather they be pink?" I asked, furrowing my brow. What little girl painted black flowers?

The hope faded from her eyes as she pushed herself to standing once more, leaving me staring after her from the ground. "I have to go."

I moved to follow, taking up a slow walk at her side as her little legs worked to make her way back to the house. She was so painfully thin that it seemed as if each step required too much energy. Still, there was a stern determination on her face that didn't belong on anyone her age.

As if she had to do it for herself, or the consequences would be dire. "What color flowers do you like best?" I asked, resolving to send her some that she could draw.

She paused, her steps halting as she hit me with a concerned stare. "I'm not supposed to talk about it," she said, biting that too-large bottom lip and staring nervously toward the house. Her eyes darted from window to window, swallowing when she found no one watching us.

"About your favorite color flower?" I asked, grinning down at her in my confusion. She was such an odd child, and if her parents truly forbid her from talking about the flowers, then I couldn't imagine what kind of life she had with them.

"I don't know," she answered. "I can't see them." She picked up her steps, quickening her pace as her lungs heaved with exertion. I was half tempted to lift her into my arms, knowing she couldn't weigh much.

"Flowers?" I asked, laughing at the ridiculousness of the notion. I'd only just seen her twirling in the fields surrounded by narcissus and never harming a single flower.

"Colors," she whispered as she reached the back door, taking the handle in her grip. She turned back to me, her eyes silently pleading for me to keep her secret. Whatever she saw on my face must have reassured her, because she nodded once and pursed her lips thoughtfully.

Looking far too old for her size and age, she turned the handle and swept into the house. She was gone by the time I followed, disappearing like a ghost in the wind.

Like she'd never been meant to exist at all.

2

THALIA

Ten months later

The knuckles of my left hand ached as I washed the blood away. My split skin moved as I flexed my fingers, watching the dark, stained water swirl down the drain. My mother hovered in the doorway, her face pinched as she watched me. "You must remember to use your right hand, Thalia."

"I know, Mommy," I said, turning to stare up at her face. It had been almost a year since I'd made the silly mistake of telling the boy I didn't know my secret.

I hadn't made that mistake twice. Even though he hadn't told on me, nobody else made me want to trust them as much as the boy who'd sat with me in the grass and hadn't looked at me like I was a broken doll.

Mommy's light hair gleamed in the overhead light as she stepped in to help me clean the sink basin. It was far easier for her to spot the red stains than it was for me to tell them apart from the dark spots of the marble.

Daddy hated when I used my left hand, because "proper girls" were right-handed. Proper girls didn't stop to think about which hand they should grab their fork with at the dinner table. Even a moment of hesitation at the dinner table meant Daddy reached across and struck my left hand.

"These will scar," Mommy said, grasping my hand in her grip and studying the wounds that never healed. Every strike, every lesson, reopened the injury until my left hand always hurt.

I thought that was the point. In his words, Daddy would beat me into being right-handed if he had to.

"Miss Thalia, Calix Regas is asking after you," one of the housekeepers said as she poked her head into the open bathroom door. Her eyes narrowed in on the injury I tucked behind my back in shame, a scowl pinching her lips together. The shadows under her eyes grew worse by the day, as if she couldn't stomach working for our family.

I knew it would only be a short while before she left.

They always did.

"Who?" I asked, turning my eyes to my mother, who set to straightening my dress. To studying the fabric and checking for bloodstains. It wouldn't be the first time that I'd wiped my injury on my dress, but I did my best not to.

Daddy didn't like it.

"He's the heir to one of the six families," my mother answered, fluffing up my wavy hair. She took my right hand in hers, tugging me out of the bathroom and pasting on that fast, easy smile that came so naturally to her. I envied her ability to smile even when she wasn't happy. She said I'd learn in time.

We stepped into the dining room where my father stood beside the already cleared table, his eyes angry when he turned his attention to us. I swallowed back my nerves, letting my mother lead me to the boy standing beside him.

The same boy who'd sat in the field with me and kept my

secret. The same one who I knew I shouldn't trust, but something in his eyes made me wish I could.

"Calix," my mother said as he leaned forward and kissed her cheek. He was just a boy, years older than me for sure, but he couldn't have been old enough to be as tall as he already was.

"Mrs. Karras," he said politely. He nodded to my father, who bit his cheek in displeasure but stepped over to my mother and took her hand. He guided her out of the room, leaving me alone with the boy when I knew it couldn't be what my father wanted.

I wasn't supposed to be alone with boys.

"I brought you something," he said, squatting down so that he was my height. He held out a single light rose, and I took the stem in hand, noting that he'd trimmed the thorns off. I drew it to my nose, inhaling the uniquely sweet smell as I bit my lip.

"Why are you here?" I asked, wincing as I thought of how my father would scold me for being so rude. It wasn't normal for a teenage boy to want to spend time with a child.

"A little birdy told me that tomorrow is your birthday," he said, standing and reaching into his back pocket. The box was small enough that he had tucked it away, but curiosity got the best of me as I reached out to take it from him.

"What is it?" I asked as I pulled the lid off. Inside the heart-shaped box were six little plastic pockets, each with a rounded ball nestled inside.

Calix's eyes narrowed as he watched me lift one into my hand. "It's chocolate, Little One," he said, grinning at the flush that warmed my cheeks. Nobody ever called me anything aside from my name.

Not even my mother.

"Haven't you ever had chocolate?" he asked, taking the one

from my hand and holding it out for me to take a bite out of. I hesitated, staring at him for a moment before I leaned forward and bit into the soft chocolate. My eyes widened as the sweetness of it exploded over my tongue, forcing myself to chew politely even though I wanted to snatch the other half out of his hand.

"No," I said softly before I leaned in to eat the other half. He chuckled as he drew his hand away and wiped the excess chocolate from his skin onto a napkin from the table. "It's yummy."

"I'll bring you more the next time I come to see you. Would you like that?" he asked. I tilted my head to the side, still wondering what could possess him to want to spend time with me and why my father would allow it.

Even the girls at school didn't want to be around me.

"Okay," I said warily as I put the lid on the chocolates and delicately placed them on the table. Without knowing how long it would be before his next visit, I felt the need to make them last.

To save them for the bad days.

I drew the rose to my nose once more, inhaling to fill the quiet that claimed the room after my admission. He didn't seem to know what to say, which I guessed was normal considering our age difference. He pushed to his feet, towering over me once more as he glanced to the door. "Do you like it?" he asked, shrugging his shoulders as if he couldn't decide why he cared.

"It's pretty, and it smells nice. Thank you," I said.

"It's pink," he answered, as if that meant anything to me. I'd never seen the color pink. There was nothing to connect to that word. "I thought it would be nice to have something different than all the narcissus flowers in the yard."

"I like the narcissus," I said defensively. "They're mostly

white. I don't—" I paused, sinking my teeth into the corner of my mouth on the inside.

"You don't what?" he asked, leaning forward to tuck my hair behind my ear. His fingers hovered at the odd point at the tip, but where others made fun of me and called me names, he gave a slight smile.

As if maybe they were cute and not freakish.

"I don't feel like I'm missing out. Narcissus is pretty even though it's just white. I don't need to see color to love them," I said.

He froze solid, staring at the rose in my hand and gave me a kind smile. "I'll bring you a white rose next time, λουλούδι μου," he said. "How does that sound?"

"It sounds perfect," I said, smiling up at him. He nodded once, turning for the door without so much as a goodbye and leaving me to stare after him as he stepped out into the night.

Grabbing the box of chocolates off the table, I tucked it under my arm and made my way for the stairs to go up to my room. My father stepped out of my parents' bedroom, eyeing the rose and the chocolates in my grip with distaste. A scowl transformed his face, the only warning before he reached forward and snatched the rose from my hand. Throwing it to the floor, he crushed it with his foot while I pursed my lips to keep from crying.

The chocolates were torn from my arm after and tossed to the side for the housekeepers to deal with. "Daddy!" I protested finally, reaching out to them with my left hand. He smacked his hand down on top of mine, the slap echoing through the hallway as I cradled it to my chest and stared up at him.

"Did you invite him here, girl?" he grumbled.

"No," I denied shaking my head furiously. He nodded once, moving toward the bedroom he shared with my mother. In the silence that followed, her pained whimpers trailed out through the open door.

"You'd better hope I don't discover you're lying," he barked, making me jolt in place as I sniffled back my tears. Stepping into the bedroom, he closed the door to cut off the sound of my mother's pain.

It was never enough.

3

CALIX

Thad pulled up at the curb to the private all-girls academy, and I peered out the window as we waited for the school to let out. Cars and personal drivers all waited to grab their charges, nannies filling the space outside the building. "I'll be right back," I said to my driver.

Hauling open my door, I stepped out into the brisk air. Spring hadn't yet arrived, the last lingering effects of frost keeping the flowers from blooming.

I wondered if Thalia still twirled in the yard when she wasn't surrounded by a black and white garden of flowers. The innocence of her youth was something I'd never known, something I couldn't remember ever having myself.

Such were the differences between the expectations put on male heirs and daughters, whose sole purpose would be to be wed and bred, I supposed. While I hadn't said anything, I'd seen the injuries on her knuckles. The scrapes and torn flesh, surrounded by various stages of healing that hinted at repeated abuse.

While I might not care for Thalia in the traditional sense, like a husband might his wife, she was still to be mine to care for. Something in the young girl would've made me want to protect her, even if she hadn't been contracted to be mine one day. Those wide amber eyes just made me want to ensure that no harm came to her.

Her innocence needed to be protected for as long as possible.

To ask the questions that needed answering, I would have to catch her without the threat of her father looming over her. I needed her to tell me how she came to be injured.

Then I would have to convince my father to back me up when I stepped in on her behalf. He wouldn't give the first shit that a girl was being abused, so it would take me some time to find a way. A bargain would need to be struck, and I hated to think of what I would need to sign over to my bastard of a father to protect Thalia.

Still, sometimes things needed to be done.

I watched as the girls finally emerged from the front of the building, chattering excitedly as they hurried through the cold to get to the nannies and parents waiting for them. Thalia was impossible to spot in the crowd, so painfully small for her age that I almost didn't see her when she stepped out at the back of the group. With her eyes to the ground in front of her, she didn't so much as glance at any of the other girls as she passed.

The innocent but lively and curious girl I'd seen in the two times I'd interacted with her in the last year was nowhere to be found, smothered by the sadness and dread on her face. Stepping toward the front of the gate, I waited for her to look up and see me waiting. For that moment where her excitement would peek out from under the quiet illusion she wore.

I didn't get the impression many people cared about her thoughts or feelings. It bothered me more than it should that this girl I barely knew was silenced by the people in her life.

She never saw the two girls reach out for her, each touching a hand to a shoulder blade and shoving her forward. Thalia's hands struck the pavement as she caught herself, and her face twisted with pain when one of the girls nudged her with a shoe and shoved her to her back. She stood over Thalia, leaning in to hiss something at her with a cruel sneer on her face.

I was already moving, closing the distance between us to stand with a foot to either side of Thalia's head. The other girl looked up at me, blanching when she saw the raw fury on my face. Thalia was small. She was awkward and she suffered from color blindness. I couldn't begin to imagine what that was like when so many people depended on color to identify and describe everything.

The last thing she needed was to be bullied by some snot-nosed kids who thought their shit didn't stink.

"Get the fuck away from her," I growled, my lips pulling back to reveal my teeth. Rage filled me as I bent down and grasped Thalia under her arms, hauling her to her feet in front of me and taking the backpack off her shoulders to carry for her.

It weighed almost as much as she did.

"You are going to forget that Thalia exists. If I ever hear you've been bothering her again, I will find you and I will make your lives a living hell, you little shits," I growled, watching as the girls nodded quickly and raced off. "Are you okay?" I asked, turning my attention back to Thalia. She nodded, keeping her eyes on the ground. "Little One?" I reached out to touch her hand with one of mine, growling when she flinched back as if I might hit her.

Any doubt I might've had that her injured hand wasn't the result of an accident fled in that moment.

"I will never hurt you," I told her firmly, squatting down

and being reminded yet again of just how small she was. I grasped her hands in mine and turned them over, staring down at the raw skin where she'd caught the pavement and the spots of blood that peppered her skin.

"I'm fine," she said, snatching her hands away defiantly. I released her right one but kept my grip strong on her left, twisting it to stare at her knuckles pointedly as I raised an eyebrow at her.

"These didn't happen today," I said, scowling down at the scarring around her knuckles "Who did this?"

"None of your business," she muttered, tugging until I had no choice but to release her. She grabbed the strap of her backpack and tried to yank it off my shoulder, but only glared at me when she couldn't. Huffing a breath of annoyance, she crossed her arms over her chest. Even in her warm jacket, her arms were far too slim, and her knees were knobby where they peeked out from her skirt.

"Let's get you to the car," I said with a sigh. "Eventually, you'll tell me who hurt you."

"It doesn't matter," she said, breathing in a more subdued way, as if she truly believed that nothing and no one could change anything about her treatment.

I'd move the earth for what was mine, and, like it or not, Thalia was my responsibility.

We stopped at the car waiting for her, and I glared at the driver. I contemplated giving him an order that Thalia wasn't to be harmed, but I refrained. I'd tell her father my fucking self. I imagined most teenage boys were afraid of the great Origen Karras.

There was nothing I hated more than a bully who picked on the weak, and it took a special kind of asshole to bully his own daughter. I swore on my life there'd be a special place in hell with his name on it.

"What color are your eyes?" Thalia asked suddenly, tilting her head to the side as that curiosity leaked back into her face.

I blinked back my impending rage, staring down at her as a smile curved my lips up. "Gray." She grinned at me, all full lips and big teeth, instantly reminding me of why she liked white flowers.

She didn't have to feel like she was missing out on the color, and for one rare moment, she could look at something and know she saw it for what it was.

4

CALIX

I strode up to the Karras home with my father's men at my back. Even though he'd neglected to show his face for the girl who would one day be his daughter-in-law, he hadn't allowed me to come unaccompanied, either.

Our lawyer glanced around the ornate entryway of the expensive house as we stepped in through the iron doorway. It was early enough that Thalia was still at school, so thankfully she wouldn't need to be subjected to the knowledge of our arranged marriage.

If I had it my way, she wouldn't need to know the truth until it came time to arrange our children's marriages. I could protect her from the knowledge that she'd been sold off to strengthen a weakening alliance, all part of the six Greek families' plan to connect us all inextricably over the course of three generations.

The woman who'd allowed us into the manor turned, making her way toward the back of the house and the office where I'd signed the contract nearly a year earlier. Following at her heels, I drew myself up and squared my shoulders for the argument I knew was coming. Thalia's father wasn't likely to take kindly to me telling him how to parent his own child.

I didn't give the first shit.

The office door was open and I didn't hesitate to step through it. Our lawyer Erasmos, an aging man with stark white hair, followed me inside silently while my father's men lingered just outside the doorway. Origen Karras sat behind his desk, not a single concern on his tight expression as he watched me stroll into the room and take the seat across from him. Erasmos dropped a briefcase on the desk in front of me, opening it before stepping out of the way.

"And what's this?" Origen asked, his focus narrowing on the stack of papers I pulled from the case.

The updated contract was stark white against the deep wood of his desk, and I found myself considering it from Thalia's point of view. Black and white and shades of grey: her world existed without warmth.

In more ways than one.

I turned to the pages where we'd added the addendum about her care and wellbeing until she'd come of age and become mine. Looking at him directly, I tapped the tabbed section where he'd need to read. "After visiting with Thalia yesterday, I'd like to make an update to our arrangement."

His eyes turned glacial as he glared at me, not even bothering to look down at the papers. "I assure you, whatever the girl has done can be remedied by the time she's eighteen. Her behavior is a work in progress," he said.

My nostrils flared as I fought back the rising anger that came with his automatic assumption that Thalia had done something wrong, when it had undoubtedly been him in the wrong.

I quirked a brow, swallowing past the lump in my throat as I leaned back in my seat and turned my attention toward

Erasmos as he spoke. "The updated section proclaims that Thalia Karras will not be harmed in any manner while under your care. She is to be given a safe and comfortable home in which to grow into the woman she will become, and all decisions regarding her discipline or education will need to be approved by Calix Regas from this moment forward. As you do not seem inclined to childrearing without harming Thalia, Calix will be an active participant in her childhood with weekly visitation."

"You would have her weak and pathetic? A sniveling and imperfect mess of a girl is all you'll achieve by coddling her. There are things you do not know about her that need to be corrected, foolish boy," Origen snapped, jabbing his pointer finger into the contract. "This means nothing if I do not sign."

"I know that she's colorblind," I said, my fingers biting into the arms of the chair as I pulled myself forward. "Unlike you, that doesn't matter to me."

He paused, his jaw clenching in shock as he glanced toward the door. Even though it was too early for her to be home, his fists clenched as if he had the driving desire to strike Thalia for admitting the truth to me. "It is a weakness. A genetic anomaly that should not exist. If I had known she would be deformed in this way, I would have aborted her before she could ever shame us. She will learn to function without revealing it to those around her," Origen warned, skimming through the contract.

"Then she will do that without your abuse," I returned with a warning growl. "You have way more to lose from this contract falling through than I do. What do you think the rest of the families will think if you allow all their plans to fail because you won't stop hitting a little girl? I saw the scars and fresh wounds on her hand. What could that possibly accomplish that's so important to you?"

"The brat is left-handed, if you must know. She ends up with ink and lead all over her hand when she writes. It's unacceptable for a girl of her stature," he said, shrugging his shoulders as he sat back in his seat. As if the repeated and casual abuse of his own flesh and blood for such an insignificant reason mattered little.

I stilled my body, leaning forward to lift a pen off the desk and set it on top of the contract. "You hit your daughter for writing with her left hand?"

"I hit her for using her left hand for anything. Eventually, she'll associate using it with pain and stop altogether." A cruel grin twisted his lips as he watched my anger rise.

One day, I'd kill him for the cruelty he'd shown a tiny slip of a girl he was meant to care for.

The Families be damned.

"Oh well. I guess I'll just have to tell the others you won't cooperate," I said, sliding my chair out from beneath me.

"You already signed the contract, boy. She's yours, whether I abuse her or not. The only requirement is that she be kept virginal for you to bleed on your wedding night. You've shown your hand and your own weakness. I should send her to your marriage bed scarred and broken for your threats," he said, standing as well.

"Do you think I would've come here without knowing the Families will back me up? All of the contracts have been updated to match the one you're looking at. Everyone else agrees, since they don't beat their own daughters. You'll be the only man to undo the plans for combining the Families." I shrugged, knowing he was trapped as his face dropped with the reality of what was coming. "What do you think they'd do with that? After years of negotiations, I think they'd do anything it takes to stop you."

"You will regret the day you decided to toy with grown

men," Origen snarled, but he dropped his hand to the pen and contract. "And what will you have to show for it? A colorblind bitch of a wife who doesn't know her place. Congratulations." He scrawled his signature on the bottom of the contract where I'd already signed, letting Erasmos scoop it into his briefcase once he was done.

"My visits will be a surprise for a while, until I'm sure you're following our agreement. I'm sure you understand," I said with a hard smile, turning back for the door.

I knew Origen would try to get even, but at least Thalia would be safe. I'd find a way to deal with her father eventually.

5

CALIX

One year later

Thalia grinned as she raced down the stairs, the sound of her tiny feet thumping against each step in her haste to make her way to me. Her mother stood at the top of the stairs, a rare, small smile on her face as she watched her daughter in a moment of happiness.

Those moments were so rare for Thalia and her mother, because even requiring that she not be physically harmed didn't mean I could control the mood of her home.

Her father was a tyrant, pushing his daughter toward perfection in a way that no seven-year-old girl should have to be. The aging and increasing tension on her mother Neri's, face led me to believe that she'd taken the brunt of Origen's inability to punish his daughter.

I chose to think that she would welcome that, given it meant her daughter had been freed from the abuse. Any true mother would.

Thalia's small figure connected with my body as she flung herself at me at the bottom of the stairs. Her face pressed into my diaphragm as she tilted her head up to look at me. "What have you brought me today?" she asked excitedly.

A grin tugged my lips despite myself, the sight of her white teeth peeking out from her always bringing a rare moment of light to the life I led. Training to become the next head of the Regas family was all-consuming, taking me to places I never wanted to go.

In the time since Thalia had entered my life, I'd killed my first man. I'd tortured and bled and maimed countless other men in the name of the six families. Somehow, she still smiled up at me like I hung the moon and stars in the night sky and gave her light in the darkness.

"Let's go outside, Little One," I teased, nodding my head to the back doors so that we could go sit amongst the narcissus flowers. The garden was still her favorite place to chat with me, where the prying eyes of her father and his men weren't so noticeable and the ears were more distant.

"Fine," she said, sticking her tongue out at me. I let her take my hand and guide me through the house, her mother's watchful eyes fading from view. Jeno stood with his arms crossed over his chest at the back door, blocking the path with a harsh set to his jaw.

Considering we were the same age, I wasn't sure why he thought he could intimidate me. Everything he'd done and learned to become, so had I.

"Move," I ordered, raising my brow. I didn't care that it was his home and his sister who I let take me to the privacy of the outdoors, not when I had the other families on my side.

"It's fucked up that you're spending all this time with her, you know," Jeno said. "Why not just wait until she's older?"

"I'll be right out, λουλούδι μου," I said, nodding my head and sending Thalia outside on her own. She looked back at me nervously before shrugging her shoulders and tugging the door open as she maneuvered her way past her brother.

She sprawled on the grass between the flower beds in the distance, the taller grass of the field enveloping her as she stared up at the sky. "The next time you make a comment that alludes to the contract, I'll feed you to my dogs," I snapped, turning a glare to Jeno. He paled briefly, his face twisting with fury as he tried to recover from the threat.

"What fucking difference does it make?" he asked. "It's part of life for her."

"She doesn't need to know that until she's older, and if you care about your sister at all, you'll make sure she doesn't. She has the opportunity to be innocent for a few years before the bullshit of our lives corrupts her. Don't you think she deserves that?" I asked, shaking my head at him. He didn't seem to care one way or another what happened to his sister, and I couldn't help but wonder why it seemed like the ones who were given such a gift never realized what they had. I shoved past him, leaving him to stare after me as I set to appreciating the light he'd been given.

Our relationship might become different as she grew, but for the time being I was her protector and the only person in her life who spoiled her.

She sat up as I approached, her dark hair spilling over her shoulders and the sunshine making her amber eyes glow. "Well, what did you bring?" she asked, picking at the blades of grass under her legs.

"What makes you think I brought you anything?" I teased, taking up a seat in the grass directly across from her.

"You always bring me something." She giggled, holding out a hand expectantly with a smug expression. Rolling my eyes dramatically, I reached into the pocket of my jacket and pulled out the chocolate chip cookie I'd snuck in for her.

I had no doubt her father knew about my tendency to bring her sweets, but the glee on her face as she dug into it was worth every bit of the wrath I might incur.

"How was school?" I asked as she took a bite of the cookie. She chewed, uttering a groan of happiness as she swallowed down the bite.

"Good," she said evasively. As far as I knew, the girls at school hadn't given her any trouble since I'd threatened them, but she largely went ignored.

I guessed it was better than being bullied.

"What's a contract for marriage?" she asked, taking another bite of her cookie while I coughed to cover up the surge of rage inside me. If Jeno had told her, I would fucking kill him with my bare hands.

"Where did you hear that?" I asked, trying to suppress my initial response. Maybe it was innocent and meant nothing.

"Girls at school," she said, raising an eyebrow and seeing far too much for her age. "Missy Galanis said her father signed her contract for marriage to Stephen Lykaios yesterday."

I heaved out a sigh of relief, handing her the napkin from my pocket to wipe her chocolate-covered fingers on. She wrapped her arms around herself, shivering lightly in the chill air.

I slipped my jacket off my shoulders and wrapped it around hers. "Some of the families believe in using marriage as a business agreement. Instead of marrying for love like in your fairytales, they marry for money or power and it's usually decided when the girl is young."

"Eew. Stephen is like old," she complained. Even though he was only a half-dozen years older than me, the unfortunate reality was that made him twenty-one when Missy was only seven.

"I agree," I said, leaning back to stare at the clouds.

"Will that happen to me? A contract for marriage?" she asked, crinkling her nose, but the shadows in her amber eyes weren't playful. Thalia knew far more than she let on, and while she might not know for sure that my place in her life was similar, she had to know the day would come.

"No, Little One," I said, my soul withering with the lie as soon as it formed on my tongue. I knew one day I would regret the words, but for now the most important thing was preserving the innocence of her childhood. "I won't let your father sell you off to someone who doesn't care for you." The addition eased the sting, because I did care for her.

Even if it wasn't in the way I should care for my wife.

She nodded, the light returning to her eyes. "Promise?"

I nodded, wishing it was a word that I could keep. She deserved to marry a man she loved one day. Instead, she'd be stuck with me.

I gave her the only words I could, sealing our fate with more lies built on childish dreams that had been massacred before they could ever flourish. "I promise."

6

THALIA

One year later

I smiled as I hurried down the stairs as quickly as I could, my left hand gliding over the bannister. As I rounded the corner toward the entryway, I was shocked to see my father standing in the doorway and looking at me with the cruel smirk he often gave my mother.

I pushed down my fear, knowing that the moment Calix had become my friend was the day my father's corrections ceased. We'd never spoken of it, but I knew he'd done something.

What a teenage boy could threaten the head of the Karras family with, I didn't even want to know.

"Come, Thalia," my father said, reaching out a hand to stroke over the top of my hair in a mockery of everything that was gentle about Calix.

"Where's Calix?" I asked, flinching away from his touch. He snatched my wrist in his hand, his fingers bruising as he gripped me tightly. His knuckles were stained dark and wet, the skin torn open. "Where is he?!" I yelled when he didn't answer, planting my feet as he dragged me out the front door.

My heart raced as I looked everywhere for Calix. He'd never once kept me waiting when he promised to visit. My father's car waited at the top of the driveway, his personal driver holding the backseat door open. My father shoved me in and climbed in beside me, making me turn wide eyes to him.

"You'll see him soon enough," he said, adjusting the sleeves of his jacket. Dressed from head to toe in black, he looked so different without the shock of a white dress shirt peeking out on his chest.

"Is he okay?" I asked, swallowing back the tears I knew would only anger him more. He hated Calix in a way that I wouldn't put it past my father to get rid of him at the first chance he got.

"Soon enough, everything will be exactly as it should. You can take comfort in the fact that you will not be punished for the mistakes of others," he said, glancing at me briefly before turning his attention back to the window. "But there will be a lesson to learn today. I hope you are smart enough to pay attention, my darling daughter," he said, staring out the window. He didn't look at me as he spoke the words, and dread gathered in my belly. His lessons always hurt, even after he'd stopped hitting me.

The streets of Chestnut Hill faded as we left the affluent neighborhood my family called home. We kept going and going until industrial buildings crowded the roads, and we made our way around the back of an old warehouse. Most of the buildings still seemed to be functioning, but despite the heavily armed security men guarding the one in front of us, it didn't seem to be used by anyone recently.

My father stepped out of the car once it pulled to a stop, nodding to me until I followed him out. He remained silent as he walked through the doors one of his men pulled open for us, letting me trail behind him even though all I wanted to do was run.

To find Calix and get out while I could.

He guided me through the main space of the building, the empty structure feeling cold. Even compared to the coolness of our home, something about it left me with a sense of dread.

Death clung to the walls. Death was on every surface and in the air, as if it were imprinted into the building itself and would never be clean. A graveyard with walls.

The doors at the back of the room opened and my father stepped through them. I hesitated at the sound of cheering voices coming from inside the new room. One of my father's men prodded me between the shoulders until I kept moving forward.

Men stood in a circle at the center of the enormous room, blocking my view of whatever might be in the middle. As my father reached them, they parted to allow him through. My feet dragged as I forced myself closer, needing to see whatever kind of Hell he'd brought me to see.

It was a punishment undoubtedly, for growing closer with Calix and not keeping him at an appropriate distance. Girls like me weren't allowed to have friends, especially not boys.

Not when my father said my allegiance would belong to my husband one day without question.

"Daddy?" I whispered, stepping up behind him. I hated the name every time I said it, knowing he'd never done anything to deserve it, but his insistence kept me from calling him anything else, even as I shook with fear of what was coming. He moved to the side, allowing me to see into the pit in front of him. Metal plates lined the walls around the hole in the concrete, leaving them with nothing but a hole where the floor must have been at one point in time. It was huge, with a dozen people standing below and plenty of space to move around.

There were bodies littering what looked like sand on the ground, and I swallowed back my rising nausea as I realized the woman kneeling at the center of all of it with her head hanging forward was my mother.

"Mommy!" I called, watching as her body twitched but she didn't raise her head to look at me. My father's hand grasped my shoulders through my dress, lifting me from the ground as my eyes connected with Calix's in horrified shock. He knelt on the ground in front of my father's men, his father and the men I recognized that worked their family's security watching in the background with their heads hung low.

Dark stains covered their clothes. Their faces. I knew even without the shock of color that it was blood.

The unmoving bodies littering the ground around the pit left no doubt to that.

My father tossed me into the pit, my hands and knees landing awkwardly in the sand as the tiny grains dug into my skin. Calix's eyes were wide as he shoved to his feet to reach me, grunting as someone wrenched his arms behind his back and secured them with rope while I pushed myself up to stand.

"She has nothing to do with this," Calix growled, struggling against the person holding him. His father knelt next to him, his beaten and bruised face a mirror of my father's torn up knuckles. Calix's bare chest was crisscrossed with bleeding wounds, one of his cheeks marked with a gash that would scar.

He'd always been inhumanly beautiful. From the moment I'd first seen him, I'd wondered how it was possible for a boy to be so pretty. The cuts on his chest and his face changed him, as well as the savage snarl on his face that I'd only ever seen when the girls at school had pushed me years before. At his side was a blade, a sword, as if he'd dropped it when he hadn't had any other choice.

I spun, my eyes sliding over the wall at my back and the weapons lining it. My history lessons flashed in my memory. My father jumped into the pit at my side, chuckling and grabbing a fistful of my hair. He wrenched my head back while Calix yelled his protest. "Leave her alone!"

"Do you like ο λάκκος, my daughter?" he asked, his voice harsh. "This is where we settle our disputes with fire and blood. This is where decisions are made and the future is shaped."

"It's a gladiator ring," I wheezed, bringing my hands up to grasp at his hand. The blood coating his skin from whatever fight he'd been a part of made my hands slick, slipping along his and unable to find a grip.

"Good, Thalia. The Italians may be useless in most ways, but at least in this they offered something of value. An entertaining way to kill your enemies and fight for power."

"What did she do?" I asked, nodding my head, as much as I could, to where my mom still knelt in the sand.

"She allowed another man to touch her. My wife let Eugene Regas inside her, when her body belongs to me alone." I didn't understand the words, not fully, but I knew enough to know that a woman belonged to her husband.

My mother would never have taken such a risk. Not with the way my father beat her for everything she did wrong. He loosened his grip on my hair, tossing me to the side so I fell to the sand.

"Let her death be a lesson to you, so that you never forget your place and what happens when a woman disobeys her husband."

7

CALIX

Origen left Thalia in the sand, making his way to his wife. Neri didn't lift her head, keeping her face to the ground until he touched her chin with mocking gentleness. He lifted her face until she blinked up at him blankly, as if she'd already withered and died.

As if watching the butchering of my father's men had killed what remained of her soul, that Origen himself hadn't beaten out of her years prior.

Thalia's father's fist struck her mother across the cheek. Blood sprayed from her lip, staining the sand as she fell to her side. "Mommy!" Thalia screamed, lunging forward as if she might try to intervene.

I pushed myself from my knees to stand, desperate to keep Thalia from interfering. There was no telling what her father would do if she got in the way, no reason to believe he would treat his daughter with any semblance of kindness, considering what she would see in a few moments.

She shouldn't have been here at all. Only men were allowed inside ο λάκκος, except for the rare occasion where a woman's infraction was severe enough to require more than one of the six families. My father being foolish enough to fuck Karras' wife qualified.

Rough hands snatched the rope at my wrist, wrenching me back to the sand. Thalia's brother, Jeno, stepped off the spot where he'd lurked by the wall, wrapping his arms around Thalia, restraining his sister as he watched his father strike his mother over and over until little remained of what had once been a beautiful face.

"Daddy, stop!" Thalia screamed, the shrillness of her voice echoing off the walls of the pit. The other families watched without a trace of emotion on their faces, no concern for the fact that they'd only just years ago moved to protect a child from her abusive father. My own father's mistake had changed the tides of power, shifting it out from under me before I was old enough to shield Thalia from the consequences.

With her mother gone, what would my father's punishment be?

"Make him stop!" Thalia snarled, turning in Jeno's arms to push at his chest.

He shushed her, his voice oddly gentle. I barely heard it over their father's savage roar as he stood up from his wife's limp body. Her lungs filled with air in a ragged breath as she turned to stare at her daughter. "Close your eyes, Thalia," she murmured, using all the strength she had to warn her daughter of what was coming.

Origen grasped one of the axes hanging on the wall, hefting the heavy weapon and moving back toward Neri's half-dead body where she lay in the sand. I lunged again, struggling against the hands holding me still. A fist connected with the side of my face, splitting the wound on my cheekbone open further and sending me stumbling forward until sand grated against my other cheek. Thalia's struggles increased, tears streaming down her face as she watched her father stare coldly down at her mother . "No!" she screamed.

"Close your eyes, λουλούδι μου," I said, and Thalia's tear-filled eyes found mine, her face twisting in horror. She was too young to understand, but just old enough to know what was coming.

She'd never see her mother again, and her final memory of her would be one filled with the shadows of blood in her mind.

Her lip trembled as she stared at me, her eyes slowly fluttering closed so she wouldn't have to witness the death of the only person she loved. Jeno moved to step away, to drag her further from the carnage of her mother's death, but Origen didn't bother to wait.

He swung the axe down. The sound of the freshly sharpened blade slicing through flesh echoed through the pit as it embedded in the sand beneath Neri's body.

Thalia whimpered as blood splashed onto her bare legs, the liquid trickling down over the skin of her shins. Jeno swayed her back and forth lightly, a rare moment of affection that I'd never seen in all the times I'd watched him belittle or ignore his baby sister. Her eyes stayed squeezed closed, waiting for the order from me. I knew without a doubt that Thalia wouldn't open her eyes until I told her it was okay.

Perhaps her mother wasn't the only person she loved after all. Perhaps she loved me in the way a girl loved her protector.

Two of Origen's men stepped forward, grabbing Neri's corpse by the ankles and dragging her through the sand as the bodies of our men were disposed of in the same way.

They'd be brought to το νεκροταφείο: the graveyard where those who died in the arena were left to rot.

There would be no tombstone. There would be no place to mourn.

Just countless bodies decaying in the catacombs beneath the building.

Only when Neri's body was dropped through the hole at the edge of the pit and added to the pile of dead did I speak to Thalia. "It's okay now, Thalia," I murmured, watching as the four other heads of family lined up at the top of the pit. Origen hiked the axe up onto his shoulder, waiting for permission to kill my father for his betrayal of what all the families held dear.

Marriage was sacred. Above all else.

"Eugene Regas, you have been accused of betraying our ideals and taking another man's wife to your bed. What do you have to say to the accusations?" the head of the Hasapis family said, staring my father down.

"Well technically I didn't take her to a bed at all. We never made it that far," my father sniped like the idiot he was.

Theodore Hasapis ground his teeth, glaring at him. "But you admit to defiling her marriage?"

"I don't think you'd have permitted my men to be slaughtered if you thought otherwise."

"Then you leave us no choice. We have determined that the Regas family will be exiled from Philadelphia. We care not where you go, but you are henceforth banished from the families," Theodore declared/ordered.

Thalia's father dropped the axe to the sand, his jaw clenching as he undoubtedly wanted to argue against the sentence.

My father's death would have been preferable for all involved, leaving me to run the Regas family with him gone. Thalia would have remained protected. But with me banished from the city....

"We are not all to blame for the actions of one fool. Would you truly punish an entire bloodline for the sins of one?" I asked. My father turned his shocked expression toward me, but there was only one thought racing through my mind.

Protecting Thalia. No matter the cost.

"A rotten apple creates rotten seeds, and we cannot allow the disease of the Regas family to spread. You will leave the city immediately, and all contracts and business deals will be severed."

Thalia sobbed in her brother's grasp as my father and what remained of his men were hauled to their feet. The man at my back tried to lift me, but I hunkered down and made my body as heavy as I possibly could.

I wouldn't leave her; not knowing that she'd have no one to defend her against Origen.

Thalia screamed out as her father's man drew a knife and pressed it to my throat. I swallowed against it, holding her eyes with mine and silently willing her to stay still. "Please no," she begged, shoving at her brother's arms until her father approached the two of them. “You can’t!” He took Thalia out of Jeno's grasp, twisting her arm behind her back until she cried out in pain.

"Get up, boy," Origen ordered. "We both know you're leaving the city one way or another."

"No," I spat, not daring to take my eyes off his. I might not have been big enough to truly fight for her, not compared to the men standing around and the sentries waiting to take me away from her, but if nothing else, Thalia would know that I fought to stay with her. She’d know I'd cared enough to protect her with my own life.

"Get him out of my sight," Theodore said, waving a hand. Another man came up to me as the original sheathed his knife, his fist colliding with my face and assaulting me with a wave of pain. Another followed immediately, the pain inside my skull thundering as the blows kept coming.

Unconsciousness crept in alongside the sound of Thalia's screams. With the final realization of just how gravely I'd failed her, blackness consumed me, drawing me to a place where nothing hurt.

Only my heart.

PART II

AFTER

8

THALIA

Twelve years later

My pencil scratched at the page carefully, methodically outlining the details of the narcissus flowers woven into Persephone's hair. Lifting my left hand up from the page, I studied the wisps of smoke floating around Hades' beautiful face. Touching the side of my palm to the page, I smudged the lines until I was happy with the way the shading blended together.

He was bathed in darkness, hidden in the shadows with only light eyes and the subtle features of his fierce snarl peeking down at the lightness of Persephone. With her white hair and fair skin, the lighting seemed to make her sparkle. I dropped my pencil to the page, heaving out a sigh as I leaned forward and draped myself over my desk.

In just a few minutes, I'd have to tuck the sketch away from prying eyes.

I leaned over the drawing, smiling down at it. A moment later, the cane sliced through the air, the sound always so similar to the memory of my father's axe. To the thudding of it striking the sand after severing my mother's head from her body.

I might not have seen it, but, even after more than a decade, that sound was firmly trapped in my memories.

Pain exploded across my back, old scars rising to ache with the injury I'd suffered through far too many times to count. "You're slouching," Lydia reprimanded as I stretched my back to ramrod straight. My stepmother moved through the room silently, leaning against the edge of my desk and pursing her lips at the stain of lead on my hand.

Her cane tapped against the scars on the back of my left hand, the skin warming instantly under her attention. "Your father won't be pleased to see you've been disobeying him again," she tutted. With a frustrated shake of her head that shook her light hair from side to side, she sighed heavily. It wasn't often that she caught me drawing; not when I did everything within my power to keep it a secret.

I knew the consequences should my father discover I'd wasted time on such a frivolous activity that a woman of my stature shouldn't partake in, but the day had been long. The wait had been exhausting.

The sun had set hours before, leaving me to wonder just how long it could take for such a decision to be made. "He called. He'll be home soon," Lydia said. I nodded, keeping my expression carefully blank.

Emotions were for the weak. Love was a lie. Perfection was demanded.

Emptiness was my closest companion, and I'd long since accepted its place in my life. There was only one person who mattered to me. One who I would do whatever it took to protect. Even allow myself to be forced into a loveless marriage that was to be determined by a trial by combat. A barbaric way to determine who would earn the right to marry the eldest Karras girl.

"Is Malva asleep yet?" I asked Lydia, turning to stare into the empty fireplace in the corner of my bedroom.

"She finally drifted off about an hour ago," she said, a hint of warmth creeping into her voice. Despite her willingness to show me cruelty according to my father's rules, Lydia loved my half-sister with all that remained of her cold, cruel heart.

I nodded, drawing in a deep breath before I shoved my chair out and strolled into my bathroom. I scrubbed my hands raw, furiously removing all traces of my sketching from my skin. "He expects you to be waiting in his office when he returns," Lydia said, clearing her throat before she ducked out of the bedroom. I breathed a sigh of relief once she was gone, lifting my eyes to look in the mirror as I clutched the edge of the counter with wet hands.

In two months, I would be married. I didn't even know the name of the groom, only that he would be an heir to one of the other remaining families. In the days, weeks, and years leading up to the spectacle that my father found so hilarious, not one of my potential husbands had bothered to get to know me.

They had done no more than give me a glance-over at parties and determine that I'd grown up well before moving about their business. I'd given them the saccharine smile that had been forced into my muscle memory, all the while wishing I could go back to being the runt of a child that nobody bothered with.

A scrawny girl had grown into a lithe-limbed woman with a too-thin body that was often painful to maintain. High cheekbones and wide, upturned "amber" eyes made me look ethereal, according to Lydia. An odd sort of beauty that required a second look to truly appreciate.

Because the first look was just odd and flawed, and I had the "type of beauty that took time to appreciate."

Drying my hands with the towel, I stepped away from the vanity and made my way into my room. After tucking the drawing with the others in the alcove in my closet, I walked out to the hallway. With calm, measured steps and a carefully straight back, I held my head high as I passed my father's men, Leon and Peter. They'd been there the day my mother was murdered, and I hadn't been able to look them in the eye after watching them restrain Calix so he couldn't get to me and take me with him.

I'd have gladly gone, and I'd waited for the day when he'd sneak back into the city to rescue me from what he had to know was a horrible life. A mother dead and murdered. A father who wanted nothing more than to hurt me to spite both her and Calix.

I'd have been better off bleeding on the sand of ο λάκκος than living the life he'd left me to.

But Calix never came back for me.

Peter slid his gaze down my body, lingering on the swell of my breasts in the dress Lydia had laid out for me that morning. I ignored him, turning the corner and descending the stairs with my hand on the railing.

My breath caught with panic, and I snapped my hand off the bannister as quickly as I'd set it there. My father didn't wait at the bottom of the stairs and there was no cold smirk on his face to taunt me, but knowing he was at ο λάκκος haunted me. Nothing would change the fact that my future husband wielded a weapon in much the same way, bleeding men and fighting for the right to wed me like I was some prize and not just a broken doll.

Like I would be anything more than another expendable toy to set on the shelf.

I turned the corner at the bottom of the stairs, walking toward my father's office at the back of the house. The door was open, the first sign that I'd taken too long before coming down.

It wouldn't please him, but I had to hope he'd had time to wash the blood from his hands and face before I'd have to look at him. But I found as I stepped into the room there wasn't a speck of shadowed grey on his suit or his skin, because he'd had no need to fight.

He owned the prize the others wanted.

I stepped in front of his desk, hanging my head and dropping my eyes to my feet while I waited for him to speak. He took another sip of his scotch before he stood, stepping around the desk to stand beside me. Leaning against the desk and crossing his ankles, he waited for me to flinch as he reached out a hand toward my face.

But there was no fear left in my body, no attempt to protect myself against the inevitable.

"Good girl." My father chuckled, touching my chin and turning my face until I looked over at him. "They fought hard for you."

I said nothing, allowing Origen to work through whatever grand speech he had planned for me. He loved nothing in this world except to hear himself talk.

He nodded, pursing his lips and moving away when he didn't get the reaction he wanted from me. "You're to marry Damianos Hasapis," he said finally, dropping into the seat behind his desk. "You should be pleased with that arrangement, I think."

I blinked once, the only sign that I'd even heard his words. I didn't know what I'd ever done to give him the impression that I had opinions of the men who might be my husband.

It mattered little to me since they were all the same. A

symptom of the archaic traditions that ran rampant in the families and needed to be dismantled from the inside out before Malva could suffer the same fate. "He would like to spend some time with you before the wedding. He wants you to be comfortable with him and to understand that he intends to treat you well." My father scoffed his disapproval, rolling his eyes as if it was a ridiculous notion. "God help me, but I cannot seem to escape insufferable fools who would treat you like a precious gem. Tell me, what exactly have you done to earn such treatment?" he asked. "Besides becoming mute as well as half fucking blind."

"You've made it very clear that I serve one purpose, and it is not to be heard. I'm uncertain why you want me to speak if you don't wish to hear me, Father," I said, keeping my voice as neutral as the empty expression on my face.

"Even when you say everything right, you somehow manage to make me want to smack the smartass right out of you," he grunted, huffing a laugh as he waved his hand to dismiss me. "At least I won't have to deal with you for much longer."

I took the dismissal for what it was and turned on my heel, anxious to retreat to the relative sanctuary of my bedroom without another word. There was no lock on my door, nothing to keep me safe from him if he decided he wanted to invade my space, but Origen didn't seek me out. If he needed me, he'd summon me like a dog.

"Thalia?" he called. I paused, turning my head to look at him over my shoulder as rage gleamed in his eyes. "Try not to do anything stupid. I would hate for you to end up like your mother." I swallowed against the reminder, nodding my head briefly and shoving down the pain.

I lived my life by a very simple set of rules.

The first was to never let them see you bleed.

9

CALIX

I marched through the house, my feet carrying me to the open-concept living room. Rafael sat at the kitchen island, typing away at something on his laptop with that grim look on his face. He knew what was coming.

He'd always known, since the moment my father had left my broken body on Miguel Ibarra's doorstep.

I'd fought like hell to stay with Thalia, to protect her from the fate I known would come in my absence. I knew she'd be punished for the fact that I'd dared to defy Origen Karras, and she'd suffer for getting close to me.

"Who?" he asked, not bothering to look up from his laptop.

My ally in Philadelphia had called me as soon as the victor was declared, but it had been a long, painful wait before I knew the name of the man I would slaughter. The man who would try to take what was mine.

"Damianos Hasapis," I growled. The son of the man who had sentenced me to banishment alongside my father. The son of the man who had taken everything from me.

Rafael nodded, finally glancing up. "That's good. His father needs to die regardless of the son's involvement in this. Perhaps the other families will be cooperative."

"Each family put forward a champion," I growled. "Would you feel so sanguine if you discovered a group of men who fought for the right to fuck Isa?" I asked, referring to the girl who had captivated him.

He watched her, much like I'd taken to watching Thalia after arriving back in the States a few months prior. The only difference was that he had the ability to manipulate and control her life.

I could not.

He glared at me with a snarl twisting his mouth, his eyes filled with loathing that promised to strangle me in my sleep. I still needed to get used to that protectiveness coming from the man who cared about no one.

"We'll take the city immediately," I said.

"The wedding is not for two months. We need time to recoup our losses before we launch a full attack on Philadelphia. The wise move is to wait and to plan. The grander the statement we make with our first assault, the more we can minimize the consequences later on. I understand your anger, Calix, but Damianos will not touch her until their wedding night," Rafe said, standing from the stool at the island and turning to face me. "You have waited twelve years for this moment. Do not fuck it up by acting impulsively now."

"Fine," I said abruptly, turning and heading for the bedroom I'd called home since we'd come to Chicago to help Matteo Bellandi win his war. I drew in a deep breath, trying to quell my rising dread. The Thalia I knew would not go quietly into a marriage she didn't want. The Thalia I knew fought and maneuvered, even as a young girl. She'd been far too smart for her own good, with a quiet rebelliousness hidden from all those who wanted to contain her.

As a child, she'd been obsessed with mythology and folklore. She'd been drawn to the beautiful creatures that hid monsters within, waiting for the right moment to devour their prey. From the ashes of those interests, she'd grown into a woman who belonged in the stories she loved so much. A beauty who smiled, giving the illusion of the perfect doll they expected her to be. But when the doors closed and the prying eyes disappeared, she morphed into the brutal woman who would cut down her enemies at the first opportunity.

The woman who held her hate within her heart, who embraced loneliness as her companion and readied herself to slaughter all who wronged her. Only the love for her sister kept her from acting on her violence, from utilizing the skills she learned in the quiet of the night alongside the man I'd planted in her security.

The ally I'd given her when I couldn't be there, who would protect her if things ever escalated past what Thalia was strong enough to handle on her own.

She'd been a girl who needed my protection. As a woman, she needed my acceptance and my love, and with it the ability to be the woman she was born to be. If I survived our wedding night, she would thrive at my side, a goddess born in the light who I would drag down to the pits of hell to make mine.

I pushed open the door, stepping inside my bedroom and glancing to the wall of monitors where I watched Thalia move around her father's house. She stepped out of his office, her face twisted into a grimace as she withheld the grief of whatever her father had said to her. In the months since I'd started watching her, I'd come to realize there was only one topic that could penetrate that shield she kept locked tightly around herself.

Her mother.

While Thalia and her mother hadn't been particularly

close, as dictated by her father, Neri'd been the only one she'd had who even remotely resembled family. The closest thing she'd known to love.

She made it to her room safely, leaning her back against the door as her lungs heaved with deep gasps of breath. Her fists clenched with the need to kill, to hurt and maim as they'd done to her. As she stepped away from the surface, she stretched her hands up to reach for the zipper at her back. Shoving the dress down her body frantically, she stripped away the layers of who they wanted her to be.

Her face transformed from that pleasant expression, hatred filling it as her amber eyes hardened into a glare she thought no one could see. My eyes moved over her body as she stepped through her room in pink undergarments. There wasn't an ounce of fat on her frame, her ribs protruding slightly from her form beyond what could be considered natural or healthy.

The strict diet her stepmother kept her on showed in every sharp edge, on the exposed hip bones that drew attention down to her panty line. She stripped off her bra and underwear, grabbing a nightgown from her dresser and frantically tugging it over her head before she moved to the bathroom to wash the makeup from her face and brush her teeth.

Watching her go through her nighttime routine, I stripped off my clothes and settled into my bed with the laptop off my desk, resting it on one of the pillows as I got comfortable. I grabbed the e-reader off my nightstand, opening the fantasy romance Thalia had been reading earlier in the day.

She did exactly as I knew she would when she returned to her bedroom, grabbing her own device and opening the protective case she kept it in. She got comfortable on top of the covers, her eyes moving as she lost herself in the world of fantasy. I alternated between reading the pages of the book and watching her, studying her face and her body as she read.

I loved every twitch of her face. I lived for every intake of breath.

I lusted for the moments when her legs rubbed together to stall the ache building in her when she approached a sex scene; watched her cheeks tinge with hesitant desire that she didn't fully understand when she thought about a man taking her body.

I'd been shocked to discover that Thalia's choice of reading —as a woman who knew what it was to be treated like property, to be owned and have no free will of her own—involved dominant men.

But they were dominant men who loved hard, who worshiped their women even as they controlled them.

As it always happened, her hand drifted down to the space between her legs as she read while biting her lip shyly as if someone could see her being naughty.

She didn't know how right she was.

I slid my hand down to grip my cock, pumping slowly as her long, delicate fingers slid down to touch her clit. Her hips rocked as if overcome with the need that one caress filled her with, the desperation for the freedom to touch and be touched written in every line of her body.

A light moan came through the computer speakers as I pumped, watching as she bit her lip to keep silent.

There had been a time when I hadn't been able to imagine wanting Thalia, when we'd been children too far apart in age for our relationship to be anything but platonic. That had changed the moment I'd seen her as an adult after sending Christian to keep an eye on her and give me video access to the house. The moment I'd seen her, the pieces had clicked into place.

She'd become mine in the way a wife became her husband's, and that was what I would be to her. Not solely a protector, but a husband in truth.

Her fingers danced over her flesh as she turned to her back, giving me an unobstructed view of the space between her thighs and the way she touched herself. I'd show her true passion soon enough, but until then I'd tolerate reading books and touching myself while I watched her.

The sight of her back arching off the bed and the soft swell of her breasts thrusting into the air sent me over the edge, pumping my cock furiously until I covered my stomach in my release.

As my heart raced and I watched Thalia come down from her high, impatience rose in me. She rolled to her stomach, revealing a fresh welt across her shoulders from her stepmother's favorite cane.

I didn't usually believe in killing women, but that bitch would die alongside her husband soon enough, for what they'd done to my woman.

10

THALIA

My hands remained clasped in front of me, carefully restrained as I made my way down the steps. Lydia's plan for a grand entrance remained firmly in place, all of them watching me as I descended slowly in my heels. The light dress hung off my shoulders, lace covering my stomach and the tops of my thighs.

I ignored the weight of my father's stare and of all the ways he would judge me and find me lacking. Keeping my gaze intent on the man who stood beside him, I forced my face to remain impassive but pleasant. If he was to be my future, then pleasing my father was no longer my main concern.

Keeping Damianos happy would be my only purpose.

He stepped forward to meet me where the stairs curved around the corner at the bottom, holding out a hand for me to place mine in. Tipping his upper body forward, he touched his lips to my knuckles. The split on his bottom lip scratched against my skin, a reminder of the violence from his fight only a few days prior.

Where he'd won me without a hint of concern for what I might think of it.

I shoved down the thought, tipping my lips into a slight smile as he stood straight. "You're as beautiful as ever, η νύφη μου," he said. I winced, only reminded of the contract that bound us together without any of the love that came with marriage in my favorite books.

It certainly didn't help that the overly affectionate name in Greek reminded me that there had been rumors of his rivalry with Calix. The two boys had been competitors before Calix was banished, but I couldn't allow myself to care. Calix was forever gone from my life, and I had to do what was necessary to find peace with the life I had.

The very one he'd promised to protect me from.

"You're too kind," I said, my cheeks heating with the lie.

"I expect her home immediately after lunch," my father barked as Damianos offered his arm. I took it, wincing slightly when his body brushed against the side of mine. I'd been so trained to expect pain with human touch that I couldn't help the reaction when presented with a new, unknown person.

I wondered if it would matter to him to see the marks on my body, and to see the welt across my shoulders that Lydia hadn't bothered to try to hide with a more modest dress. Instead, only the curtain of my dark hair offered any cover.

"Of course," Damianos said, grinning at my father's attempt to control the man who had recently taken over as the head of the Hasapis family. His father's battle against the cancer that had riddled his body in the last year had made the transition of power necessary, and with it came the knowledge that Damianos was not a man content to remain one of several in power.

He'd start a war if the other families didn't keep him in check, and I'd somehow had the misfortune to find myself the glue between the two factions. The last time such an alliance had been struck, it had ended with my mother dead.

I had to hope I wouldn't follow in her footsteps.

Damianos guided me out the front doors, not pausing when I turned my face up to feel the sun on my skin. My seclusion had worsened after my mother's death, the result of private tutors who did their best to keep me trapped inside for all the daylight hours. Without my mother's attention, my father had allowed her field of narcissus flowers to wither and die in the yard, and I couldn't bring myself to step outside there in the rare moments I snuck away.

To feel the death of everything I loved so poignantly. That garden had been where I'd felt closest to my mother. It was where I'd met Calix.

It seemed fitting, in a way, that it too would be dead.

His car waited, and I regretfully let him fold me into the passenger seat. His eyes fixated on the expanse of my thigh as my dress rode up, making me swallow back the bile that came at the thought of his hands on me. I squeezed my eyes shut as he closed the door and walked around to the other side.

Damianos wasn't an unattractive man. While his dark hair might have been longer than I suspected was my personal preference, he had a ruggedly handsome quality to his face and broad shoulders, as if he was truly a gladiator and didn't just engage in battle because of some ridiculous competitiveness.

We remained silent as he started the engine of his Porsche, pulling away from the home's entrance to turn down the long driveway. I wrung my hands in my lap, shoving down the feeling of horror that started to rise inside me. In my brief interactions with the other girls my age, I knew Damianos was considered a great catch.

Several wanted nothing more than to be contracted as his wife, given that there were no rumors of cruelty toward the women he slept with or the escorts the families employed.

Still, the knowledge that he would touch me in less than two months' time made something insidious slither over my skin.

"Do you—" I paused to swallow down my nerves before starting over. "Is there anything you wish to know about me?" Perhaps if I could find a way to believe this was more than a business arrangement, then I would be able to find him more tolerable.

He glanced at me out of the corner of his eye as he drove through the streets toward the restaurant that wasn't far. "Like what?"

I bit my lip to fight the surge of anger that rose at his blatant dismissal of everything that was me. It was the only confirmation I needed that he was just like all the rest. I would be his breeder, his trophy, tucked away and all but forgotten until he had the desire to use my body for his own pleasure.

I turned to look out the window, tugging my dress down to the best of my ability as I felt suddenly exposed in a way I hadn't even moments before.

"Your father mentioned you liked history," he observed, as if the fact that he knew one small fact about me would ease whatever hurt he'd caused. He just didn't understand that he wasn't capable of hurting me. Not in that way. "He says you spend your free time buried in a book."

"Yes," I said, not bothering to admit that more often than not I read romance or fantasy books. "Ancient history specifically. Mythology. That sort of thing." The fact that he only knew my more acceptable hobby was salt in the wound.

My father wouldn't advertise the parts of me that he saw as flaws in the pristine image he hoped to create of me.

"I enjoy artwork as well. Sketching, mostly," I said, watching as he clenched his jaw.

"But you have such lovely, soft hands." He reached across, taking mine in his grip and running his thumb over the smooth skin and eventually to the scars on my knuckles. "Wouldn't such a thing ruin them?"

I forced my best impression of the sultry smile Lydia had taught me, raising my right hand to run over the back of his where he held mine. Turning it over, I separated our hands and ran delicate fingers over the rough skin on his palm. "You have calluses, but you are far from ruined," I murmured softly, watching as his hand twitched in my grip.

Turning my eyes up to look at him through my lashes, I watched as his eyes slid to mine. They darkened, as if I'd made a mistake and awoken something I couldn't have predicted would come so quickly. "I would much rather your nails dig into my shoulders than your calloused fingers," he said, deftly bringing us back to the reality that I was nothing but an inexperienced virgin who had no place playing games with a man.

I swallowed as my cheeks heated, moving to withdraw my hand. He clutched it in his as his attention refocused on the road. Resting the back of my hand against the top of his thigh, he seemed oblivious to my discomfort. "I think we should come to understand one another to prevent misunderstandings later on."

"Okay," I whispered, tugging back on my hand.

"I'm not a man to toy with. I will not fall for manipulations through sex and teasing as your stepmother likely tried to teach you. Such things are done to catch a man, but you already caught me, sweetheart. We have no need for games between us, because in just a few weeks I'll spend my nights inside you." His voice was cold and impassive as he said the words, but there was no cruelty or taunting to them. Just a bleak picture of my reality.

He deftly pulled the Porsche into the parking lot, pulling up to the valet. "I understand," I whispered.

He made no move to get out, only releasing my hand and

shifting in his seat to touch his to my bare upper back. His fingers skimmed the welt from Lydia's cane, gently prodding the skin. "But this is unacceptable. You will not suffer at my hands in this way," he said, pulling his hand away finally.

"I won't?"

"No, η νύφη μου. I will not harm you, and in return you will do what I expect of you as my wife," he said. "Can you do that for me?" I nodded slightly, holding still as he raised a hand to cup my cheek. Even if my instinct was to back away, to avoid the touch at all costs, I let his thumb trace over my cheekbone.

He shoved open the car door, walking around and pulling me out to escort me inside so that we could have lunch together. The fortunate reality was, after we were married, he'd likely spend very little time with me.

My days would be my own, even if my nights belonged to him.

11

THALIA

One week later

Christian lurked in the corner behind my mother's gardening shed, the same place he always hid when he needed a cigarette break. We'd never discussed why he helped me, or what his motivation was in risking my father's wrath to give me the outlet he did.

Slipping my shoes off, I crept around the corner behind him. Keeping my body as still as possible, other than my toes that dug into the ground with every step, I restrained the breath in my lungs.

Crouching low quickly, I swept a leg at his feet, groaning my frustration when the bastard hopped over it. "What the fuck!" I exclaimed with a laugh, straightening as he turned smiling eyes my way.

"You still breathe too heavy," he chuckled. I pursed my lips at him in a pout, straightening my dress as he put out his cigarette against the edge of the gardening shed and tucked it away in the vase he kept tucked beneath the shrubbery. "What do you want, Monster?" he asked with a sigh.

"I need a favor," I said, holding my head high as I prepared to ask for the one thing I thought even Christian wouldn't give me. If anyone ever discovered the truth, which seemed like it would take careful planning on my part to avoid, he would be punished right alongside me. He'd pay the consequences with his life.

Guilt consumed me at the thought, making me hesitate to voice the favor. It'd be stupid and selfish, and pointless in the end.

"What is it?" he asked, his brow furrowing in concern.

"Nothing," I said with a smile.

"Thalia," he said, reaching out a hand very slowly to take mine in his. "You know you can ask me for anything. If it's within my ability, I'll give it to you."

"I want a night. To be free to choose who I want for my first time," I said with a swallow. "If there's a way to do it without getting caught, then I have to try. But I need to find a way to do that without involving you. I won't let anyone else suffer for my choices."

He leaned back into the shed wall, crossing his arms over his chest and staring at me with wide eyes. "You want me to help you get laid?" He swallowed as if the thought was insufferable, and I pushed down the old hurts of being an awkward girl who nobody ever looked at twice.

"No. I want to choose for myself. I think I can manage to convince one man to fuck me." I laughed. "I just need the window for it to be possible."

He sighed, running his hand over his face. "Okay. Give me a week or two to figure something out and make the arrangements. I can't guarantee anything, but I'll see what I can do," he said, nodding back toward the house where Lydia poked her head out to look for me. "You get your ass back to the house and act like you didn't just ask me to help you commit suicide. Fuck," he groaned.

I flung my arms around him for a brief hug before making my way back to the house, keeping with the shadows until I could come up into the still-living gardens at the side of the manor and pretend I'd been sitting among the flowers.

Nobody could know.

12

CALIX

My cell vibrated on the desk as I looked over the reports Enzo had sent to the house. The Bellandis wouldn't leave me to fight my war alone; not after Rafael and I had given everything to help them in theirs.

By the time Thalia's wedding came, we'd be ready. We just needed to develop the perfect strategy in the meantime. I picked up the phone when Christian's name flashed on the screen, knowing that he would be safely tucked away in his tiny apartment at this late hour. "What's wrong?" I asked, jolting to my feet as every muscle in my body tensed. The thought of Thalia being harmed at all was enough to send me into a furious rage, but for her to be hurt severely enough that he would risk his cover to contact me?

It was unthinkable.

"She's fine," he reassured me quickly. "I promise. No one has hurt her in the last few days from what I've seen."

"Then what the fuck do you want?" I snarled, dropping my weight back into my chair.

"She came to me with a request today. It isn't something that I'm comfortable dealing with on my own, so you might have to move up your timetable." He gave an uncomfortable chuckle, and I could just imagine the man rubbing the back of his neck with his other hand.

"What are you talking about?" I asked, exhaustion creeping into my tone. Every waking hour had been spent making arrangements and contacting allies in the region who would be willing to go up against the five remaining families to have me reinstated.

Or to kill them all and take the city for myself. Either option worked just as well for me.

"She doesn't want to lose her virginity to Damianos," he said suddenly. "She asked me to help her get a window where she can find a man and..." He trailed off, the hesitance in his voice making me grind my teeth together.

"Don't you fucking say it," I warned with a growl.

He ignored me, continuing on. "She wants to find someone to fuck her, so she can say at least once she had a choice in who she took to bed. I'm going to go out on a limb and say that you aren't down with that idea, so how would you like me to handle it? I saw the look on her face, man. If I say no, she'll just find another way."

My chest vibrated with the need to rip his vocal chords out of his throat for planting the image of Thalia with someone else in my head, but as much as I hated his insistence on telling me what I didn't want to hear, I knew he was right.

She was nothing if not rebellious at her core, and was never going to go quietly into a loveless marriage.

"Set it up. Get me a day and a time, and I'll fucking be there," I said, gripping the edge of the desk with my free hand.

"You're going to stop her?" Christian asked, his voice full of questions. We both knew Thalia knowing I'd returned would ruin all our careful planning.

"No. I'm not," I snapped, pulling the phone away from my

ear and jabbing the screen with furious fingers. I stood from the desk and moved to the screens to watch Thalia sleeping peacefully in her bed.

She was beautiful, peaceful, as she lay there curled up into a ball beneath her blanket. Like an angel of death, just waiting for me to defile her.

If she was so desperate to be ruined, I'd happily oblige.

13

THALIA

Two weeks later

I paced back and forth in my room in the ballet flats I'd slipped onto my feet. I didn't own anything even remotely resembling sneakers, at my father and step-mother's insistence.

With my shoes for the night packed into the designer tote slung under my arm, my lungs heaved with the panic that threatened to overtake me. By the end of the night, I wouldn't be a virgin.

By the end of the night, I'd have experienced what it was to be normal for just a few hours. To do something foolish and impulsive purely for the sake of it, because I wanted to.

Glancing at the watch on my wrist, I blew out a breath as the time finally reflected ten at night. The quiet knock on my door came promptly, leaving me to move toward it as quietly as I could and slowly pull the door open. Christian's kind face stared back at me on the other side, and he waved a hand at me to step out. "You've got everything?" he asked, looking down my body with a furrow to his brow. "Where did you get that dress?"

"Lydia has been filling my closet with clothes more appropriate for pleasing my husband," I whispered. "Is there something wrong with it?" The dark and fitted dress hugged what I had for curves, extending down past my knees except for the slit up the thigh.

He rolled his eyes to the ceiling, muttering to himself before grimacing and shaking his head. "Nope. Great, let's go," he said, turning to stroll down the hallway for the stairs.

"Wait, we're just going to walk out the front door?" I asked.

"Yes, hurry up or we'll miss our window," he grunted, taking my hand in his and hurrying me down the stairs. One of my father's security men stood there, facing the wall on the opposite side and diligently pretending he didn't see us as we pulled the doors open and stepped outside.

"What about my father?" I asked.

"Gone to the stables for the night. They brought in a couple girls from New York, so he'll be occupied until morning," Christian said as he shoved me into the backseat of the waiting car. He climbed in beside me, tapping the back of the headrest and signaling the driver proceed down the driveway as I fought back the surge of nausea at the thought of my father being occupied with the escorts.

"What about Lydia?" I asked. "If she wakes up and notices I'm gone, this will all be for nothing."

"Sleeping pill in her wine. No one will notice you're gone as long as you get back before morning. We should be safely back on the property by four a.m. Understood?" he asked, nodding to my watch. "Can you set an alarm on that thing?"

I took my phone from my bag, setting an alarm for three in the morning just to be safe as the driver made his way down the road. Without a single glance toward the backseat, he seemed determined to pretend he hadn't seen me. As if I wasn't in his car, and he wasn't defying my father's very strict orders that I be kept at the house with very few exceptions.

Namely, when he or my step-mother accompanied me to required outings.

We pulled up to a hotel in the center of the city, and I quickly changed out my flats for heels before allowing Christian to pull me from the car. "Aren't we too close?"

"We can't go too far if we want to get you home in time. Nobody will recognize you here. I've cleared the guest list, and aside from you, only hotel patrons will be allowed tonight. It may limit your—" he swallowed down his distaste "—options, but it will keep you alive."

I nodded, biting my lip hesitantly before lunging at him for a quick hug. "Thank you," I mumbled.

"Don't thank me just yet," he said, his voice catching with emotion. "Just be safe, yeah?"

"Of course," I said, watching as he got back into the car and waited. Turning and striding into the hotel, I made my way to the elevators to go to the rooftop bar. With my heart in my throat, I almost couldn't hear the quiet melody of the elevator music. The numbers on the panel rose one by one, lighting up as if counting down my last chance to change my mind.

There would be no backing out for me; not if I wanted to be able to look myself in the mirror come morning.

Having an adventure meant taking risks. I would just have to do whatever it took to make sure that I was the only one who paid the price for what I would do.

As the elevator doors opened, the steady thrum of jazz filled the night air. Stars twinkled vaguely overhead, drowned out even on the rooftop by the light pollution of the city. Deciding to make my way to the center of the space, I headed straight for the bar with my nerves threatening to tear me in two. The bartender's eyes met mine briefly as I approached, and she smirked once before she went back to her work and poured a glass of white wine.

I sat on a stool, curling my hand around the glass of wine that landed in front of me. "I didn't order this," I said, pushing it back toward her with a shy smile.

"It's on the house, honey. I know when a woman just needs a drink," she said.

"Is it that obvious?" I asked, raising the glass to my lips and taking a sip. The bitterness of the liquid caught me by surprise, coating my tongue in a dry flavor that wasn't entirely pleasant.

"Not a fan of wine?" she asked with a chuckle, and I shook my head shyly.

"Not a drinker of anything, to be honest," I said, forcing down another sip. I knew people swore by the way alcohol made them relax, and if anyone needed that tonight? It was me. I was about to lose my virginity to a stranger and risk certain death if I was caught.

"You should be careful of your surroundings if you aren't used to drinking, Little One," a male voice said behind me. I spun in the stool, the name that fell off his lips nearly making me tumble to the floor with the suddenness of the movement. My eyes landed on his the moment he reached out his hands to catch me around the waist, steadying me so I didn't topple to the floor. His hands seared me through the fabric of my dress, an inescapable heat that sank beneath the surface of my flesh and dug straight into the core of who I was.

"Sorry," I mumbled, sliding my ass further onto the stool. His hands never left my waist, one of his thighs tucked between my knees ever so slightly. Still, his gaze stayed focused on mine. Not on the heaving of my breasts as they shoved higher with each lungful of air I sucked back in my nervousness.

"Exactly how much have you had to drink?" he asked, his lips quirking to the side with the barest hint of a smile. Those stunning metallic eyes shone down at me, making my heart race in my chest. While I had no doubt that they were blue or some other enviable color, I couldn't help but be reminded of the silver of Calix's eyes.

Of his boyishly handsome face as he'd made me believe that someone in the world cared about me.

"It wasn't that," I admitted with a flush as I tore my eyes from his. My hand slid down the fabric of his suit jacket, clasping his forearm in my grip. I started to grip him so that I could push away his touch, but stopped at the last moment with a twist of my lips. "Nobody has called me Little One in a very long time. You surprised me, is all."

"Hmm," he hummed thoughtfully, grasping the stool next to me in one of his hands. He tugged it closer, settling on the seat and enclosing my legs inside his until I felt trapped. The movement didn't fill me with fear as I might have expected, though, only serving to give me the sense that he would protect me from whatever dangers might be lurking around the room.

I took another sip of wine to steady myself, wondering how on earth women understood the rules of picking up a man. He might have been interested, but he also could have merely acted out of interest in being gentlemanly and keeping me from making a foolish mistake.

Perhaps he simply saw through the bravado I'd tried to don the moment I'd walked into the bar.

"So not Little One, then," he murmured, and something inside my chest eased. I wouldn't have been able to go to bed with a man who called me the same pet name as Calix. It would have felt like a betrayal to all that he'd meant to me once upon a time. "So what should I call you?"

I wrinkled my nose, running my finger over the base of my wine glass to calm the urge that wanted to make me fidget in my seat. "Nothing," I said softly. "No names."

He raised his brows at me, huffing out a light, shocked laugh. He paused for a moment, studying my face as he tried to understand my motivation. I knew it must have seemed ridiculous not to give someone even my first name, but I needed to stay detached.

One night of sex. One time to feel like maybe I was using the man just as much as he used me.

"If I don't tell you my name, what will you scream when I make you come tonight?" he asked, his full lips tipping into an arrogant smirk that caught the breath in my lungs. I bit my lip, turning my face away as my cheeks heated. "That is what you're looking for, isn't it, my beauty?"

"I haven't even told you my name, and you already think to own me?" I said with more snap than intended. Doubt coursed through me, wondering if it was even possible to have even one pleasant experience. People did it all the time, so I had to believe there was someone in this bar who would be able to give me what I wanted.

He just might not be quite as breathtaking as the man in front of me, with his dark hair and sinfully light eyes shining down at me. "For tonight. I am not a man who plays games or beats around the bush when it comes to what I want," he said, leaning forward to rest his palm on the bare skin just above my knee.

"And what is it you want?" I asked, staring down at that hand.

"The same thing I expect brought you here, sitting in a bar alone and swearing off names," he chuckled. Another man stepped up to us, opening his mouth to speak briefly before a single glare from my handsome stranger sent him scurrying away.

"That was hardly necessary," I said with a laugh.

"I don't share," he growled in warning.

I lifted his hand off my knee, standing in the small space between his legs and grabbing my wine glass. "Well, I suppose it is fortunate for me that you don't own me. I'll seek my entertainment elsewhere." Moving to step out from the trap of his spread legs, I winced when he didn't budge. Even with the crowd of people filling the rooftop and the bartender behind me watching us with rapt attention, dread filled me at the thought of having to deal with a forceful man.

I'd had enough of men who thought to take from me without giving a single thought to what I might want.

"Release me," I hissed, watching as his eyes lit in response to the challenge in my voice.

"If I were to do that, we would lose out on a very valuable opportunity that we are now presented with," he said, flashing me his perfect teeth in a broad grin. "You're angry with me. I would very much like to have all that fire wrapped around me while I fuck you, my beauty," he added, stretching out a hand to cup my cheek in his hand. I jerked back from the contact, glaring at him as his hand followed and settled against the side of my neck. His thumb stroked over the delicate cord of my throat, leaving me with a feeling of vulnerability that I was all too used to. But whereas when my father hurt me all I felt was pain and fear, the stranger's touch evoked something different altogether.

Heat bloomed between my thighs, my body warming in the way it did when I read romance novels in my bed at night. Biting my tongue to stifle my reaction and the moan that threatened to surface, I stared up at him in shock. I hadn't pictured a hate fuck for my first time, not with being a virgin.

I'd imagined someone gentler, something sweeter, but there was no denying the reaction in my body and the appeal of his words. When I read, it wasn't the sweet lovemaking scenes that forced my hand between my legs to relieve the ache, but the rough and passionate ones that left me breathless.

His touch promised all the things I'd read about; the very desire I'd only ever dreamt of having. He was silent as he watched me process my choices, studying the features of my face as if he could see every thought as it floated through my mind. I should have said no.

I should have called Christian to take me home before I made a mistake that I could never undo.

"Do you have a room?" I asked instead, my pulse thumping against his thumb where he stroked over it with gentle pressure.

He nodded, his light eyes turning wolfish as he drew his hand away from my neck and tucked it around my waist. The moment I was pressed into his side, he strode toward the elevators, guiding me to the place where he'd take what I would give and seal my fate.

For better or worse.

14

CALIX

My hand at her waist felt like it had always belonged there. Like the more than a decade of separation had changed both of us in synchronization somehow, and we'd grown into the perfect match for the people we'd grown to be as adults.

On the other side of our tragedy, she was mine and I was hers.

She just didn't know it yet.

Her silence grated at me, and I knew I needed to try to be mindful of her virginity. While I'd watched her fingers dance over her clit at night and slip inside her tight heat, she'd always been cautious. The knowledge that her betrothed would expect her to be a virgin, and she'd been saving that for him, only served to drive my need higher to claim her and make her mine. By the end of the night, I alone would know what she felt like on the inside.

As I shoved open the door to my suite, I tried to convince myself it didn't matter that she hadn't recognized me. There was no shame in that, because she'd only been a girl when I'd left. Even if I'd have recognized her anywhere, life hadn't been kind to Thalia. I didn't know what it was like to go through life in shades of gray, but I imagined it made people less recognizable. All light eyes looked the same. All dark hair looked the same.

She stepped inside hesitantly, her back straighter than a rod and her head held high to look every bit the princess her father had tried to mold her into, but Thalia was never meant to be a princess or a queen. She'd been born to be a warrior.

To bathe in the blood of our enemies.

I closed the door behind me gently, moving into the suite to stand behind her. She stilled at the feeling of my chest against her back, her breath hitching in a way that I instinctively knew wasn't in desire. It would take time to get rid of those impulses, of her instinctual expectation of pain.

Gathering her dark curtain of hair in my grip, I pulled it over one shoulder and revealed her smooth olive skin to my gaze. There wasn't a blemish marking the top of her shoulder, only the faint remainder of a welt across her shoulder blades that made me grit my teeth. She moved as if she might step away, freezing when I gripped her hair tighter and pulled her head to the side. Careful not to pull, only to put her where I wanted her, I moved slowly until my lips touched her skin.

A gasp escaped her, making me wish I'd positioned her in a way that I could see her face. Instead, I trailed my lips over the delicate flesh, touching gentle kisses and working to start preparing her to take what I would give her.

She allowed it for a few moments, her slim body writhing against me as desire built in her. "I thought you were going to fuck me," she murmured softly, a teasing challenge to the words that made me smile against her skin. Spreading my mouth open, I sank my teeth into her shoulder to suppress the fight.

She moaned, her voice breathy as I released her and spun

her to face me. With a hand still buried in her hair, I tilted her head back until she had no choice but to look up at me. When her pouty lips parted slightly, the desire to taste her came over me. Leaning forward slowly, I brushed my lips against hers. She held my stare, and I willed her to feel me.

To see me.

Her hands came up to rest against my chest as I pulled away, touching my forehead to hers and wondering what it would take for her to see me as I was. For who I was. Would she remain oblivious until the moment I revealed myself? The thought bothered me more than it should.

I leaned forward, touching my lips to hers again and tracing the parted seam with my tongue. She moaned for me, opening wider as I slid inside and claimed her mouth as mine. The first part of her to be possessed by me, the first part of her that I would take. As she adjusted to the softness of my kiss and the slow and erotic tangle of our tongues, I exerted more pressure.

Her eyes drifted closed finally as I plundered her mouth. She inhaled suddenly when I released her hair, dragging a hand down over her arm to grab the zipper at the back of her dress. Slowly pulling it down, I waited for the moment when she'd come to her senses and realize the dangers of being so reckless.

For the moment when she'd walk away, not knowing that what would happen between us was inevitable. Whether it happened here and now or on our wedding night was her choice, but in the end Thalia would be mine and mine alone.

Instead, she pulled her lips away from mine and brushed the straps of her dress off her shoulders. The forest-green fabric dropped to her waist, bunching around her hips until she slid her hands down to it and shimmied out of it. She stood nearly naked in front of me with a tease in her eyes as she backed away a step, unconcerned with the fact that it was the first time she'd been nude with a man. Only a scrap of lace covering her pussy hid her from my view, her small breasts high and perky on her frame without a bra.

The high heels on her feet made her legs look even longer, and she bit her lip as a trace of insecurity filled her face when I didn't move. Wrongly assuming I might not want her, when the reality was that I couldn't move or take my eyes off her.

Finally shrugging my jacket off my shoulders, I tossed it over the back of the armchair at the side of the room. Thalia's eyes narrowed in on my fingers as I worked open the buttons of my shirt one by one. I smirked at her when her eyes heated, throwing my shirt to join the jacket and then stripping off my shoes and pants. "Last chance, my beauty," I murmured. Every second that the words sat between us made my deception worse. Every time I used the name that didn't belong to her, it struck against the deepest part of me. We were finally reunited, but still so far away.

I left my boxer briefs on for the moment, closing the distance between us again. She tilted her head up to accept the kiss I didn't give her, instead taking her waist in my hands and tossing her onto the bed behind her. She giggled as she bounced against the surface, the sound trailing off as I climbed up and spread her legs to slip my hips between them.

My cock nestled against her pussy, her heat like a brand through the only clothing remaining. With the warmth in her amber eyes, I leaned my weight over hers. Pebbled nipples rubbed against my chest, driving me mad with the need to drive inside her.

I kissed her, groaning when her cautious hand slid between us to touch my cock. She nipped my bottom lip before pulling away. "If I wanted gentle, I could have picked a dozen other men," she said. A warning grumbled in my chest;

the very idea of her choosing anyone but me would have been disastrous for all involved.

I'd kill anyone who dared to touch her.

"Fuck me," she ordered.

"I'll hurt you," I returned, raising an eyebrow at her. I couldn't say any more than that, because the knowledge that she was a virgin wasn't something a stranger would have. As much as I'd wanted Thalia to recognize me, it was truly for the best that she hadn't.

She nodded. "I want it to hurt," she said, a questioning hurt filling her gaze. She couldn't understand that there was nothing wrong with having desires like that, and she'd never be able to fulfill them in a safe way with a husband she couldn't trust, but everything about our first time would be wrong if I gave her what she asked for.

She deserved so much more than to be brutally fucked by a stranger in a hotel, and everything inside me rebelled against what had become of her, and that this was how desperate she was for the ability to make her own choice even once. It seemed like such a simple thing to anyone else. Her right as a human being.

But for her it was an act of rebellion at best. Suicide at worst, because if her father found out what she'd done, if Damianos rejected her if he realized the truth?

Origen would have no use for her.

It was very fortunate for my Little One that she would never marry Damianos.

I leaned forward, nipping her bottom lip before surging inside her mouth. I kissed her like I wanted to consume her, painting every corner of her with my possession. With only our undergarments between us, she squirmed beneath me. Rolling her hips against the outline of my cock, she gasped into my mouth at the pressure it put on her clit. I was overwhelmed with the need to feel her slick heat rubbing against me, to glide through her parted lips and drive her mad with teasing thrusts long before I ever slid inside her. But Thalia would need to know who was in charge, and her very demand for me to fuck her before I was ready went against everything I knew about myself.

As my wife, she'd need to know exactly what to expect from me, and there was no time like the present to start with her education.

I pulled her hands away from my body, pinning them to the bed beside her hips as she narrowed her gaze up at me. "I think you've misread the situation," I purred, gliding my lips away from her mouth and toward the sensitive skin of her neck. I trailed them over her skin, feeling her squirm and press up against me as her body was lost to the instinct that lurked inside her. "You aren't in charge of anything when you're in my bed, my beauty."

"Unless you live in a hotel, I'm not sure how that's relevant," she said quickly. The comeback came with such ease that I chuckled hoarsely. The very fact that she had one after being so beaten down by the life I couldn't protect her from proved everything I'd always known about her.

She was stronger than anyone imagined.

"If you're in it, it's my bed," I murmured, biting her ear briefly before gliding down over her collarbone to touch my lips to the swell of her breast. She shuddered beneath me, her body going taut as she prepared for the contact she'd so desperately craved. With my hands occupied with pinning her down, all I had to work with was my mouth.

It was enough.

"I think your logic is faulty," she gasped as I sank my teeth into her flesh, biting harder than I should in my desperation to mark her. "Don't," she warned, seeming to realize the dangers of returning home to her stepmother with bruises. It took everything in me to pull back and gently run my tongue over the mark.

Releasing one of her wrists, I gripped her breast in my palm as my mouth found her other nipple. Her back arched off the bed as her free hand plunged into my hair. Grasping and pulling at the short strands, she kept me pressed tightly to her as I worshiped her and every inch of her torso with my mouth. By the time I'd slid down between her legs, she quivered beneath me with desperation. Her eyes met mine as I tugged her underwear down her thighs and tossed them to the side.

She spread her legs wider for me without me needing to ask, her body bared to me without a hint of hesitation. She didn't need to care what I thought of her when she thought she would never see me again, and she most definitely didn't want to waste the opportunity to feel what she probably never would again.

Men like Damianos had no need to make sure their wives enjoyed their sex life. Not when they were already paid for and unable to escape.

Pinning her arms to her sides once more, I moved slowly into her, holding her eyes as I ran my tongue from her entrance to her clit in a smooth glide. She moaned, shoving her hips up at me harder in an attempt to get more pressure as I kept the touch of my mouth against her soft. "What do you want, my beauty?" I murmured.

"More."

"Manners," I reprimanded her, gently biting into the soft flesh of her thigh.

"Please," she groaned. Smirking into her flesh, I dove forward and gave her everything she wanted. I devoured her with intense sweeps of my tongue, shoving it inside her and fucking her with it while she gasped and moaned. "Fucking please," she begged again, squirming until my mouth returned to her clit. I wrapped my lips around it, sucking it lightly and working it with my tongue until she shattered beneath me. Her eyes squeezed shut, separating me from her in those intense moments of her orgasm. I determined in that moment that her next one would be with her eyes on mine. That I'd watch as the pleasure consumed her.

When her breathing relaxed and she opened those stunning eyes, I released her hands and crawled off the bed. I wanted nothing more than to pretend the condom waiting in my pants pocket didn't exist, so desperate to feel her pussy wrapped around me with nothing between us. But a one-night stand would wear a condom, and I wanted there to be no doubt that our future child was conceived when she was already my wife.

Tearing the packet open with my teeth, I watched the first tendril of caution settle over Thalia's features that I'd come to recognize as well as my own in the time since I'd started watching her obsessively. "Last chance," I said, a challenge in my tone.

Daring her to back down was the fastest way to ensure she followed through, because there was no possibility of her leaving my bed as a virgin. Not after what we'd started.

She raised her chin, watching as I shoved my boxer briefs down and rolled the condom onto my cock. Her lips parted in shock for a moment, the reality of what was about to be inside her giving her another moment of pause.

Prowling onto the bed between her legs, I settled over her and spread her wide. With the wet heat of her pussy searing me even through the condom, I slid through her oversensitive flesh as I watched her face. The smart thing would be for her to give a stranger a warning. To tell him that he was about to fuck a virgin so he might have a chance to be more gentle with her.

But even as I gave Thalia the opportunity to be honest with me, she kept her lips firmly clamped around her secret.

With a ragged groan, I notched myself at her entrance and watched her face. Even though I wanted to have my lips on hers when I first slid inside her, I forced myself to keep separated, to watch her face and give her the chance to tell me if it was too much or too fast.

I drove inside, shoving through her tender tissue more quickly than I should, given what I knew. Even with the force of it, I couldn't get far. Not with the way she was choking the life out of my cock. She groaned, bending her neck so that she curled in on herself as a startled scream caught in her throat. "Something you need to tell me, Beauty?" I asked, pulling back and then pressing forward again. "Because this feels like something I should know."

"Fuck you," she hissed, baring her teeth at me as she reached down to grab my ass. She pulled me closer, impaling herself on my cock as I pressed through that barrier inside her, then yelped, leaning up to press her mouth to my shoulder. Teeth sinking into my flesh, she marked me in the way I wanted to mark her.

When she finally settled back onto the bed, I moved inside her with slow but firm thrusts, taking her in the way I wanted and touching my lips to hers. Our breath mingled as she wrapped her legs around my waist.

Slowly the pinch of pain on her face faded to something else entirely, shock flooding her features as she realized the depths of pleasure that could be found with me inside her. With one hand wrapped around to hold the back of her thigh, I slid the other beneath her neck and held her exactly where I wanted her. She took me deep, accepting the pounding pressure as her pussy spasmed around me with a coming orgasm.

I wanted it. Wanted to keep it for myself.

"Eyes on me," I ordered, touching my forehead to hers. The intimacy of the moment was something I'd never dreamed to have, because it wouldn't have made sense with anyone but Thalia. She'd always been meant to be mine.

Her breath caught in her throat as she came with nothing but the movement of my cock inside her, her amber eyes turning molten as her pussy choked the cum out of my cock and I followed her over the edge in a blinding release of my own and filled the condom.

She lay beneath me, panting for breath as I dreaded what came next.

Knowing she would walk away from me wouldn't stop the sting when she actually did it.

15

THALIA

The loss of the stranger immediately settled over me as he pulled out. He left me in the bed to dispose of the condom, and that empty hollowness that had threatened since the moment my mother had died claimed me once more.

I'd been foolish to risk everything for one night with a stranger who didn't even know my name. I'd risked leaving Malva entirely vulnerable if anyone discovered what I'd done. Considering that I had to behave for the right to even spend time with my younger sister, my father wouldn't hesitate to remove me from her life entirely.

I'd be a bad influence on her, and in that moment, my father's voice that echoed in my head was right. I would never have allowed her to do something like this. Not knowing what the cost might be.

I sat on the edge of the bed, curling my fingers around the edge of the mattress as the sore place between my thighs throbbed with pain.

And for what?

Pushing to my feet, I grabbed my underwear off the floor

where he'd tossed them and tugged them up my thighs. I winced when the wet mess between my legs touched the fabric, but using the bathroom was the last thing on my mind.

I needed to get home before someone noticed I was gone.

"You wound me, trying to sneak off without even saying goodbye," the stranger said as he stepped out of the bathroom. He hadn't bothered to cover his manhood, leaving it to swing indecently between his legs. Even softening after his orgasm, the length caught my eyes and I couldn't help but wonder exactly how that had fit inside me.

"My apologies, I know you care about my manners," I spat, turning to give him my back as I grabbed my dress off the floor.

The air around me went still as I stood straight, and I glanced over my shoulder to find him staring at the scars criss-crossing my back and the flesh of my ass intently. His nostrils were flared, his jaw tightly clenched.

I shut mine briefly, drawing in a deep breath as I realized my mistake. The light from the open bathroom door illuminated the faint white lines that had faded over the years. It had been a long time since I'd done something to earn a caning quite like those.

Raising my arms to pull my dress over my head, I winced as rough fingers ran along the thick scar on my lower back. "He will get what's coming to him," he said, leaning forward to touch his lips to the scar. My skin twitched beneath his mouth, the gentleness and care in the contact drawing a shiver from me.

I would never know such a sweet touch again.

"Who said it was a he?" I asked, trying to deflect from the well of emotion surging inside of me. My father wasn't the only abuser in that house of nightmares, and even though the worst of the blows had come from his steady and unrelenting hand, my stepmother had never been innocent.

Neither had the many guards who'd watched my father abuse and humiliate me, getting off on the searing pain that split my skin in half.

The stranger took my dress in his hands, tossing it to the chair at the side of the room as he grasped my chin in his grip and turned me to face him. "You're beautiful, even more so now."

"Sounds like you have a kink for hurting women," I snarled, flinching back as his lips came closer to mine. The heat of his breath against my swollen flesh reminded me of all the savagery in his kiss when he'd taken me, bringing a flush of heat to my sore core that I wished I could deny.

Nothing about this conversation should have been a turn on. Talking about my caning with a stranger who would never be able to understand the misery of a life that wasn't my own should have cooled all the impulses that seemed to drive me toward him relentlessly.

I couldn't explain the connection or the feeling that I'd met him before. That I somehow knew him or that he meant the words when he said that the person who hurt me would get what was coming to him.

Those plush lips of his brushed against my cheek as his light eyes drifted closed. "I have a lot of kinks, but that is not one of them," he said with a smirk. "A mysterious, strong woman who bears the scars of her abuse without fear however..." He slipped a hand around the front of my hip and between my thighs. His fingers slid inside my underwear and through the wet mess he'd left, a groan rattling in his chest when my hips moved of their own accord and my ass pressed into his hardening length. "That, my cock can't seem to get enough of."

He dipped a finger inside me, watching my face for the pain he knew I must have felt. I didn't give him a reaction, keeping my face as stoic as possible. While I didn't think he would hurt me or use my pain against me, I needed the distance between us. My scars out in the open had left me feeling vulnerable, knowing that I'd dreaded the moment the rejection came from any man who saw me without my clothes.

Who wanted to look at an ass covered in white lines?

"How sore are you?" he asked, walking forward and maneuvering my body so I had no choice but to move with him. The bed loomed closer and the breath caught in my lungs from the implication that I wouldn't be leaving the room just yet.

I still had time, but was I able to take him back inside me so soon? With all my old vulnerabilities in the open? The scars made me more *me*, not just a strange girl in the night who would be gone by morning.

My knees and thighs hit the edge of the mattress, and his hand touched the space between my shoulder blades. He pressed me forward, bringing panic to the surface as memories threatened to overwhelm me.

I whimpered, and his hand stilled so suddenly I knew he must have understood that it wasn't a whimper of anticipation. My heart thumped in my chest as I squeezed my eyes tightly shut, trying to chase away the phantom hands of my stepmother tasked with putting me into position, pinning my hands to the surface and reminding me that it was my own fault.

Trying to remind myself that the softness of the mattress was different than the cold wood of my father's desk.

"It's just me, my beauty. I will never hurt you," he murmured, sweeping my hair off my neck. He paused, waiting for a moment to allow me to catch my breath and chase away the shadows of my nightmare. "You didn't answer me."

His voice took on a teasing lilt, pushing back the demons as that inexplicable urge to argue with him rose in me.

Not because he was wrong, but because I could.

He wouldn't cane me for talking back or tell me to remember my place; he'd take anything I said with a grin and enjoy the banter for what it was. I hummed, considering my answer as I tried to embrace my last moments of freedom before I went back to my gilded cage.

"I'm not sure you fucked me hard enough for that," I murmured. His deep chuckle vibrated the air behind my back, his hand returning to my shoulders and pressing me forward until I bent over the bed. When my nipples brushed against the bedding, they pebbled in response to the friction as his hand trailed down over my spine and made me arch my back.

His weight disappeared from behind me for a moment, and the crinkle of a foil packet sounded. When he returned, he peeled my panties down and let them bunch around my knees. The swollen head of his cock slid between my legs and rubbed against me as he groaned. "We'll have to fix that then," he said, not bothering to call me out on the lie. He trusted me to know my body better than he did, and even though he was a stranger that made something pang inside my chest.

A dull ache that reminded me of all I'd lost, and everything I would never have again.

He slid inside me, pounding deep enough on the first stroke that I cried out as the ache flared to life. "But I thought you weren't sore, Beauty?" he asked, gripping my hips in his hands and tugging me back further onto his cock. He brushed against the end of me, threatening to fuck through me if he got any deeper.

"I think you're terribly full of yourself," I said, my voice arching higher as he drew back and pounded inside me again.

"No, Little One," he said, his voice dropping lower as my heart seized in my chest. Even as a coincidence, the name was wrong to hear a man say as he moved inside me. A bastardization of everything Calix had meant to me.

But Calix was gone. He'd left me behind and moved on with his life without once trying to come back for me to save me from what he knew must have been a miserable existence. The man who slid his cock through my pussy was real flesh and blood, and warm.

Making me feel for the first time since I'd lost Calix and my mother to my father's vindictiveness.

"You are the one full of me," he growled, wrapping my hair up in his hand and pulling back. I rose up to my hands, moaning as his hips slapped against my ass and he set a punishing rhythm. He didn't seem concerned about the scars covering my skin or anything other than chasing his release inside me. The weighted stare of his eyes on those marks on my ass should have made me uncomfortable; instead it only drove me higher. Being seen for who and what I was and still found beautiful was heady. "Touch yourself," he ordered.

When I didn't move to do just that, he reached between the mattress and my body. Pulling me back from the edge of the bed slightly, he slapped his fingers against my pussy just hard enough that I jolted in his grip. "What the hell?" I asked as he shoved deep and held still.

With his head pressed against the end of me, the pressure felt endless. "When I tell you to do something, you fucking do it," he growled. His hand left my pussy, gliding up to where I grasped the bedding tightly and grabbing one to position between my legs. "You expect me to believe that these beautiful fingers don't dance over your pretty little pussy when you lie in bed at night?" he asked, guiding them into a slow roll over my clit as he drew his length out and then drove back in sharply. "You're going to need the pleasure when I'm done with you."

He abandoned my hand there, pausing for a moment to make sure that I did as he told me. His hand traveled up to my throat, grasping me around the front and pulling my back into his chest as he fucked me. My breathing restricted, my head going light until all that remained was the feel of him pounding up into me. His warm breath on my cheek as he panted and groaned his pleasure.

Still, my fingers circled my clit frantically, driving my pleasure higher to combat what would undoubtedly make me very sore come morning. "Fuck," I whispered as my vision blurred, the shadows of the room fading into bright white light that overtook my senses.

My ears rang with the force of my orgasm, only faintly aware of the driving thrusts of his cock still moving inside me and the brutal roar of his orgasm as he pulled me down onto his cock and came.

When he released my throat, I fell forward. My body went limp and languid, and I cherished the moments when there was no consequence. When there wasn't the threat of nightmares looming on the other side of sleep, and I could just curl into the bed he placed me in peacefully.

He left for a moment, returning quickly and curling himself around my body. "Sleep, Little One."

Sleep evaded me, knowing I needed to leave shortly enough, but I allowed myself to enjoy the way his breathing evened out as he found his own rest.

It was only after he'd fallen asleep that panic seized my lungs and sent me hurrying from the bed as quietly as I could.

My heart wanted to let him in, to accept him as someone I could care for when I could never.

But that wasn't what had made me panic.

He'd somehow known to guide my left hand between my legs.

16

THALIA

"Thalia!" Malva hissed in a whisper, drawing me out of my distracted musings. The eleven-year-old rolled her eyes at me as I startled and pressed a hand to my chest. "Are you living in a dream today?"

"I'm sorry," I said sheepishly, a blush tinting my cheeks. "I don't know where my head is today." The night before had played in my brain on repeat since I'd managed to tuck myself safely back inside my bedroom in the early morning hours with no one the wiser that I'd ever been missing.

I alternated between heat-inducing thoughts that made me crave my stranger's touch once more, and the terror that something had gone horribly wrong. Had he somehow known I was left-handed?

It wasn't possible for him to have seen something and drawn that conclusion in our night together. To use my right hand when people were there to witness was deeply ingrained in me.

The only time I used my left was to draw, and even then I began with my right and shifted because I just couldn't sketch properly with my right.

I shoved the thoughts aside, knowing if there were to be some consequence for my rebellion, it would come with or without me fretting over it.

With the wedding only a month away, I intended to enjoy the limited time I was allowed with my sister before it became even harder to see her. In truth, if it hadn't been for Malva's safety hanging over my head, I would have run long ago.

I'd have freed myself from the chains of my life and what this marriage promised to be for me. It wouldn't have mattered if I needed to take out my father's men to gain that freedom, but I couldn't risk Malva.

I couldn't take her with me; not without risking her being harmed or worse in the crossfire. Leaving her behind just was not an option, because I knew what happened when my father lost an outlet for his abuse.

My mother's death had shifted the entirety of his focus to me for the time before my stepmother came and embraced his darkness.

"Did you have a bad dream again?" my sister asked, concern twisting her features. It wasn't uncommon for my screams to wake the house and for an urgent banging at my door to startle me awake. The sleep aids they made me take to prevent that usually kept the nightmares at bay.

"I just couldn't sleep is all," I said evasively. She pursed her lips but nodded before prattling on about her day at school. I smiled through the bitterness that our lives in the same household were so vastly different. She was the treasured daughter, the one who knew no harm and could do no wrong.

Whereas I'd been born defective and punished for it every day of my life.

After my mother's death, I hadn't even been allowed to leave for school, having private tutors brought to educate me without the corruption of outside influences. "And what did

Percy do after Cassandra threw the stone at you?" I asked, humoring the crush she seemed to have on the boy she saw infrequently at the gatherings of the families. If my father ever learned of her feelings for him—fleeting and innocent as they were, considering they were both children—there was no telling what he would do.

"He threw it back at her and told her to stop being a nasty hag," Malva said, bright laughter tinting her sweet voice.

She was older than I'd been when my innocence was stripped away, and the mistake I'd made the night before only made me more resolved to make sure she kept that for as long as possible.

Malva could never know what a pool of blood looked like or the sound of a blade cutting through flesh.

I'd die before I let anything stain her in the way I'd been ruined. Because in a life of misery?

She was the only thing I loved.

17

CALIX

One month later

Christian climbed into the backseat of the SUV beside me, the cane clutched tightly in his grip. He handed it over the moment the door closed and Lex pulled away from the driveway. Christian accepted the towel I handed him, wiping his blood-stained hands on it and glaring at the red caked underneath his fingernails. "Any survivors?" I asked, not bothering to take my eyes off the weapon in my hands.

By the time I finished with Origen, he'd be lucky if I hadn't shoved it so far up his ass it came out his mouth.

"Everyone who was in the house is taken care of," he said. There wasn't a hint of remorse for killing the men he'd been forced to work alongside in his time watching over Thalia, but he also didn't dare disobey my orders in the slightest.

I'd known Thalia suffered at her father's hands, but I'd never known the extent he'd gone to correcting her "unsatisfactory" behavior. The whiteness of her scars made me believe that she'd had them long before I'd planted Christian.

That was the only reason he still breathed, because I couldn't expect him to protect her from something that had happened before his arrival. That responsibility fell on my shoulders alone.

Having him retrieve the cane had been a risk. If anyone in the Karras Estate had managed to contact someone, my plans would've gone out the window quickly. But I couldn't explain the need for the cane, beyond the need to get Thalia the revenge she so desperately deserved.

And that cane would be a part of it.

"The church?" Lex asked from the front.

"Yes. Is everyone ready and waiting?" I asked, holding his gaze in the rearview mirror.

"All are in position," Rafael said, turning to look back at me. "You ready for this? For her to know who you are?"

"The next time she comes on my cock, it will be my name on her lips. What do you think?" I asked, raising an eyebrow at him. Rafael chuckled, that deep, twisted laugh that made men quiver in fear.

I had no doubt he was occupied by thoughts of the girl he'd left in Chicago. Watching and waiting for her to be old enough to claim.

We pulled onto the street where the church waited. "Has it started?"

"Just about to get to the 'I do's," Rafael said, glancing down at his phone and the updates he received regularly from our contact inside. Not all of the five families had been pleased by the turn of events twelve years ago that had led us here.

I nodded as the SUV pulled up directly in front of the church, watching as my men poured out of the vehicles lining the street and emerged from alleys.

By the time we were done, the church would be bathed in the blood of everyone Thalia knew.

And she would be my wife.

18

THALIA

I was going to die. If my heart didn't give out and my body didn't crumple to the floor in a pile of flesh and blood right there at the altar, Damianos would kill me when he realized I wasn't a virgin. My stranger's somehow intimate knowledge that I was left-handed naturally had left me feeling like I'd walked into a trap. Like this entire thing was a stage, and I'd end up in the pit where my mother had died.

I couldn't even look at the man next to me, and he was about to be my husband. Only minutes separated me from being Thalia Hasapis, and his dark eyes were inquisitive as he stared at me in his peripheral vision. The priest continued with his rambling rant as if anyone cared about God's wishes when I was in a church filled with murderers and thieves.

"Do you, Thalia, take Damianos to be your lawfully wedded husband?" The room seemed to vibrate around me, a buzzing sound filling my ears as I tried to process the words I'd known were coming. Still, I went rigid. My world ended, narrowing down to the memory of a stranger's hands on me, of his mouth and his body against mine.

Did I take the man I'd never wanted? I didn't know if I

could live my life knowing that real passion was out there, but never being able to reach out and grab it for myself.

My mouth dropped open to answer, the only words I could ever truly give in the situation. The choice had been taken from me before I'd even known what marriage was. The name and the face of my husband were irrelevant.

The result would be the same.

I should just be grateful that he didn't appear to be an overly cruel man. He had high expectations of me, but he wasn't the same kind of monster as my father. He'd be a step up from my life at home.

Of all the men who might have won the right to marry me in ο λάκκος, Damianos was arguably the best of my choices. Even still, I couldn't make my lips form the words.

Damianos clenched his jaw as he watched my reaction, his anger palpable in the air as he waited. I knew every second of hesitation was an embarrassment that I would likely suffer for, both from my soon-to-be husband and my father. His hand tightened on mine as he turned me to face him, his face transforming with a brief understanding. "I will protect you, η νύφη μου."

I raised my eyes to his finally, my heart filling with a moment of hope. Perhaps he wouldn't kill me when he discovered the truth. "I—"

My voice cut off as a scream tore through the chapel, and I craned my neck to face the door. Something hot and wet splashed against my cheek, and I nearly fell to my knees as Damianos dropped to the floor. His grip on my hand nearly dragged me down with him, and I gasped as his head struck against the wood floor. The gaping hole where his eye had been stared back at me, his other eye staring up, blank and unseeing.

Prying my fingers free desperately, I reached up to wipe

the wetness from my face. They came away stained with dark, viscous fluid. I'd seen enough of it, felt enough of it on my skin, to know exactly what it was.

Blood.

The blood of the man who would have been my husband. I spun to face the doorway and the crowd of men filling the back of the chapel with assault weapons in their grips, but it wasn't the crowd or impending death that stole the breath from my lungs.

It was the shockingly familiar face tucked just behind the barrel of a pistol with a silencer attached to the front. The light eyes that studied me intently, cold and unyielding. No trace of the teasing amusement or dominant lover I'd met a month before remained, but there was no doubt that they were one and the same.

Damianos's mother screamed, lunging to her feet in the audience and finally drawing my eyes to her and away from the man I'd never thought to see again. Her chest shook as my stranger turned his gun to her, firing two shots into her breast. Inky black bloomed on the fabric of her dress as she staggered and then fell to the floor, the rest of the people in the chapel finally vaulting to their feet in panic.

Jeno and my father pulled out their own weapons as the five families erupted into chaos and bullets exploded everywhere. Despite the gunfire, the stranger from the hotel lowered his gun and stalked up the center aisle toward me. His eyes never left mine, leaving no doubt to his intent as the lightness in them shone with fury.

I darted forward, snatching Malva's hand in mine and yanking her away from her mother where she huddled in the pews. She cowered, clinging to me as I lifted the side of my dress and ran for the door at the back of the chapel. The priest ran in front of us, leaving the people of his congregation to their fate as he saved himself.

I supposed my father's donations meant nothing once he was dead.

Just as we reached the door, a familiar grunt sounded behind us. I spun, looking to confirm the sound I would never forget. Even when we'd been children, the sound of him when he was hurt had been imprinted on my memory in a time when I'd wanted nothing more than for him to love me as a brother should. But he hadn't, and he'd deserved every bit of punishment he got.

Jeno's eyes widened as he touched the wound in his chest. A knife protruded from it, my stranger staring him down as he pulled the knife free.

"Run, Thalia," Jeno begged, his voice rasping out his final breath as he collapsed to the floor. My stepmother's scream echoed behind me, her body curled over my father where he sat clutching his side while the stranger stalked toward me.

I shoved a sobbing Malva forward, fleeing from the chapel and into the back. Down the hall, to the right, we moved as quickly as we could. The door at the back loomed large and welcoming, the priest's hand only inches from grasping the knob as he turned back to speak to us urgently. "My car is back here," Father Yiannis said. I had no faith in his desire or interest to keep us safe, but if we could just get away from the massacre then maybe there would be hope.

The back door opened, two men stepping into the church and staring us down as they closed the door behind the priest. I came to a stop, backing away a step as they walked closer. "Miss Karras, I have to ask that you and your sister return to the wedding," one of them said, his lips tipping up in amusement.

"What wedding?" I hissed, shoving Malva behind me. "They killed the groom!"

“There will still be a wedding, λουλούδι μου” a voice behind me said. My flower. My blood froze, turning to solid ice in my veins as I slowly turned around. The voice was familiar, the same raspy one that had murmured orders to me while I writhed beneath him.

His face was the same, breathtaking and rugged in a way I didn't often see with the proper men of the five families.

But that name? That name was something from the past. A ghost who had left me to the fate my family had chosen, when I'd been too young to understand he wouldn't come back for me.

And all that he'd left me to suffer.

As soon as my eyes connected with his light gray stare, I wondered how I hadn't seen it. Calix had been my protector. My everything.

An arrogant smirk twisted his lips as he watched the breath expel from my lungs in sudden shock.

"Hello, Little One."

19

THALIA

My heart raced, feeling as if my chest might implode with the force of it. I felt every pulse of blood surging through my veins, my fingertips tingling as I grappled to find the words to speak to the man who had deceived me.

To the boy who had left me and never looked back.

"Calix?" I whispered, my voice barely a breath. It hovered between us, Malva's stare shifting back and forth between the two of us as she tried to process how I might know the man who had murdered my fiancé and led the slaughter at my wedding. I couldn't spare a glance down at her, even though her hand tightened on mine.

I couldn't take my shocked eyes off of Calix, where he stood staring at me with his head held high as if he had nothing to be ashamed of. As if he hadn't torn my world apart and ruined the only good memories I'd had of my childhood.

I fought back the burn of tears, shutting out the echoes of screams and shouts trailing through the closed door to the sanctuary of the church and echoing in the silence that hung between us. Calix didn't speak, looking back at me with his brow tensed and that intense light in the gray eyes I'd never thought to see again.

That I'd convinced myself I never *wanted* to see again.

"You knew," I said finally, the soft accusation cracking through the space like a whip. He didn't so much as twitch in reaction to the hurt in my voice. I'd wanted one reckless night with a stranger before resigning myself to a life of misery where I was nothing more than a walking corpse. I wanted one person who desired *me* and not the family name that came attached to the space between my legs.

Instead I got another game, another manipulation in a long line of twisted, ugly half-truths that dominated my life. As if it hadn't been bad enough to feel used by the very system I'd wanted to escape, even after all these years, Calix was the one person who had the power to hurt me.

I sank my teeth into the tip of my tongue, clenching my jaw to keep the tears at bay.

Never let them see you bleed.

I wouldn't die with tears in my eyes, but with the promise of haunting him until his very last day on this earth staring back at him. "Did it entertain you? To know that you fucked me before you'd kill me?" Malva gasped at my side, completely unfamiliar with that kind of language coming from me. Even if she hadn't been, the admission of what I'd done would have been a death sentence only moments before.

Now, it hardly mattered.

He stepped toward me, those long, muscled legs closing the gap between us until he towered over me. He reached up, his thumb touching my bottom lip and tugging it to the side. The metallic scent of blood reached me, a fierce reminder of who he was and what he'd done. His eyes gleamed as he looked at my mouth, transfixed on the place where he touched me before he raised his silver gaze back to mine. With the knowledge of who he was revealed, the faint white scar on his cheekbone shone in the light streaming through the windows. I hadn't noticed it before or drawn the similarity to the injury Calix sustained in ο λάκκος all those years ago; not until I knew I was looking at the very same person.

His full lips were set into a harsh line, his square jaw tense as he stared down at me. His dark hair was parted messily just to the side, framing his face in a way that would have made him look the part of a gentleman, if it hadn't been for the blood staining his hand. His fingers painted my chin with it before he slid his grip down to grasp the column of my throat. He wrapped his hand around it, squeezing either side gently as his lips tipped up into another smirk. There was no doubt he was thinking of the last time he'd cut off my breath, depriving me of air as he fucked me into the bed of the hotel room we'd shared for a few short hours.

Malva trembled at my side, curling around to my back and pressing herself tighter into my body, but there was nowhere for her to hide. Not with the guards lurking at our backs to keep us from leaving the church.

"I've no intention of killing you, λουλούδι μου. As I said, there will be a wedding." He tilted his head to the side, leaning forward until his nose brushed against the end of mine in a mockery of something affectionate. "And I find myself in need of a bride."

I snapped my head back, stumbling as my body hurried to catch up. I nearly fell over Malva, catching myself on shaky limbs just in time to prevent further embarrassment. I took another step away from him, shaking my head in denial. He didn't move to follow me, instead staring at me with the calm assurance of a predator who had caught his prey in a well-maneuvered trap they had no chance of escaping.

I shoved Malva toward the guards at the back door anyway,

racing for the slight space between them. They stepped together in a synchronized move, blocking our path without a word. "Let us out!" Malva shrieked, kicking one of the guards in a move that might have made me proud if it didn't make me fear for her very life.

Once upon a time, I'd known Calix better than I'd known myself, but he was no longer the knight in shining armor who protected me from my father's violent impulses. He was the villain from my nightmares, the thing that could kill everything I loved with only a twitch of his fingers.

As one of the men reached down to haul her off her feet, I lunged. The icy breath of panic filled my lungs, burning me from the inside out. The thought of a world without Malva, without the only bit of light that existed for me, felt unimaginable. I'd follow her to the end of the world and the depths of Hell to save her if it came to that. Protecting her would always come first. She was the only thing that mattered.

I grabbed at his arm, sinking my nails into his suit as if I could bleed him through the fabric. He hadn't hurt Malva, not yet, but the sight of his thick hand on her was too much for me to bear.

An arm wrapped around my waist, pulling me back as I fought to stay by Malva's side. I thrashed in Calix's grip, shoving at his arm to try to get free as he lifted me off my feet.

The sound of a gun cocking next to my ear made me freeze, watching in horror from the corner of my eye as Calix lowered it to his side. He didn't point it in Malva's direction, didn't do anything to even motion toward her, but the threat was clear. *"NO! Not her!"* I screamed.

Calix's grip around me twitched, tightening as his breath sighed into my hair. He paused as if in thought when I froze in his grip.

"I have no need for two Karras girls. What is her life worth to you, Little One?" he asked, the cruel set to his words and lack of anything human in his voice making my heart throb in my chest.

It was all the confirmation I needed that the boy I'd loved as my protector was dead and gone, as lost to me as my mother was. "What are you doing?" I asked, my voice cracking as I shifted in his grip, trying to turn to look at him.

"What will you give me if I let her live?" he repeated, loosening his arms as he finally allowed me to turn and face him. Staring up into that impassive face, tears pricked my eyes.

"Anything," I whispered on a broken sob. "I'll give you anything."

He nodded, shoving his gun back into his holster and nodding to the men behind me. I spun to watch as one lifted Malva onto his shoulder, carting her shrieking form through the back door and disappearing from sight.

"No! Please, she's just a child. You can't hurt her," I begged, touching frantic hands to his chest. The need to claw at him was nearly overwhelming, but I fought to restrain the urge.

Only for Malva.

I stared up at him, willing him to turn his attention back to me and to *see* that this would be the moment that broke me. I'd survived losing my mother, survived losing him, but if he was the one to take away from me the only thing I had left to cling to, I would wither and die on the spot.

He didn't have to pull the trigger to destroy all that remained of me.

"I never said I would. You jumped to that erroneous conclusion all on your own. But that doesn't mean that I cannot take her away from you and send her somewhere you will never be able to reach her without my permission," Calix said, raising an eyebrow. As harsh as the words seemed, the confirmation that he hadn't intended to kill her soothed something inside of me. As if it was a hint of whatever humanity might remain inside of him, even if he was using the only person I loved as leverage.

At least she'd live.

"Bring her back," I pleaded. "She's scared."

"Jorges won't hurt her. He is merely taking Malva to stay with my mother for the time being," Calix explained, lifting a hand to touch my cheekbone.

"Her home is with me," I said, my shaky voice shifting into something more resolved as I twisted my head away from his grip.

"Perhaps when you've settled into your new life, then we will be able to arrange for Malva to come and live with us. For now, I suspect we'll need some time to ourselves for you to come to terms with your place by my side," he said, his hand lingering where my face had been, hanging in the air as if I might press back into his touch. "She's far better off with my mother until we know that you don't intend to try and kill me in my sleep."

"You'll keep her locked away from me so that I can't murder you without risking her," I snapped, flinching away when his hand finally dropped and his fingers touched the tips of mine. He laced them together, entwining our hands until he used his grip to guide me toward the doors to the sanctuary where the massacre awaited. "Why are you doing this? I didn't do anything to you."

Calix paused at my side, staring down at me with a gentle look on his face, but his eyes glimmered like steel, all hard edges and cold retribution as he glanced toward the door. "They took *everything* from me. I'm taking it back."

"You can't take my friendship by force and expect things to go back to the way they were. I adored you because you protected me from men like you," I said, tearing at my hand to try to get it free from his grip.

"It was not your friendship I sought with my cock between your pretty thighs, λουλούδι μου. You are no longer a child, and I am no longer a boy waiting to become a man."

"I preferred the boy," I snapped when he tugged me closer to that looming door and what waited beyond it. The thought of my family lying dead didn't horrify me and the idea of seeing my father lying in a puddle of his own blood made satisfaction course through me.

But there was a wedding lying in wait, and I couldn't help but feel like the sacrifice he tore from me would be far greater than the one I would have given to Damianos.

"I'm sure you did, all wrapped around your finger and expecting nothing in return. I have always done what I could to protect you from the men who sought to abuse you; now my protection comes at a price," he argued, placing a hand on the knob and turning it. He spun to look behind us, nodding his head at the remaining guard where he shoved the priest forward. They stepped around us as Calix hauled open the door, stepping through into the carnage on the other side.

Bodies littered the room, the stain of blood on the wooden floor slithering across the planks.

"It hardly counts as protection if you are the one who wants to abuse me!" Calix turned to me, tugging my hair over my shoulder. His fingers trailed over the scars on my upper back, on the reminder of just how cruel the people in my life had always been.

"I'm not a good man, but I am not capable of something like this, either," he said, his lips twisting into a grimace as he pressed his fingertips into the sensitive, white scar tissue gracing my shoulder. "You won't know this kind of pain by my hand."

His other hand held mine tightly as he turned back toward the door, tugging me after him. My feet moved sluggishly, as if they couldn't process what my brain had already determined. It would do me no good to fight what was coming; not when he had Malva to hold over my head.

So many bodies.

The pews were stained with the splatter of blood and gore, the sanctity of the church desecrated with more death than I'd ever thought to see. Damianos's mother lay on her stomach, blood pooled beneath her with her face turned toward the altar as if she'd tried to run when they gunned her down. Wives and women were usually exempt in the power struggles between the families; harming one of them was considered something of a sin amongst The Six.

To see one of the mothers of a council member gunned down at her own son's wedding was unfathomable. It was a line that none had dared to cross. The last time a man had violated the understanding that wives and daughters were off-limits, the Regas family had been banished from the city.

Her blank eyes stared at the altar where her son lay in front of it. Half of Damianos's face was covered in blood where Calix had shot him. Jeno lay crumpled in the aisle between the pews, his white shirt covered in dark, inky stains.

He'd been a terrible brother. He'd let our father abuse me in the name of crafting me into a woman he could marry off easily. But he'd also been the one to shield me from our mother's gruesome death, and sometimes when he'd heard me crying at night in the weeks that followed, he'd stepped into my bedroom and sat in the chair beside my bed until I fell asleep.

I sank my teeth into the inside of my cheek and turned away, following the path that Calix set for us. My father leaned against the wall opposite the doorway, clutching a gunshot wound in his side. Lydia had torn a scrap of fabric from her dress, pressing it into the wound as he paled, as if she could prevent the way death called his name. It wouldn't be long before my father was gone from this world if the fading of his skin was any indication.

Eugene Regas lingered over my father, a gun held in his hands as he glared down at the man who had been responsible for his banishment by bringing it to the council. The guard led the priest to the altar, resuming the place he'd taken when I'd thought I'd be marrying Damianos.

Instead, Calix Regas stepped over the body of my former betrothed, kicking his corpse out of his way. His dark shoes glistened with the wet sign of blood as he moved into the place a groom would occupy, pulling me with his grip on my hand until I faced him and gave my back to my father and stepmother.

"Thalia," my father rasped, shuffling sounds accompanying the words as I turned to look at him over my shoulder. He tried to sit up; tried to get his feet underneath him as if he could control what I did in these next precious moments. "If you even think about it..."

Calix grabbed my chin with gentle fingers, turning my face back around to meet his stony gaze. "You don't look at him. He doesn't get the satisfaction of your attention ever again; do you understand me, Little One?" he asked, holding my gaze until I gave him my nod of understanding.

"You little fucking bitch!" my father rasped, trying to override the command Calix had given me. But with my father's death certain, I didn't even so much as flinch away from the venom in his voice.

Calix lifted a hand, gently cupping my cheek as he tilted his head thoughtfully and looked over my shoulder at where my father was slowly bleeding out. "A long time ago, I promised you this day would come," my childhood friend and more recent lover growled, his jaw clenching as he gritted out the words. "Your only son is dead. Your eldest daughter will be my wife and your youngest, my ward. I will wipe your very name from the face of this earth while you watch. Only then will I allow you to die for what you've done to *her*."

Shock claimed me at the vehemence in his voice, and the growl that twisted his words into something brutal. It wasn't from discussing his retribution for being banished, but in the abuse I'd suffered at my father's hands. "I will take everything that was yours and make it mine."

I swallowed against the nausea swirling in my gut. With my brother dead, I'd stand to inherit everything of my father's when he was gone.

His money. His properties. His territory.

Despite the hint of pretty words hiding behind Calix's threats, I was nothing but a conduit for more power. Nothing but a way to get more of everything he already had in abundance.

Used.

I fought back the trembling in my hands, reminding myself that the face of the man standing across from me hardly mattered. I'd been prepared to make this sacrifice to keep Malva in my life when it had been Damianos. I would do it with the boy from my memories lingering at the back of my mind.

"Get on with it," Calix said, instructing the priest to look down at the Bible placed on the altar in front of him. He lifted it into his arms, stepping around to the other side to stand directly in front of us.

"The union into which you are now about to enter—"

"Does it look like you have an audience for all the bullshit?

I'd like to be married before my soon-to-be father-in-law croaks," Calix said, his voice droll.

The priest cleared his throat, swallowing loudly as he fought to turn the page in his Bible. The pages stuck together, coated with the inky stain of slowly drying blood. "Calix Regas, will you have Thalia Karras to be your wife, to live with her, respect her, and love her as God intends with the promise of faithfulness, tenderness, and helpfulness, as long as you both shall live?"

Calix held my gaze, my throat closing as his hand tightened on mine. "I will," he murmured. He lifted it into the space between us, pulling a wedding set from his pocket. He slid the metal bands onto my ring finger, the glimmer of an ebony diamond encased in the center of a black, diamond-studded lotus flower. The tiny diamonds on the flower petals twinkled in the light shining through the stained glass windows of the church, making me swallow as the rings settled around my finger. They felt heavy, weighted down with far more than metal and stones, the smooth surface wet with smears of death.

"Thalia, will you have Calix to be your husband, to live with him, respect him, and love him as God intends with the promise of faithfulness, tenderness, and helpfulness as long as you both shall live?"

"I will beat you until you forget how to breathe," my father snapped, his words chasing away the fear I felt. They pushed back the terror in my lungs and the way my mouth couldn't seem to form the answer I needed to give.

Defiance pushed me forward, forcing me to set aside my fear of what had yet to come. I wouldn't be a prisoner in my father's home any longer, and I'd be damned if I'd change my jailor for the same man with a different face when I'd only just escaped the promise of a life with Damianos.

My future had been set in motion, and one day soon enough, I'd be free. I raised my eyes from the rings on my finger, accepted the simple black band Calix placed in my hand, and tentatively gripped his palm in mine so that I could slide the band down his ring finger. His eyes gleamed with satisfaction, probably never suspecting the thoughts of escape that swirled inside of me. I sealed my fate and my path forward.

"I will."

20

CALIX

The ring settled against my finger, heavy in a way that felt as if it had always belonged there. Like an invisible tether ran from her ring to mine, uniting us as one despite the way the fates had tried to intervene, driving us apart over the years with thousands of miles between us.

I felt the red strand of destiny connecting us, and the way it wrapped around my finger and stretched inside of me, consuming me, as Thalia stared up at me. Our love was written in blood, our dream of vengeance born in the death of nearly everyone Thalia knew. She would rise from the wreckage like a spirit that the underworld couldn't contain, and learn to stand by my side as Persephone did with Hades.

I reached up, cupping her face in my hand and letting my warmth sink into the chilled skin of her cheek. Her eyes fluttered shut, like the dance of a butterfly's wings against her high cheekbones as she stripped me of that intense amber gaze. For just a moment, it felt as if she pressed into my touch, as if she could sink into the moment of affection that she'd been deprived of since they'd torn me out of her life.

I leaned down, brushing my nose against hers and willing

her to give me the beauty of her eyes once more. They sprung open, a sharp gasp filling her lungs as she froze solid. With her eyes so close to mine, the streaks of brown that radiated out from her pupil were that much more noticeable.

She'd been an oddly pretty child, standing out among the girls who all fit the same mold, but as a woman, Thalia stood out in ways they could never hope to achieve. She'd grown into her features,

"Breathe, Little One," I murmured, sinking my teeth into my bottom lip. Her gaze fell to the motion, snagging on it with a nervousness I didn't like seeing on her face. She didn't need to doubt me or fear me in the same way she would the others. I resolved to show her just that, leaning forward to gently touch my lips to hers. "I won't bite you...just yet." My words made my lips move over hers, the moment feeling incredibly intimate as the scent of blood and death around us faded into the background. Her father didn't lurk just behind her, watching and picking his daughter apart for every weakness she exhibited; her brother's body didn't lie just a few feet away with the blood of her previous fiancé staining my shoes.

There was only Thalia, only the taste of her in my lungs as her breath finally returned. It felt like the first breath of fresh air I'd had since she'd snuck out of my hotel room. It felt like *living* in a world dominated by the dead and all that they demanded from me.

"You have thus consented in holy matrimony and have witnessed the same before God, family and friends; by virtue of the authority vested in me as an Officiant and the laws of this state, I now pronounce you husband and wife. Therefore, what God has joined together, let man not separate. You may kiss the bride!" the priest said, his dismay echoing in his voice as he slammed the Bible shut and stepped away from us.

I slid my hand farther, gliding it over the skin of her cheek and jaw to cup the side of her neck until my fingertips wrapped around the back. The blood of our enemies covered her skin, painting her in the retribution she'd been owed since she was a child. Pulling her closer, the breath stalled in my lungs the moment her chest collided with mine.

Curving my body over hers, keeping our mouths only just separated from one another, I shared breath with the girl who had always been my destiny. With the woman become.

With my fucking *wife.*

My lips danced over hers, moving slowly and teasing her to try to bring out the mischievous woman who'd met a stranger in a hotel for one night of pleasure. Those distrusting eyes stared up at me with defiance, refusing to concede what we both knew.

I would be in charge of the how. I would control the when. And when I so much as gave a hint of what I wanted, Thalia would bend. She would never break, never shatter to a thousand pieces and cover the earth with what remained of her, but for me, she'd learn to submit, and it would mean more because of the uniqueness.

I smiled into her mouth, a chuckle rising in my throat as I took her hand in mine. The cool metal of her ring touched my skin, a placating icy brand that reminded me how far I'd already come. I laced our fingers, raising our hands to my neck so that the back of hers touched my skin.

"Do you intend to kiss your husband, λουλούδι μου? Or should we stand here all day surrounded by the carnage of your past life and stare at one another?" I murmured, my lips tipping into a smile that she couldn't see but must have felt against the plump flesh of her mouth.

"I'd prefer not to have your mouth or hands anywhere on my body," she said, her voice breathless as her eyes fluttered shut.

"That isn't what you said the last night we met," I murmured, lifting a brow at her in challenge. Her stepmother gasped behind us, but the reveal of Thalia's lack of virginity hardly mattered. She'd given it to the very man who should have owned the right to it in the first place, walked right into my waiting arms in her desperation to escape what she knew to be wrong.

Somewhere deep down, even without the knowledge of our betrothal, she knew as well as I did that her virginity belonged to me. Even if she didn't have the faintest understanding of it and there had been a time when it seemed unfathomable, the adult Thalia was mine in every way.

"What have you done?" her stepmother asked, making Thalia squeeze her eyes shut. Shame heated her cheeks, the archaic system she'd been raised in making her believe that she truly had something to feel guilty for. I wanted to say it should have been her choice all along, but that wasn't true, or wouldn't have been if it was me she'd tried to skip out on before our wedding day.

I pressed my lips to hers with gentle force, molding the seam of my lips to hers. My tongue darted out to touch her mouth, coaxing her to open for me. Somewhere beneath all that resistance, the woman who needed me as badly as I needed her waited. Her lashes fluttered for a moment before she sighed, her complete and utter starvation for a touch that wasn't cruel overriding her sense as her lips parted slightly. I used the moment to my advantage, angling her head and taking what I wanted. My mouth opened and we shared our breath in truth, as the air in my lungs made its way inside and became a part of her.

There was nothing to stop me from taking and claiming every part of her, from filling her with my very essence. I kissed her as if she was the air I needed to breathe, trying to give her the reassurance that I couldn't say until I trusted her.

She'd be safe so long as she was mine.

When I pulled back from her mouth, Thalia's body leaned forward into my chest as if she wanted to follow. As if she needed more as much as I did.

I touched my mouth to her forehead as she tried to remember how to breathe and reminded herself why the feeling coursing through her was wrong after everything she'd learned about me. She rebuilt the walls surrounding her heart up brick by brick as I waited, giving her the moment to compose herself before I asked more of her.

"Do you love your wife?" I asked, combing my fingers through Thalia's dark hair as I looked over her shoulder at where her father lay bleeding. "Would it hurt you to see her in pain?" I ghosted my fingertips over the scars on Thalia's back, caressing them lightly with heavy meaning. She twitched away from the touch, the movement so slight I doubted anyone but me could detect it.

"Of course it would hurt him!" Lydia protested, her face twisting as she stared up at me. Rafael Ibarra, my ally who had given me shelter after I was banished from Philadelphia, stepped up beside me, Lydia's favored cane from the Karras house held in his grip. Thalia twitched as if to run from the sight of it, swallowing as she forced herself to be still. "I have been a good wife to him."

"You always did think you were more important than you were," Thalia said, her voice soft but her body as rigid as stone. Rafe placed the cane in my outstretched hand, the wood feeling worn and heavy as I wrapped my fingers around it.

"Perhaps Lydia should know just how little she means to you before I slit her throat," I said, raising a brow as I nodded to Rafael. He moved slowly, with the deft, confident movements of a man who did not hurry for anyone's schedule but his own. Despite the carnage around us, the Spanish man from Ibiza was the epitome of composure. There wasn't a wrinkle on his suit, not a single hair out of place, as his multicolored blue and green gaze fell on Lydia with a coldness that made grown men cower.

"Up," he grunted, glaring down at the woman who huddled into her husband's side. She looked to Origen as if he might save her from the fate she thought Thalia deserved. Lydia didn't move, her mouth dropping open and brow furrowing when Origen didn't so much as twitch to protect her. "You can either take your punishment with dignity, or you can be a pathetic, sniveling woman who is capable of causing unimaginable pain to a *child* without ever being strong enough to handle it herself. The choice is yours, but the end result will be you bent over that altar, even if I have to force you there."

Thalia's bottom lip trembled as she turned a questioning stare up at me. The emotions danced clearly on her features as she wondered if I could do what had been done to her without any stain on my conscience.

I could, because I didn't have one, but that didn't mean I would.

I held my unwavering attention on my wife, keeping my touch gentle as I brought her hand down to the cane in my grip. Wrapping her fingers around the wood that had torn open her skin more times than I wanted to think about, I let her feel the weight of it in her palm.

"What are you doing?" she asked, the harsh whisper hanging between us. Behind her, Rafael tore Lydia from Origen's side, forcing her to the altar beside us as the priest backed away with a swallow and a hand covering his mouth.

"Did you cry when she struck you?" I asked, covering Thalia's trembling hand with mine and offering silent support as tears pooled in her eyes and her face showed strain while she tried to understand what I was offering. Rafael tore the dress down Lydia's spine, leaving her with only enough fabric to stay covered.

He muttered something to her as Lydia's body wracked with sobs, her fingers clenching around the edge of the altar as she hung her head forward.

"At first," Thalia whispered, her eyes darting over to her stepmother's bare skin. It was unblemished by the abuse her father had always shown to Thalia and her birth mother.

"Did she care?" I asked, clenching my jaw to keep the rage I felt from showing in my voice. Thalia needed guidance in taking what she deserved and claiming the vengeance that was rightfully hers for all she'd suffered, but she was as skittish as a frightened animal, threatening to bolt at the first sign of aggression from me.

"She told me I wasn't allowed to cry anymore." Thalia hung her head forward, raising the cane in her grip. "This isn't me. I can't strike her."

I smiled softly, knowing the day would come where that would change. "I know, but you deserved to make that choice for yourself," I said, taking the cane back as she handed it to me. Lydia heaved a sigh of relief, clearly believing that if Thalia wouldn't be the one to wield it, she would be safe from the pain coming her way. I turned to her husband, my smile broadening. "We both know that you won't walk out of here alive. I have a proposition for you, my dearest father-in-law. You can beat your wife as you instructed her to beat your daughter, or I can beat you for the command."

"I wonder which he'll choose," Rafael muttered with a dark laugh. Origen didn't hesitate to force himself to his feet, holding out a hand for the cane. I placed it in his, keeping Thalia sheltered behind me with his threats regarding our marriage hanging between us.

Thalia didn't watch as her father made his way to Lydia. She didn't look as the cane cut through the air and filled the church with a whistle. She flinched the moment it cracked against Lydia's spine, the force of it tearing her step-mother's skin open as her screams flooded the air.

"Origen!" she screamed, and I watched as blood dripped down her back from the wound he'd given her. I stepped back in front of Thalia and pulled her into my chest, offering her the comfort she should have always had after her father's abuse, trying to stem the trauma that was necessary for Lydia to get what she deserved.

For her to understand that she had never meant anything to Origen Karras, a man who cared only for himself.

"Why?" Thalia rasped, the tears that had gathered in her eyes dripping down to wet the front of my suit. She sniffled, turning her gaze up to me as I looked down at her. I balanced on the precipice, wanting to memorize the way Lydia's blood dripped to the floor and wishing I could convince Thalia to draw it for me one day.

"Because you deserve nothing less than to know that, even for just a few moments, she understood what she did to you. Now she knows what that pain feels like, what it is to have a man who should love you abuse you. She has lived as nothing, and now she will die knowing that."

21

THALIA

My father struck Lydia over and over again, the sound of the cane colliding with her flesh echoing through the open chasm of the church. Her screams and whimpered pleas filled the space, following the arc of the wood each time it cut through the air. Surrounded by blood and death, by the waste of life the people surrounding me had been even before their deaths, all I could do was wait for it to end.

I'd wanted my revenge, but that didn't mean I needed to reduce myself to their level. "Enough," I said, the quiet whisper of the word sounding like a lash in itself. My father ignored it as he always had, continuing gleefully in the torment that so pleased him. But Calix stilled, his fingers tightening on my waist as he pulled me closer.

With the next crack of the cane against Lydia's spine, Calix's voice rang out through the space. "She said enough."

My father turned, dropping the cane as he stumbled and clutched his side in pain. "You always were a little bitch for her," he snarled, his lips peeling back from his teeth in something that looked more animal than man. I wanted nothing more than to watch Calix wipe the look off his face, to remind him that all semblance of control he'd thought he possessed had been erased in one day.

Within a few moments, Calix had stripped him of everything he valued, and soon enough, he'd take the very last thing that mattered to him.

His life.

Calix released me, unwinding his arms from where they'd fallen around me while I'd fought back the memories of those first times I'd felt the fire of Lydia's cane. I immediately felt bereft, the absence of him like a cold splash of loneliness sinking into my heart.

His few steps toward my father were painfully languid as his long legs ate up the distance between them. He strolled straight past my father, ignoring him entirely in favor of Lydia. She stared at the wall, her face blank as tears streamed down her face. "You genuinely thought he cared for you?" Calix asked her, commanding her attention as she turned pale eyes up to my new husband. I swallowed with that realization, the term sounding far too foreign, considering I'd known I would have one soon enough.

I just hadn't in my wildest dreams imagined a massacre like this at my wedding.

"You were nothing but a tool, just like the wife he murdered in cold blood. I hope you die knowing that you sacrificed your humanity for *nothing*." He pulled his knife from his pocket, the blade already covered in the dark, inky stain of blood. He wiped it clean on the folds of her dress that hung around her, placing the edge to her throat as she swallowed against it. Her throat bobbed with the motion, a plea rising to her lips as Calix stared down at her thoughtfully. "There was a time when I thought I wouldn't be able to kill a woman," he said, shrugging his shoulders as he pressed the tip of the knife into her skin. Blood welled, dripping down as he grasped her by the hair and pulled her head back to get a better angle. "There really is a first time for everything."

He dragged the knife across her throat, releasing her as soon as he was done. She collapsed to the floor, her mouth moving as she gasped for breath. My eyes tracked down to the wound at her throat and the way her flesh parted, revealing the dark mess of muscle and gore inside. She gurgled, the sound erupting from her mouth something that would haunt my worst nightmares. Her body twitched as she raised her hands to her throat, slowly covering the wound as if her body had already started to cease functioning. Her fingers pressed into the wound as her blood soaked them, pumping out of her body in violent waves.

Calix stepped over her body as she bled out, her eyes clouding as she fought for her final breaths. Making his way toward where my father waited under the supervision of the other man, Calix shoved the knife back into his pocket. Placing a hand on top of my father's shoulder, Calix pushed him down to his knees. He knelt in the pool of blood, the black blending in with the pants of his tux as he turned a sneer up at Calix.

"Do you see her now?" Calix asked, his eyes falling on me. He shoved a hand into my father's hair, grasping the graying strands in harsh fingers as he turned his face to look at me. It took me that moment to realize he spoke of seeing *me,* not his dead wife on the floor of the church. "Does she look like the broken doll you were so determined to turn her into?"

I lifted my chin, refusing to wipe away the stain of tears on my cheeks. My father spit at Calix, narrowly missing the lapels of his suit in a move that made Calix sneer in disgust.

"She'll be the last of the Karras family after you're gone," Calix said, his lips curving into a cruel smirk.

"The Karras family dies with me and Malva. That traitor is no daughter of mine," my father said, his face twisting as his glare finally met mine.

"Betraying you would imply that you were ever on my side in the first place. Call me opportunistic, but you are *nothing* to me. I cannot betray a man who has always been my enemy," I said, fighting back the urge to flinch away from the venom in his glare.

"You saw her as weak all her life, faulty and broken, but she brought you to your knees," Calix said, wrenching my father's head back for good measure. "Thalia is the reason you will die alone, with only the bodies of your family to keep you company as you make your way to the afterlife. She was never weak. She terrified you, because you saw what she could become."

Calix pulled the gun from his holster, cocking it for good measure. "Calix," I said, unsure why I stepped forward. My father was far from my family, far from anything I cared enough to save.

"This is the part where Rafael can take you to the car, λουλούδι μου. Otherwise you'll find out what your father's brains look like splattered across the altar," Calix said, pressing the barrel against my father's forehead.

"Wait," I said, uncertain why my voice seemed to have a mind of its own. I couldn't process what I was doing, my body moving as if in a daze as I closed the remaining gap between us. I squatted down, wrapping a trembling hand around the cane that my father had used to beat Lydia. The same one that had tormented me for years, breaking my skin open at his order. The wood was slick with blood, forcing me to wrap a second hand around the base as I spun on my heel back to face my father.

Calix's eyes tracked over me as I spread my legs to shoulder-width, raising the cane over my right shoulder like a baseball bat. The breath wheezed in my lungs, torn from the darkest part of me that wanted my father—no, Origen's—blood as payment.

It might have been Lydia who'd wielded the cane in more recent years, but my father had been the one to scar me. My father had been the one to order my beatings when he couldn't be bothered to give them himself.

As much as I hated Lydia, she'd been another victim of the life designed to make us obedient.

I swung the cane, the whistle of air making my father's head jerk as Calix pulled the gun away in the same moment. The wood clapped against the back of my father's neck, his entire body sprawling forward as the wood vibrated in my hands. They throbbed in tune with the vibrations, an ache spreading up my wrists and to my elbows as I raised it again.

Calix raised a brow at me as my father fell forward, landing face-first on the floor slickened by blood. He pushed up to his hands and knees in a daze, his body as I raised the cane over my head.

I brought it down over and over again with a shrill scream, all the force in my body going into the movements. The wood split as it crashed against his spine a final time, splintering down the center as he flopped onto his stomach and didn't move.

I panted for breath as I stared down at his unmoving body, wondering if I'd killed him or only knocked him out. I didn't know which I preferred, thinking I'd been the one to end him, or that I'd be able to move forward without that stain on my conscience.

My fingers shook as I gripped the cane tighter, the hand that came down on my shoulder startling me into motion. I spun, swinging what remained of the cane through the air.

Calix caught it a breath from the side of his neck, gripping it tightly as he raised an eyebrow at me in question.

"Don't touch me," I hissed. My breath continued to come in wheezes, hard fought and hard won as I tried to pull the cane free from his grip.

He raised his other hand slowly, grasping my fingers and peeling them off the wooden shaft one by one. "Let it go, λουλούδι μου," he murmured, his voice soft despite the fact that I'd nearly struck him with enough force to truly harm him.

I couldn't decide if I would have regretted it.

When he'd finally pulled all my fingers off the cane, he took it from my hand, twisting it around so that the sharp, broken point pointed down. He never took his eyes off of mine as he drove it down into my father's back, the thick squelching sound filling the room as he twisted it in the older man's body.

The space where my father's heart might have been, had he possessed one, was nothing but a gaping hole by the time Calix pulled the broken cane free and tossed it to the side.

"Time to go home, Little One," he said.

22

CALIX

Thalia ignored the hand I offered, her gaze stuck on the hole in her father's back. She took a single step closer, lifting her wedding dress up with blood-stained hands. The red marked the white fabric with handprints as her foot encased in a diamond studded heel peeked out from beneath the hem. She kicked her father in the side once, staring at him as if she expected him to move.

When he didn't so much as twitch, she wedged that foot beneath his torso and heaved with all the strength in her leg. The heavy weight of Origen Karras's corpse flipped to its back, eyes staring up at the ceiling with the glossed-over film of death. Thalia crouched down, staring at her father's face with something like disbelief etched into her features.

The cane had driven straight through to the front of his chest, a much smaller hole evidence of the exit wound. Thalia touched her fingers to the edges of it, the vivid red covering her manicured nails. She pressed them into the wound, the wet sounds filling the church as I watched her. My head tilted to the side as I observed the woman I loved while she stared at the pulverized mess of what had been her father's heart.

She lifted her hand from the wound, turning it over to stare at the blood as it dripped down her fingers toward her palm. Rubbing two fingers together as if she needed to test the viscosity of the liquid to know it was blood, she looked down at her father's face once more. "I can see you bleeding, Father," she said, her voice hollow and low as she spoke to the man who would never have an answer for her.

I swallowed, emotion clogging my throat as I tried to imagine what meaning her words held to her. There was some clear emphasis in her mind, something that had been drilled into her head time and time again, I had no doubt. I held out my hand again, my face turning soft as she turned tired eyes up to me. "Come home, Little One."

"I don't have a home," she said softly, glancing back down at her father's corpse before she turned her gaze to the carnage around the church. "I never did."

"Your home is with me," I said, reaching down to grasp her hand. I pulled her to her feet slowly, letting her get her footing in the red pool that made the wooden floors of the church slick. She stepped toward me hesitantly, holding perfectly still when I raised my hand to cup her too-thin cheek.

Blood covered her flesh, the stain of red a shock of color against her olive skin as I traced my thumb over her high cheekbone. Her wide, angled eyes drifted closed as I painted her face in the death of our enemies. I hoped one day she would come to understand that the bodies surrounding us were my sacrifice to her, my atonement for the way I'd failed her when she'd been a child looking to me for protection.

I touched my lips to hers briefly, withdrawing before she could protest the kiss, as if she didn't need it just as much as I did. When I pulled back, I slid a hand behind her back and another behind her knees, scooping her into my arms. I wouldn't force her to step over the carnage littering the floor, not with the way her dress would trail through the mess and risk getting caught.

I hadn't been able to give her the dream-like wedding she deserved, having to settle for a union born in death and vengeance instead, but the least I could do was carry my bride over the bodies of her family.

She squirmed as I settled her against my chest, her head coming to rest against my shoulder as all the fight drained out of her. She cradled her hands in her lap, positioning them carefully as if she both didn't know what to do with them and they caused her pain.

I stepped over the bodies carefully, leaving Rafael to supervise the cleanup and disposal while I tended to my new wife. Perhaps one day, I would return the favor if things with Isa didn't go as planned.

My slate gray *Koenigsegg* waited for us at the front of the church, allowing me to lower Thalia to her feet at the passenger side. I reached down, grasping the hidden latch and lifting the door forward so that it slid on its hinges. Thalia raised an eyebrow at me as she watched, as if to say *really?*

"I like pretty things," I said with a shrug, my gaze intent on her face. My meaning wasn't lost on her, her cheeks flushing pink as she swallowed.

"We'll get it all bloody," she said, glancing into the interior of the very expensive vehicle. I'd already thought it through, covering the fabric of the seats temporarily. It might have been easier to just take one of the SUVs waiting back to my home, but something in me wanted to drive off with my wife in my car, leaving her abuse in the past.

I wanted the first car she rode in as my wife to be *mine*, to look over at her empty seat when I took the *Koenigsegg* to conduct business and have the memory of her covered in blood like an avenging fury imprinted on my brain.

I guided her into the car and settled her in the seat, bending down to lift her legs and pivot her into the car. She glared at me as I stuffed the train of her gown into the vehicle with her, the overly formal monstrosity only appealing because it was on her.

Pulling on the door so that it slid into place, I walked around to the driver's side. I'd expected Thalia to fight going with me. I'd thought she might try to run, but she stayed put as I slid into the driver's seat and started the engine. It rumbled to life with a loud purr, and I pulled out away from the curb in silence.

The Regas estate was in what had once been our corner of the city. I'd remodeled it to my exact specifications, avoiding color wherever I could for a distinctly neutral space where Thalia wouldn't feel like she had to question anything. She would know exactly what her bright, white and gray home looked like.

Only the fact that the rest of the families avoided the Regas Estate like it was a plague that could have them banished from the city had allowed me to perfect it without anyone being the wiser.

"Why did you do it?" Thalia asked suddenly, drawing my attention to where she wrung her hands in her lap. I couldn't see through the blood covering her palms to examine the skin beneath, but I suspected she'd hurt herself with the swing of that cane, from the delicate way she handled herself.

"Kill your family?" I asked, glancing at her with a furrowed brow. I would think my motivations for the slaughter would have been obvious.

"Why did you have to use me to do it? Why marry me? You already have everything you could possibly want," she said, looking at the car that surrounded her as I navigated the streets of Philadelphia.

"I married you because you belong with me," I said simply, not giving her any more. I could make professions of love, could tell her all the ways I intended to worship her throughout our lives together, but she was still reeling, and processing the fact that she was not Thalia Hasapis but Thalia Regas.

"And what about what I want?" she asked, her gaze feeling heavy on the side of my face. I glanced at her, holding her intense stare for as long as I dared while driving. "What if I want to be free? To leave this twisted city behind me and go out into the real world?"

"What do you know of the real world, my flower?" I asked, attempting to keep my voice soft. Irritation leaked into it; the reality was Thalia didn't understand that ugliness like this city was everywhere. She would never escape her family name and her ties to the city that had birthed her.

She would never escape me.

The bottoms of her eyes filled with moisture, the threat of tears pulling a sigh from me. I didn't want to be harsh with her; not when I understood better than anyone that her entire life had been flipped on end.

She'd never had a job. Had no real skills, no licenses. She'd been completely at the mercy of the family that had raised her to be a wife and mother, but that was no fault of her own.

She turned her heated, teary stare away from mine suddenly, depriving me of her eye contact. It was probably for the best until we got to the estate, but I felt the loss within me nonetheless. I turned up the winding drive, through the trees that guarded the way to the Regas Estate just outside the busier part of the city.

I hadn't changed the cobblestone driveway, even though the red hue would be lost on Thalia, suspecting she would appreciate the stonework of the circle it formed at the center.

Left to her own devices, she was fond of textures and patterns that her eyes could process, lending interest to things that could have otherwise felt flat.

Pulling up to the dark gray front door surrounded by white, Greek-inspired columns, I brought the car to a stop and cut off the ignition. The white cladding of the house wrapped around the two upper decks that overlooked the driveway, a perfect place for security to keep an eye on anyone approaching. A man stared down at us from each platform, watching as I exited the vehicle and made my way around to pull Thalia from the car.

She stared at the house with wide eyes, and I realized that even with all that we had meant to each other as children, she'd never visited the Estate. She wouldn't know I'd made changes to it for her sake, or even that it had ever been anything but the modern and comfortable home I'd transformed it into.

I placed a hand at the small of her back, guiding her toward the front doors as one of my security men opened them for us to enter. The foyer sprawled out before us with gleaming lines of white marble on the floor, light gray walls, and black, wrought iron railings ascending the staircase.

I guided her through the vast, open space to the kitchen at the back, her dress leaving a trail of blood behind her as we walked. I needed to get her changed out of it before my housekeeper threatened to kill me in my sleep, but tending to her needs was more important.

"Are you hungry?" I asked, making her look at me as if I'd lost my mind. I left her side in favor of moving to the kitchen island, leaving her standing in the center of the open-concept main room.

"How could I be hungry after that?" she asked.

"You need to eat something. You're too thin as it is," I said, wincing as soon as the words left my lips. She was too thin because of the diet her stepmother kept her on.

Thalia tore the shoe from her foot with frantic hands, hurling it across the kitchen at me. I ducked out of the way, narrowly avoiding the heel that had been aimed straight for my face. The vase on the island shattered across the counter, water flowing free while the narcissus flowers fell to the white-flecked onyx marble.

"I'm so sorry my body is a disappointment to you, you fucking *dick!*" she yelled, the rasp of her voice evident as she raised it. I had no doubt the scream in the church had taken something from her, as the agony of beating her own father with that cane had been torn from the deepest part of her.

"That wasn't what I meant," I said with a wince, raising placating hands to try to calm her down as she bent down to grab her other shoe.

I only had so many vases.

"What could you have possibly meant, then?" she asked, raising the stiletto in her grip and waving it at me in warning.

This was a trap.

I moved quickly, surging to close the distance between us. She gasped as she threw the shoe, narrowly missing my head as she spun and made to run away from me. The predator in me rose to the surface, the need to chase her down surging through my blood.

But it was far too early for any of that—Thalia's trauma too recent. When I chased her down and took what was mine, she'd be an entirely willing participant in the games we would play. I wrapped my arms around her stomach, her body squirming tightly to get away from my grip. "I meant that they *starved* you, λουλούδι μου," I said, my voice harsh as I held her tight to contain her thrashing body.

Her desperation to get away was far worse than I could

have imagined, as if she was trapped in the trauma response where she expected violence to follow her outburst. I had no doubt her father would have beaten her bloody if she'd ever thrown something at him.

I lowered to my knees, keeping her encased in my grip as her legs slipped out from under her. Turning her around and laying her out on the marble floor, I placed a hand on either side of her head and leaned my body over hers. She reached up with panicked hands, aiming for my face with nails crusted with dried blood. Pinning her hands next to her head, I tried to shut out the way her throat worked to swallow as she closed her eyes tightly.

"Let's get one thing straight," I said, the fury tinting my voice the exact opposite of what she needed to hear from me in those moments. But the very thought that I might have hurt her, that she expected me to abuse her, set my blood on fire and threatened to make me boil over until I destroyed everyone and everything in this godforsaken city. "I will *never* hurt you."

She opened her eyes slowly, peering up at me between long, mascara-covered lashes with those amber eyes that seemed to belong more on a wolf than a human woman. "You say that now."

"You just threw a shoe at my head," I said, raising a brow as I leaned down and rubbed my nose against hers. "I think if I was going to hurt you, it would be now."

"I'm not hungry," she whispered, the words soft in the space between us. The fight went out of her, the stubborn woman who'd thrown a shoe at me all but disappearing as exhaustion claimed her. She looked so damn tired, as if she could fall asleep on the spot, and sadness lingered on her face as she turned her head away.

I wasn't sure what I'd said to put her over the edge, but I

slid my fingers free from her hands and glided them over the bare skin of her forearms as I sat up.

Sitting back with my ass on my bent legs, I dropped my palms to my thighs and stared at the limp body of my wife as she lay on the floor, probably waiting for me to take what most men in the six families believed was our right. "Alright, Little One," I said, standing and holding out a hand to help her to her feet.

She took it hesitantly, as if sealing her fate, and let me pull her up and use that hand to lead her back to the foyer so we could go up the stairs. She lifted her wedding dress off the floor as we made our way past the trail of blood she'd left when we entered, much more conscious of the mess she was making.

Like I cared.

The way she lifted her dress with perfect poise to ascend the stairs, her posture straight despite how tired she must have been, was more reminiscent of the photos I'd seen of royalty than anyone who existed in modern day Philadelphia. Her face was a blank mask, carefully shielding every emotion from me as I guided her up to the bedroom we would share.

Christian had already had her belongings delivered, a team unpacking them while we were occupied with our wedding vows. Thalia glanced around the room as we stepped inside, taking in the sight of the book that had been carefully perched on her nightstand at home.

Books were splashes of dark ink on white pages. Entire worlds at her fingertips that she could experience the same as anyone else.

In all the months I'd spent watching her, I'd never seen her without one.

"This is mine," she said, stepping over to the nightstand on the side of the bed that she preferred to sleep on. She ran her fingers over the cover that was covered with a splash of red leaves, her eyes turning longing as she spun to look back at me in question.

"You'll find all your belongings are here," I said, clearing my throat. "The ones you would want to keep anyway, which wasn't much, I must admit."

There was a moment of silence as she sank her teeth into her bottom lip, her face ambivalent as if she couldn't decide if she wanted the answer to the question forming inside her head.

"How would you know what I want to keep?"

23

THALIA

"I think it's probably best that we save that conversation for another time," he said, unfastening the buttons of his tux jacket. He moved with the lethal grace of a predator, but all the refinement I would have expected of a man raised by royalty.

I didn't know where he'd gone in the years after being banished from the only home he'd ever known. Only that wherever life had taken him had guided him away from me in a way that the man who'd finally returned was nothing like the boy I'd known.

He folded his tux jacket carelessly, grabbing a garbage bag out of one of the drawers built into the base of the wide, cushioned seat that lined the bay window of the bedroom. He shoved it into the garbage bag, dropping it to the wood floor at his feet as he lifted a hand to his tie.

Like a businessman shedding his skin, revealing the monster waiting underneath, his fingers that were stained with the dark, crusted memory of death tiredly worked the silk open until he dropped that into the bag, too.

I swallowed when his eyes came to the train of my dress

where I gripped it in my hands and to my bare feet that touched the cool floors.

Never in my life had I wished for a third foot until his gaze raked over my wedding dress, sliding up my body until it landed on my face with heat filling his cool gray stare.

"I don't think that's your choice to make," I said, crossing my arms over my chest as my fear of what was coming reached a crescendo. I'd already felt Calix's body moving inside me; had already felt him cover me with his weight and the way he could demand things from me in the throes of passion.

But that was before I'd known he was the boy I'd never thought to desire—the boy who was meant to protect me from men like him.

He smirked, toeing off his shoes one by one and kicking them to the side. He moved forward, slowly closing the distance between us until he stood so close his light button-up shirt nearly brushed against the crystals sewn into the lace of my wedding gown.

"Everything is my choice to make, Little One. Every decision you make for yourself is because I indulge you in it, because I *allow* it. You are my wife, and it would do you well to remember what that means in the Six Families" His deep voice grated against the wounds in my heart like lash marks beating against my chest, a reminder of everything I would never be.

Free.

"I'm to be your property, then? Mindlessly doing as I'm told?" I asked, swallowing past the burn in my throat. I'd foolishly hoped for something more; some semblance of affection that would remind me of the Calix I'd loved as a girl.

"That's not what I said." He raised a hand, sliding it beneath the curtain of my hair and gripping the side of my neck. "But you should remember how things could be, so you can fully appreciate just how treasured you'll be with me."

I caught my breath, peering up into the intensity of his stare as he murmured the words. He touched his lips to mine for barely a whisper before he pulled back and his fingers went to the buttons of his shirt. He undid the top one as I swallowed back my nerves, reaching behind myself to pull down the zipper of my dress.

The sound of it broke the silence of the room, making his fingers pause on the button as he studied me with his head cocked to the side. I brushed the lace straps of the dress off my shoulders, letting the heavy fabric slide down my arms. It fell to my waist, leaving me to pull my arms free so I could wiggle from side to side until the fitted lace finally pushed over my hips and fell to my feet.

The bare back of the dress had left me no choice but to go braless for the wedding, leaving me standing in only a pair of white lace underwear. Lydia had told me they were white, drilling in the essence of my purity until the final moments before my new husband would take what was his.

What I'd already unintentionally given to that husband.

I bit back the whimper that tried to escape at the cruel twist my life had taken, stepping out of the fabric pooled around my feet and feeling Calix's eyes heavy on my body. I stepped toward the bed, reaching out to touch the dark fabric patterned with light narcissus flowers. I stopped before I could touch it, the sight of my blood-crusted hands giving me pause.

I was fairly certain that wasn't what Lydia had meant when she'd talked about the bloody sheets on my wedding night.

"As much as I love seeing you covered in the blood of our enemies, I don't want to bring them into our bed," Calix said, making me glance back at him as he continued to take his shirt off. He tossed it into the garbage bag along with his suit jacket, bending down to fight with the fabric of my dress to squeeze it in alongside them.

I tore my eyes off his broad shoulders, facing the bed once more as I fought for the composure to deal with what we both knew he wanted.

"Then where do you want me so we can just get this over with?" I asked, fighting back my wince when I looked over my shoulder at him and found his gray stare had hardened. I turned to face him fully and lifted my chin high.

I wouldn't play the simpering bride, desperate for her husband's touch. Not when I wouldn't have chosen him in a million years. I'd have rather tolerated the touch of a man I couldn't stand than ruin the memory of the only boy who'd ever shown me kindness.

"Get it over with?" he asked, his voice carefully controlled as he reached up and grasped my chin between harsh fingers. "Is that what you think of me? That I would lay you out and fuck you until I was done, not giving the first shit whether you wanted it?"

"You've hardly given me a reason to expect otherwise," I said, jerking my chin away from his grip. "You used my sister to make me agree to this sham of a marriage."

"Oh I promise you, λουλούδι μου, nothing about our marriage will be a sham," he warned, a cruel, bitter smile transforming his face. "But that doesn't mean that I'll take you when you're anything less than begging for it."

"Begging for it?" I asked, a huff of laughter erupting from me. "That is not going to happen."

"Whether I use your body or not, I own it now. If I cannot take pleasure in it, then neither can you. So I hope you're ready to forego all your late nights spent alone in bed with those pretty little fingers dancing between your thighs," he said, his voice a smooth purr.

My cheeks flushed, the need to deny the truth of his words flowing through me. But I couldn't force the words to come, choosing instead to keep my head held high and pretend the thought of someone knowing about when I touched myself didn't bother me.

"I'll miss those nights far more than I would ever miss *your* touch," I snapped as he took a step away from me and put a tiny bit of distance between us.

He dropped his hands to his belt buckle, smoothly unfastening it and the button on his slacks. "One of these days, we'll see which one of us can make you see stars, λουλούδι μου."

He shoved his pants and boxer briefs to his ankles, stepping out of them with more masculine grace than should have been possible. There was no shame on his face as he stared at me in challenge, his skin gleaming under the lights overhead as the sun set outside. It wasn't dark out just yet, though that would come soon enough.

He took my hand in his, tugging me away from the bed once he'd shoved his pants and socks into the bag with all our bloody clothes. I crossed an arm over my chest, trying to cover my breasts as my bravado faded.

If he wasn't going to get it over with, then I'd prefer to spend our conversations clothed.

He guided me into the bathroom as I held my gaze steady on the back of his head. The space light and airy and far too massive for what a bathroom really needed. I glanced around the room, looking at anything but his naked body. The memory of it kept me awake at night, his image filling all the fantasies that came after reading in bed since our one-night stand. Even just the line of muscle that extended over the curve of his shoulders, flexing as he turned his neck to look back at me, was enough to remind me of the way his skin felt against mine.

A cushioned settee was next to the deep claw foot tub by the windows overlooking the back gardens. Reaching in to start the water in the adjacent shower enclosure, he turned back to me with mischief playing on his face. "Are you intending to shower with your underwear on?"

"I'm not showering with you," I declared, wrapping my other arm around my torso.

"Water preservation is of the utmost importance, Thalia. I would think you'd want to do your part to save the planet. Especially when I've already had my tongue between your legs and explored every part of you that you could possibly try to hide now," he said, reaching behind me and touching a hand to the small of my back. He guided me into the shower, underwear and all, the rainfall showerhead pouring water down on me as I sputtered. I retreated to the back corner, stepping out of the spray and wiping the moisture from my face.

He stood beneath the cascading water, tipping his head back as he ran his hands through his dark hair, smoothing it back over his head as the water slid over the features of his face.

When he tipped his face back down, the gray of his eyes seemed to lighten with the piercing gaze he settled on me. The stains on his skin lightened as the water washed the blood away, and for once I was grateful that I couldn't see the tint of red to it or watch the color of life itself swirl down the drain and disappear.

My father's crumpled body flashed in my mind, Lydia's split throat following shortly after. Worry for Malva coursed through me and I huddled into the tiled wall, which felt cold at my spine as steam filled the shower between us. Calix moved toward me, his steps slow as he crossed the distance. I couldn't help the way my eyes tracked down his body, where water dripped over his chest and the defined muscles of his abs, clinging to the grooves in his hips that seemed to mimic carvings of the Greek gods.

He placed a hand on the wall next to my head, leaning his body over mine in a way that made me feel far shorter than I was. "Don't," he murmured, water dripping off his face and onto the swells of my breasts.

"Don't what?" I asked, keeping my eyes on his. His other hand touched my bare hip, his gaze dropping to the place that he touched me as he studied the way his fingers splayed out over my skin.

"Don't waste another moment of your time on the people who never deserved you. Don't spend a second of your life regretting the fact that they finally got *exactly* what they deserved," he said, shifting his gaze back to my face. His fingers toyed with the lace strap of my underwear, bunching it up in his grip as I swallowed.

His nostrils flared slightly as he lowered to his knees in front of me, his other hand trailing lightly over my torso to grasp the lace strap on the other side of my hip. "What are you doing?" I asked, hating the panic that had leaked into my voice.

"Relax, Little One. You will always be safe with me," he said, tugging the fabric down my thighs. I clenched them together, fighting the loss of that last coverage that hid even the slightest part of me from his view.

He tugged them down past my resistance, leaving me naked and huddling against the shower wall as he tossed the underwear to the other corner. He stood, leaning a forearm against the shower wall and keeping his body carefully separate from mine, allowing no part of him to touch me. "Breathe," he said finally, staring down at me with a face full of everything gentle.

With patience and understanding.

"You said you didn't want—"

"I just want to take care of you, λουλούδι μου. Let me help you get the blood off. You shouldn't have to spend another night wrapped in their sins," he said, touching a gentle hand to my cheek. He rubbed it lightly, washing away what I had no doubt was the spatter of Damianos's blood from when he'd shot him.

"I can do it," I protested as he reached for a bottle of body wash and squirted some into his hand.

"You've been taking care of yourself your entire life. It's my turn now," he said, using a gentle thumb to continue washing my face with a tenderness that brought tears to my eyes.

"Calix," I said, unsure what was supposed to follow. He stepped back toward the water, guiding me with him.

"Let the water run through your hair while I get the blood off your skin," he said, positioning me beneath the rainfall shower. The water fell onto my head, forcing me to tip it back if I wanted to avoid a deluge in my face. Calix dropped his hands to my forearms, grasping them gently and tugging them away from my torso where I'd attempted to cover my breasts from his prying eyes. I closed my eyes, trying to ignore the foreign feeling of another person's touch on me.

He started at my neck and shoulders, working the blood off until he managed to get those clean. I opened my eyes, shifting closer to him until the water ran over the back of my head and I could have a more relaxed angle. The thought of my eyes being closed while he touched me in less appropriate places terrified me, making me wonder what images I would conjure behind closed lids.

I couldn't afford to wish for the night we'd shared or to want the man that I knew I needed to escape as soon as I could.

He washed me efficiently, recognizing my discomfort with

his touch on my breasts. He didn't comment about the little gasp that came free from my lips when he ran his thumb over my nipple, or my rough inhalation between parted lips as he moved over my stomach to the space between my legs. He slid his fingers between them slowly, keeping his eyes on mine, and I fought back the little whimper as he washed me.

A groan rattled in his chest, vibrating as I dropped my forehead forward and rested it against his chest. Any sane woman would have given him anything he asked for with the gentle care he took to clean me and the self-restraint he showed when he pulled his hand free and knelt at my feet to clean my legs and feet free from blood.

He stood when he was finished, spinning me in place and filling his hands with shampoo. He rubbed it through my hair, massaging my scalp and rinsing out the gore from our wedding. He finished with conditioner, the floral scent of cherry blossoms mixing with vanilla as he took tender care to work the conditioner into the ends of my waist-length hair. Tears stung my eyes, my throat clogging with emotion as his fingers worked gently through the strands.

His touch felt like another lie—another promise to cherish me made by a man who had brought me some of the greatest pain I'd ever known. I knew what to do with agony. I knew how to survive abuse.

But what was I supposed to do with this?

He pushed me farther under the water, running his hands over my head to rinse my hair the same way he had wet his own. I felt like a new woman by the time he was finished with me. I stepped out from beneath the spray, letting him wash himself with far less tender motions.

"There's something for you to sleep in laid out on the chair in your closet," he said, dismissing me as he sank his teeth into his lip and watched me make for the shower door.

I paused with my hand on the handle, turning back to look at him and finally allowing my eyes to drop below his waist. His cock was long and hard, his shaft swollen and angry-looking as if it might explode if he didn't come. "Are you going to—" I broke off, shaking my head as I kicked myself for even thinking to ask that question.

What business was it of mine?

"No, Little One. I'm not about to jerk off to thoughts of your pussy wrapped around me. The next time I come, it will be inside of you," he said, making my cheeks heat as I pulled open the door and escaped the suddenly stifling heat of the shower.

He chuckled behind me, finishing with his shower as I stepped out and dried myself off hastily. I walked back into the bedroom with a towel wrapped around me, moving to the other door he'd mentioned.

The closet was painted in light shades, soft and feminine to contrast all the strong prints and patterns of the clothes hanging on the racks. They were nothing like the clothes Lydia had picked out for me, rather textured and vibrant in a way that even I could appreciate. I turned to the cushioned chair at the center of the walk-in closet, lifting the nightie he spoke of and tugging it on over my head without hesitation. The dark silk settled on me comfortably, the shine of white hydrangeas on it drawing my fingers to touch them.

Grabbing the towel and drying my hair off, I moved to the vanity on the other side of the closet. Lifting the comb from the top, I pulled it through the ends of my hair carefully, staring down at the dark locks in thought.

"Let me," Calix said, pulling the comb from my hand as he stepped up behind me. I looked up at him in the mirror, watching as he very carefully worked the comb through the knots at the back of my head.

"I can comb my own hair," I said, twisting my lips as I fought the urge to take the comb back from him.

"I know you can," he said, continuing to comb it until he worked the last of the knots free. He tipped my head back, parting my hair slightly to the side in the same spot I always did.

"And yet you are doing it for me anyway," I said as he smoothed it down the sides and combed it back until it settled behind my ears.

"I don't do things for you because I think you're incapable of taking care of yourself. I do things for you because you shouldn't have to," he said, setting the comb on the vanity.

I stared down at it in confusion for a moment, spinning on the stool suddenly to face him. My knees bumped into his bare legs, as only the core of his body was covered by the pair of boxer briefs he'd apparently slipped on after getting out of the shower.

"Where am I sleeping?" I asked, raising an eyebrow at him as he grinned at me. He shook his head, amusement on his face as he leaned forward and plucked me off the vanity stool. I squeaked as he lifted me into his arms, holding me carefully as I fought to make sure my pussy stayed hidden. I hadn't found underwear to put on, and I already regretted it, even if he had just had his fingers *there.*

He deposited me onto the bed where he'd already pulled back the covers, the smooth, expensive sheets touching my bare skin and seeming to try to drag me under immediately.

"You're my wife. Even if I'm not spending my nights inside you, you spend them in my bed," he said, moving to the other side of the bed and climbing in next to me. He pulled the covers up over us, turning to hit the light switch on the wall. After he touched a button next to it, the curtains pulled shut across the windows in an automated system.

"Aren't you worried I might kill you in your sleep?" I asked, looking over at him briefly. I could barely make out his features with the sudden darkness in the room.

"You're welcome to try, λουλούδι μου. Fair warning, though," he said, pausing to lean his body over mine. His lips dropped to mine gently, coaxing me to open for him so he could take the goodnight kiss he wanted. The heat of his mouth was like a brand inside of me, filling my lungs with fire. He pulled away slowly, tucking a lock of wet hair behind my ear. "I may enjoy it."

I turned my back on him with a glare, scooting to the very edge of the bed to put some distance between us. It was *not* normal for him to like the prospect of me trying to hurt him, but I couldn't get the image of his amusement out of my mind when I'd swung the splintered cane for his neck.

My husband would definitely like it.

He wrapped an arm around my waist, hauling me to the center of the bed until his chest brushed against my bare upper back. He slid a hand beneath my pillow, holding me steady with his arm draped over my side and sliding it between the valley of my breasts to nestle in there. His fingers splayed around the base of my throat, pinning me still without ever threatening my breathing.

He surrounded me, holding me still with the heat of his body at my back. "Calix," I protested, squirming as if to get out of his grip.

"If you keep moving like that, you might find my cock has a mind of its own when I'm asleep," he murmured into the back of my neck.

I stilled immediately, sinking my teeth into my bottom lip, something between desire and terror inside of me.

"Go to sleep, λουλούδι μου," he said, snuggling deeper into

the pillows and burying his nose in my hair. He breathed deep, taking me into his lungs.

As if I could ever sleep with a wolf at my back.

But his warmth sank into me, surrounding me in an embrace like nothing I'd ever known, and as his breathing steadied into a rhythmic pattern, my heart seemed to slow to match his.

And my eyes drifted closed.

24

THALIA

Sometimes, I dreamt of what it might be like to experience a garden in color, but every time I reached for a rose in the hopes of seeing it, and of holding something vivid in my hands, it faded away. Withering to the ashen dust of gray in my hands, it dissolved as if it decayed while I watched.

I woke, my eyes opening slowly to the foreign room that surrounded me. The curtains were still pulled closed, the room bathed in dim light from the open doorway to the hall.

I sat up, feeling the cold expanse of bed at my back and knowing that Calix had been gone for some time. Suspicion rose in me, the reminder of the fact that *I* wasn't allowed to touch myself, and yet he could sneak out of our bed before the sun finished rising.

I forced myself not to care. Every moment he spent in another woman's arms was a night of freedom for me. Every minute he spent away from me was another chance to remind myself how wrong my twisted feelings for him were.

Swinging my legs over the edge of the bed as I pulled back the covers, I ran my hands over the narcissus-covered bedspread. I wished I could see the orange at the center of the flower, so I could know what *warmth* looked like in a world filled with cold.

My eyes stung with tears as I stood from the bed, crossing my arms over my chest and crossing to the bathroom to brush my teeth. When that was done, I walked toward the open bedroom door.

My thirst drove me down the stairs toward the kitchen, my stomach pitching with something between nausea and hunger. I was far too familiar with the feeling, from never feeling satisfied with the meals I was allowed to have.

My hand touched the iron railing as I stepped down slowly, the sound of someone moving around in the kitchen reaching me as I made my way to the curved landing at the bottom and moved toward the dim light filtering in through the enormous windows at the back of the house.

My feet were cold as I padded across the marble floor, crossing to the wooden planks in the kitchen. Calix stood behind the kitchen island, slicing tomatoes on a cutting board. His body was encased in a dark suit, his hair drying from the shower he must have taken before I woke up. He was the perfect image of a gentleman, getting ready for a day of business and ready to conquer the world. There wasn't a mark on him from the violence of the day before, nothing to signify that he and his men had slaughtered an entire church full of people—all but eradicating two family lines from existence.

"I didn't think you'd be up so early, λουλούδι μου. I meant to bring you breakfast before I left," he said, finishing with the tomato and wiping his hand on a towel before he stepped around the island. He approached me without hesitation, leaning over me as he dropped a quick kiss to my mouth.

"You're leaving?" I asked, raising an eyebrow at him. Only a made man would leave his new bride in a home she'd never even gotten a tour of, on the day after their wedding.

"As much as I want to spend our day together, I have business to tend to before the Council summons me to deal with the consequences of yesterday. It's important that everything is settled on my end before then, and I thought you might like the day away from me at any rate. I know you like to be alone to process," he said. His words were another reminder that he seemed to know things about me, almost as if he'd never truly left the city.

But that wasn't possible, and I would have known if I'd seen him before that night in the hotel.

He nodded toward the doorway to the back patio where a pool overlooked a secluded garden and yard. The man who stepped into the doorway made my breath catch in shock.

Christian stepped into the house, his hands tucked into the front pockets of his slacks as he strolled in a manner far more casual than I'd ever seen in my father's home. "Hey, Monster," he murmured, the guilt in his voice erasing any confusion I'd felt in the moments after he'd stepped into view.

Torn between pure elation and absolute betrayal, I looked back and forth between him and Calix while the two men waited for me to speak. I couldn't find the words to articulate what I was feeling or to express the heartache that the man who had treated me as something more than a pathetic damsel had ulterior motives, too.

"I can't believe you!" I gasped suddenly, spinning to pin Calix with a glare. My throat burned with the tears I refused to shed, my teeth grinding together as I realized just how long Calix had been working toward this goal. This manipulation and massacre.

Christian had been employed in my father's home for years.

"Where are the others from the house? Were they all working for you, too?" I asked, trying to think of every man who had treated me horribly, who had refused to even *look* at me for fear of angering my father.

"They're dead, Monster," Christian answered, shrugging his shoulders as he moved farther into the kitchen. "I made sure of that."

"Christian will be overseeing your personal security while I'm away. You're not to go anywhere without him," Calix explained, closing the gap between us. He dropped a hand to the small of my back while I tried to digest the fact that Christian had murdered the men he'd worked alongside for years.

He'd slaughtered the men who had been his friends, in a way, all for Calix.

Calix, who led me to the patio doors, bringing me to the stone pavers surrounding the pool, where we stared at the gap in the trees as the sun rose to the left of the house. "I know this is probably another shock," he said, brushing my hair over my shoulder. He ignored the bedhead that I hadn't bothered to brush out after waking, dropping a kiss to the back of my neck and lingering there. His breath tickled my skin, sending a shiver through me despite the torrent of emotions I couldn't seem to grasp. He sighed when I didn't answer. "I'm going to go make you some coffee. I'll be right back."

He turned back to the house, leaving me to watch the sun rise in a moment of peace that felt anything but. The silence pressed in on me, weighing heavily as I fought to restrain my anger. I didn't *understand* any of it.

I made my way to the steps of the pool, placing my foot on the first one as the cool water slid over my toes. My other followed, gliding down the steps one by one until I was waist deep in the shallow end of the pool and watching the sun rise over the horizon in the distance.

The cold shock of water against my skin contrasted with the humidity of the summer air around me. With the silk of my nightwear floating around my hips, I dropped my hands and held it in place, half wondering why I bothered.

Nothing was a secret from Calix, anyway.

I felt the moment he stepped out onto the patio, and the rage that seemed to pulse through the air when he thought I'd tried to run. He sighed when he found me in the pool, and I moved to the edge and laid my forearms on the ledge. Leaning onto it and ignoring Calix, I tried to restrain the tears that threatened and refused to turn to look at him.

"I thought you'd tried to run," he admitted, the clank of a coffee cup setting down on one of the patio tables echoing across the open space.

"What would be the point?" I asked, knowing the truth in the words. Running would be futile, because Calix had long since had more power than the rest of the families gave him credit for.

"You don't have to seem so dejected about that, you know. You'll be treated in ways you can't even begin to imagine," he said, and I could just visualize him running his hands through his hair. Even after all these years, even after all this time, there were hints of the boy I'd known in the mannerisms he had.

They only made it more painful to look at him.

"Another pretty cage," I whispered, running my tongue over my teeth. "You shouldn't have wasted it on someone who can barely fucking see it." All my life, I'd been surrounded by pretty things, but none of it was for me. It was everyone for *else;* it was just the wrappings on the gift I'd make for one man.

"We'll discuss it later after you've had some coffee," Calix said, his knowledge of my morning crankiness only serving to drive my rage higher. He turned to walk away, the sound of his steps shuffling over the stone pavers making me spin to face him.

"What happened to you?" I asked, the rage fading from my face as I thought of the boy who had never been anything but sweet to me. Of how much I missed him.

He stopped, his steps faltering as he slowly turned to face me. His eyes were trained on the water surrounding me, glowering and hard by the time he raised them to my face. "They took me from you," he said, his jaw clenching as if it irritated him that he even had to explain himself to me. "So I became the man I needed to be to find my way back."

My hands clenched and unclenched, fighting with the urge to scream, and to remind him that he'd stayed away for nearly two decades. "You left me here with them!"

"They dragged me away unconscious, λουλούδι μου. What would you have had me do?" he asked, crossing his arms over his chest.

My voice softened, the hurt showing even as I tried to hide it behind the rage of a woman abandoned. "You never came back for me."

"I was no good to you dead," he said, running a hand over his face. "And if I came back before I had any power or ability to take a stand, that was exactly what they would have done to me. Killed me and laid my body next to your mother's in o λάκκος."

"You promised me I would never be forced to marry—"

"Someone who didn't care for you," he finished, stepping toward the edge of the pool. He lowered himself to a crouch beside it, staring at me as if he could will me to see things his way. "I remember every word I ever said to you. I slaughtered an entire church full of people to keep that promise. You would do well to remember that, because if you doubt everything else you've ever been told about me, *never* question that

I am a man of my word, Little One. Never doubt that I would slaughter the entire world just to fucking keep you."

He stood smoothly, rolling his head from one side to the other as I gaped up at him. Then he spun on his heel, storming through the doors to the house and disappearing from my sight. Something shattered in the house as I hauled myself up over the ledge of the pool, grabbing the coffee off the table, ready to chase after him and throw it in his face.

The scent that wafted off the cup made me pause; my favorite brew with what I suspected was the perfect creamer to sugar ratio made me drop it back to the table as if it had scalded me.

Christian leaned his shoulder against the doorway, crossing his arms over his chest as he raised a brow at me. "Things are going well, I take it."

25

CALIX

I shoved open the front doors of the church, stepping into the open space. No longer were the floors littered with the bodies of my enemies. No longer were they tainted by the gore of my massacre, but the scent of death and decay clung to the walls, filling the air with the macabre of what waited for all of us. Our spirits may or may not move on to an afterlife—it could be paradise or the underworld—but our bodies would always be left behind to rot.

Rafael and Ryker spun from their places next to the altar where the priest had married Thalia and me. He'd had very little hesitation or concern for the innocent woman he must have believed himself to be assigning to a life with an evil, twisted murderer, given what he'd seen of me.

He'd known me when I'd been a child. He'd watched me grow in the pews of the church, listening to his sermons about the importance of repenting our sins. I would die long before I repented what I'd done in his church the day before.

There was nothing sinful about ridding the earth of the cockroaches that had stained it and had abused my wife. If that got me sent to Hell, I would walk willingly into the flames.

"I wasn't expecting you so early," Rafael said, furrowing his brow. He looked over my body, over the taut lines of my face, and a knowing grin spread across his. "I do believe the newlywed phase is supposed to last longer than the wedding night."

I grunted, walking up the aisle at the center of the church. The floor was stained with blood, with the carnage of having bodies dragged from the space one by one, but I was certain I recognized the blemish specifically left by Thalia's brother where I'd left him to bleed out.

He should have protected her from the violence of their father, and if he had, we could have moved forward into a new era as allies. Instead, he'd died with the rest of them.

Rafael and Ryker, Matteo Bellandi's executioner from Chicago, exchanged a look as I approached. Something sinister lingered behind the amusement of their attention as I closed the distance between us. There was only a hint of it, as if they were truly more interested in my first night with my wife by my side.

I supposed it hadn't been all that long since the hatchet-wielding, muscular Ryker had snatched his wife and children and moved them into his converted warehouse in Chicago, and Rafael still waited for his Isa to be ready for him to claim.

"If I didn't know better, I would think you were almost disappointed there were no bodies left for you to kick," Ryker said, crossing his arms over his chest as he smiled.

"I was thinking more along the lines of stabbing, actually," I said, piercing Bellandi's executioner with a withering glare and sardonic smile.

"You know Calix gets irritable when he doesn't get to look

at dead people for a few hours," Rafael said, running his fingers over the Bible the priest had left on the altar the evening before.

"Listen, I like it when they scream as much as the next guy, but your fixation on them after they're dead is just a little disturbing," Ryker said, shaking his head and moving to the cleaners waiting to scrub the floors now that the bodies had all been dealt with. He spoke to them in hushed tones, pretending to ignore the response he would receive.

"What good is any form of art if you don't take time to appreciate the masterpiece at the end?" I asked, making him scoff and pinch the bridge of his nose between two fingers.

The splashes and smears of blood were our paint, the wood and stained glass of the church our canvas. There was beauty in everything.

Even in death.

"What's with the concerned face?" I asked, turning my attention to Rafael, where the man furrowed his brow and steepled his hands on the altar in front of him. He leaned onto the Bible, and for a moment I wondered how the devil himself didn't burst into flames touching the supposedly holy document—in a church, no less.

"We're missing two bodies," he said, making my fists clench at my side. The thought of any of the Hasapis family making it out alive was enough to make me murderous.

"Who wasn't here?" I asked, running through the memory of the faces staring back at me the day before. Admittedly, I'd been distracted by thoughts of Thalia, and trying to get to her before she could be caught up in the bloodbath that followed. My flower had gone above and beyond though, abandoning all but Malva and trying to escape.

The sight of it had filled me with both pride and rage.

"Damianos's younger brother Tobias was evidently conducting family business outside of Philadelphia at the time of the wedding. It's only a matter of time before he hears of what you've done and demands the blood debt be paid in o λάκκος. You'll need to work quickly to form alliances with the other families to see that does not happen," he said.

I ground my teeth together, turning my head away to stare at the spot where I'd shot Damianos for daring to try to marry my woman. His worm of a brother was even worse than the original Hasapis heir, a power-hungry prick, and it amazed me he hadn't slaughtered his older sibling years before. "That was one. You said there were two."

"We cannot find Jeno Karras's body," Rafael said, raising his brow at me.

"That's impossible. I stabbed him myself," I said, shaking my head as I looked back at the place where his blood had coated my hand, the hot pump of it thick against my skin with the final beats of his heart.

"And yet he is undoubtedly missing. Unless someone managed to steal his body, it would appear that you didn't finish the job properly," Rafael said, a smile making his lips tip up at the corners. The fucker knew how much it would both irritate and entertain me to know Jeno had escaped alive.

Surely no one would have any use for a *dead* Karras.

"You shouldn't look so pleased when your enemy escapes with his life," Rafael said, crossing his arms over his chest as his look turned scolding.

"Maybe, but do you honestly mean to tell me you wouldn't relish the opportunity to take your time with someone who'd hurt Isa?"

"Did Jeno ever hurt her?" Rafael asked, his lips pursing in thought.

It was a fine line to walk between standing back and watching it happen and actively participating. I believed Jeno was just as responsible for Thalia's suffering. I'd have preferred to slowly murder her father.

But the son would have to do.

26

THALIA

The silk of my robe settled onto my shoulders as I ran my hands through my hair in frustration and stared around the closet. The varying fabrics around the room were all new—all unfamiliar.

I gritted my teeth as I tried to think of what I could possibly do to get dressed without looking like a fool. I would *not* ask Christian for help where he waited downstairs, but the constant reminders of the fact that I couldn't even dress myself without memorizing what matched and went well together during Lydia's lessons made me sink down onto the tufted ottoman in the center of the room.

Christian knocked on the doorway to the closet as he peered in, his gaze not even hesitant. He'd known damn well I wouldn't be able to dress myself in this situation, so had little fear that he might discover me naked. He'd seen it all anyway when they'd forced him to supervise my more severe punishments, so I doubted my privacy mattered much to him.

"You won't find any color in your wardrobe aside from jeans, Monster," he said, stepping into the space. He grabbed one of the dresses off the rack, draping it over his arm delicately so the fabric didn't wrinkle. Carrying it over to me, he peeled back the neckline to reveal the silk tag sewn into the inside of the dress.

Light gray.

I reached out, running my fingers over the tag. "No color whatsoever?" I asked, bringing a smirk to his face as he took the dress back to the rack and hung it carefully while I asked, "How could Calix want his wife to exist in black and white and shades of gray? That's not exactly feminine."

"How could Calix want his wife to wear something she wouldn't choose for herself?" he returned, raising a brow as he retreated from the closet. He pulled the door closed behind him, giving me the illusion of privacy for a few moments. Moving to the drawers beneath the shirt racks, I pulled one out to find a variety of bras staring back at me. The next drawer was filled with underwear.

Going to grab a white pair from each, Lydia's words that I should "wear white for as long as possible after the wedding to remind Damianos of the innocence he'd taken" rang through my head.

I grabbed the darkest black I could find, the small rebellion filling me with the need to see it through as I stripped off the robe and hurried into the set. I walked to the pant section of the closet, grabbing a pair of jean shorts off the shelf.

The tag read *dark gray denim*. I knew enough from the fashion magazines I'd had shoved down my throat all my life that people wore just about everything with jeans, but I'd never been allowed to wear them. I couldn't even remember the last time Lydia had let me wear pants.

I tugged them up my legs, letting the heavyweight fabric settle against my skin as I shimmied from side to side and buttoned them at my waist. They fit me perfectly, and I tried not to think about the implications of that as it all added up.

Grabbing a black tank top off the rack, I shrugged it on over my head. Trying to adjust to all the skin that showed on my arms and bare legs, I padded to the closet door and pushed it open. Shoving through the doorway and ignoring where Christian lingered in the bedroom in wait, I hurried down the stairs to the main living space.

"Would you like a tour?" he asked.

"I don't want a fucking thing from either of you," I snapped, spinning to glare at him before I took myself into the kitchen to find something to eat. I tugged open the fridge, finding it fully stocked and ignoring the tomatoes and mushrooms Calix had been slicing on the counter.

"You could have been eating an omelet if you hadn't pissed him off," Christian said, pulling out one of the stools on the other side of the island. He sat in it, leaning his elbows onto the countertop and placing his chin in his palms as he stared at me with amusement. "Do you even know how to cook?"

I grabbed a yogurt from the fridge, popping the lid off and licking it clean. "I am fairly certain this day will be *slightly* less miserable if you stop speaking to me. Otherwise, you may find out what it feels like to have someone shove a spoon down your throat until you choke on it," I said, giving him a saccharine smile as I pulled open one of the drawers to look for said spoon.

Christian chuckled, tilting his face down until his palm rubbed over his cheek. "You can spew whatever bullshit you want to make yourself feel better, Monster, but I've been in your father's house for years."

"I'm aware, thank you," I said, closing the drawer harshly. The soft-close feature caught it before the drawer could slam, and the feature enraged me further when I couldn't take joy in the resulting noise.

He lowered his arms to rest flatly against the countertop,

leaning forward with his eyes gleaming playfully. "So I have seen the way you looked cowed out of fear. You never would have dared to act this way in your father's home, because you knew just what would happen if you did. Say whatever you want about Calix, call him your enemy all you need to, but you would never act this way if you thought he would hurt you."

I tore open another drawer, hating the truth to his words. I wouldn't have dared to speak out against the comforts my father gave me or storm around the house in a fury. I'd stayed tucked away in my bedroom and feared the consequences of wandering.

What would I have done if I'd woken up in Damianos's house this morning?

I'd have been grateful for him leaving me for the day, because it would've meant he wouldn't touch me and I'd have some peace and quiet to come to terms with my thoughts on what had happened the night before.

I might not have even woken up this morning if I'd wed Damianos and he had realized I wasn't a virgin. I swallowed, shoving the spoon I'd found into the plastic container of yogurt and forcing myself to scoop a bite into my mouth.

I sighed, placing the container on the counter as my hunger fled. Tears burned the back of my throat as I considered just how close to death I'd really come for my foolish attempt at a moment of freedom.

And it hadn't even fucking mattered in the end. I'd still ended up in bed with the man who would become my husband. I just hadn't known it.

"The honey is in the pantry," Christian said, nodding his head toward the two cabinet doors that extended from the ceiling to the floor. I retreated to them, taking the moment to put a little distance between us. Christian's betrayal and involvement in my deception hurt almost as much as the loss of the boy I'd loved when I'd been a girl. I couldn't let him know that there was even a part of me that was grateful to be alive—to be in Calix's home and not Damianos's, suffering the ramifications of however he'd seen fit to punish me for my indiscretion.

I tugged open the cabinet doors, my eyes widening when they parted to reveal a walk-in pantry. Foods of every type lined the shelves, perfectly organized like in a model home. I had to wonder if it was Calix who required such order or if there was a housekeeper with a penchant for it.

I found the honey in a prominent place, snagging it off one of the smaller shelves at eye level. It would seem I wasn't the only one in the house who liked to enjoy *straggisto* in the more traditional way.

Taking a deep breath before I walked back out, I tried not to even glance at the chocolate treats organized in clear bins on the shelf below the honey. The rebellious part of me wanted to eat every last one, to enjoy the sweets in a way I hadn't been allowed since my father had destroyed the ones Calix had given me as a girl.

I turned my back on them, the haunting memory of a cane cracking against my hands making my fingers ache when I even considered it.

I stepped back into the kitchen, closing the cabinets behind me to hide the pantry once more. Christian's eyes were heavy on the side of my face as I moved through the space, turning the honey over and squirting a small dollop into my yogurt. "You good?" he asked, sliding off the counter stool. He didn't move to step around the island between us, staying on his side as if he feared I may strike him if he wandered too close.

Thanks to him, I could probably make a single hit count—at least a little bit.

"I'm fine. I don't have much choice, do I?" I asked, scoffing at him.

"Why are you so angry with *me*? Calix I can understand. He deceived you that night in the hotel..."

"Why am I so angry with you?" I asked, my voice rising in disbelief as I dropped the spoon into my yogurt. "I *trusted* you!"

"How have I broken that trust? Because I work for your husband instead of your father? My job was always to keep you as safe as I could. That was true regardless of which man signed my paycheck at the end of the day, Thalia," Christian said, keeping his voice gentle. But I could hear the note of irritation.

The fucker thought I was being unreasonable.

"You knew when you made the arrangements for me to go to that hotel. You and Calix set me up," I protested, crossing my arms over my chest and glaring at him.

"I told him you would be there. I didn't make you fall into bed with him, Monster. Did you really think I'd allow you to skip out on Damianos if you were going to be his wife? Fuck's sake, you might as well have asked me to just kill you myself," he argued.

I threw my spoon at him, narrowly missing his forehead when he twisted to the side. The metal clanged against the floor in the dining room behind him. "Fuck you," I growled.

"You went there to get laid. You got what you wanted, and because of Calix you are still *alive* in spite of it. Everyone who has ever hurt you lies dead and rotting now, and you complain about broken trust? What kind of trust could you have had in me, if I'd allowed you to continue to suffer?"

"The kind where I would at least know exactly where you

stand. I would know you were loyal to the man you vowed to serve, even if I hated him with a passion that rivals the wrath of Ares himself!" I snapped, watching him warily as he stepped around the island and approached. All the fight drained slowly out of me slowly, the next words tearing free from the deepest parts of me I wanted to hide. "I thought you were my friend in a world where I couldn't have them."

Christian's face gentled, and he cautiously reached out with a single hand to tuck my hair behind my ear. "I still am. I know all about your interest in the flowers and the way you cry when you look at the fields behind the house and think of the narcissus that grew there when your mother was alive. I know about all the nights you draw in your room when everyone else is sleeping. I know you have a fucking mean left hook that I wouldn't want you to land," he said, his words trailing off into a chuckle as he dropped his forehead to mine and stared at me meaningfully. "I've learned everything I could about you, all the little things that make you who you are. I just didn't learn them for me—not really. They were for Calix, the man who waited for you to be his."

"Why did he wait so long?" I asked, hating the way the statement betrayed the real reason for my upset. I wouldn't have been nearly as sad if Calix had come for me years ago, if he'd rescued me from my life of abuse sooner.

"He couldn't, Monster. I swear to you; he came as soon as he possibly could. When they banished him, they stripped him of all his family money and every bit of influence he could have hoped to wield to save you. He had to work his way up from the bottom all over again, but believe me when I tell you there wasn't a moment that passed where he wasn't worried for you. Where he wasn't dreaming of the day that he could give you your vengeance and free you from them," he said.

"Some freedom this is," I argued, huffing as I stepped back and glared down at the yogurt I no longer wanted. My hunger had indeed fled, the stress threatening to consume me as I wondered what my new future would look like. More years of living for Malva's sake, certainly.

"Give it time. Philadelphia is a dangerous place for you right now until Calix can finish taking control of the council and the city, and he has to protect you," Christian said.

"He has to protect his interest in using me to gain access to the Karras seat, you mean," I said, grabbing the yogurt and tossing it into the garbage can.

"Now you're just being deliberately obtuse. I can't wait to watch you eat your words," he said, laughing as he walked toward the sliding glass doors to the back patio and the pool.

He always had needed to get the last word.

The shit.

27

CALIX

I strode into the house, the paper bag filled with Thalia's favorites tucked under one arm. It had been a long day away from her, but my text messages with Christian confirmed it was probably for the best. Her newfound penchant for throwing things hadn't lessened since the night before. I supposed I should be grateful she hadn't taken to throwing knives just yet.

I gave it a week.

The kitchen was empty as I stepped into it, setting the paper bag down on top of the island. Christian was the first to enter from the back patio, snagging an apple out of the fruit basket on top of the counter and taking a bite. The sound of it echoed through the silent kitchen and he turned his nose up as he chewed.

A smirk tipped his mouth up as he studied me. "Kiss ass," he chuckled, opening the bag to peer inside. "Do you really think *tirokroketes* will get you lucky?"

"Of course not," I said, crossing my arms over my chest as I looked over his shoulder toward the pool. I watched through the open doors as Thalia took the first step and rose slowly from the water. The black bikini clung to her thin frame, her breasts pushed high as strings wrapped around her waistline. She held my stare, the amber of her eyes piercing as the rest of her figure emerged.

There was a challenge in her gaze, a defiance that I felt nothing but pride in. I just wished she could have rebelled in a way that left her wearing more clothes around Christian.

"Really?" I asked, shifting on my feet as my cock hardened. Thalia turned her side to me, bending forward to grab a towel off one of the lounge chairs beside the pool. Her back arched as she straightened, running the towel over her hair and drying the ends. The scars on her back were visible, and it filled me with disgust that she'd been harmed that way, and simultaneous pride that she wore them like scars she'd earned in battle.

"I'm fairly certain she would have gotten in naked if I'd asked her to put on something more modest," Christian answered, quirking a brow. He didn't even glance back at her, confirming that the man knew damn well how I would feel about Thalia being practically naked around another man while I was gone.

"Just so we're clear—"

"You'll dismember me slowly and then use my corpse as a canvas for your next artwork. I'm quite aware, thank you," he said, turning and waving quickly to Thalia. She raised her chin proudly, not returning the gesture as she continued to dry off.

I grabbed the bag of takeout off the counter, giving Christian my back as I made my way toward my wife. She watched me approach, finally wrapping the towel around her waist to cover the tops of her thighs. She raised a brow in challenge, clearly expecting me to fly into a rage about her propriety.

One day soon, she'd come to understand her body was

mine to command, no matter how she dressed it. She'd understand that true ownership of her body would come when she surrendered it, not from a man who demanded it without ever earning that submission from her. "Were you expecting something from me, Little One?" I asked.

She crossed her arms over her chest, glaring at me in response. "What if I was hoping you and Christian would tear one another apart so I could walk right out the door? What would you have to say to that?"

"I would say that would be a very foolish thing to hope for. I am the only thing keeping you alive right now. Without me, who knows how the rest of the families will seek their vengeance? If they find out you and I connected before yesterday, they just may blame you for the chaos, too. I don't think I need to tell you what they would do to you before they killed you if they thought you betrayed them," I answered, shrugging my shoulders.

Thalia's jaw clenched, the truth of my words settling over her. As much as she and I both hated Origen Karras for what he had done to her mother for her affair with my father, there were many among the families who thought she'd gotten off easy. There were those who thought she should have been treated as a whore for days by the families before they allowed her to die.

I would die long before I ever allowed them to give λουλούδι μου the same fate.

"What a lovely consolation prize it must be to know that you are a *slightly* better prospect than being raped by the rest of the families," she scoffed.

I ignored the stab of pain that lanced through me at the harsh words, knowing without a doubt that her anger drove them and not how she actually felt. She'd had no complaints about my hands on her body before she knew who I was. Her choice didn't lie as easily as her mouth did.

Thalia desired me as much as I wanted her.

I hummed thoughtfully, stepping toward her and depositing the bag onto the coffee table on the patio. "Do you think they'll bring you *tirokroketes* and chocolate?" I asked, lifting a brow as she froze. She turned her eyes toward the bag on the table, pursing her lips and running her tongue over her bottom teeth as she turned her attention back to me.

"That's cheating," she said, but she took a step toward the bag as if she couldn't help herself. Chuckling, I retreated into the house to grab napkins and forks. "I see Christian's been talking!" she called after me, bringing a smile to my lips that I hid before I turned back to face her.

I returned to the patio, placing the napkins on the table before I grabbed the closest chair and pulled it out for her. She watched me cautiously as she lowered herself into it, allowing me to push it in for her until she sat as close to the chair next to it as possible. I took the seat next to her, reaching into the bag and pulling out the containers of food one by one. Thalia's eyes widened as she stared at the sheer amount I'd brought for the two of us, and something inside of me ached for the fact that she'd never once known a meal of overindulgence.

She'd never had the privilege of ordering so much takeout that she'd have to eat it for lunch the next day because her eyes were bigger than her stomach.

I dropped a hand to her thigh, nudging the towel out of the way so I could touch her bare leg. The soft olive of it gleamed with the dampness of her skin that she hadn't been able to wipe away, and I watched as her cheeks stained with pink. She stared down at my hand, pursing her lips but never removing it from her body.

She focused on the food instead, carefully pulling the lid off the first container. She opened the *tomaotokeftedes,* staring down at the tomato fritters as I leaned forward. Taking one in my hand, I tore a chunk off and dipped it in the yogurt at the center of the platter. Lifting it to Thalia's mouth, I touched it to her lips until the plump flesh of her bottom lip was dotted with white. "Open, Little One," I murmured, holding her stare with my intent gaze.

She blinked, slowly parting her lips to allow me to slide the fritter into her mouth. Her eyes drifted closed as soon as it touched her tongue, and I let her mouth close around my fingers as I withdrew them to allow her to chew.

"To answer your question, yes. Christian has told me all about your favorite things, though the chocolate was no secret," I said, hinting back to all that I'd known about her when she'd been a girl. It shouldn't have been a surprise to her that I would remember them, but her eyes opened and confusion clouded her features. "But there are plenty of things he didn't need to tell me."

"Things you remember from when we were younger?" she asked, swallowing down the bite of food as I popped a bite into my mouth. She reached for the fritter to take her own and glared at me when I swatted her hand away. "I can feed myself."

"Can you?" I asked, humming as I chewed and fed her a second piece. She opened in spite of her protests, her desire for the food I offered far greater than her need to be spiteful. "Some things I remembered from when we were younger. Others I learned by watching you."

She swallowed abruptly, a tiny cough escaping her lips as she sat back in her seat and watched me open up the second container. Taking out a *tirokroketes,* I took off the lid and tore a fried cheese ball in half. She barely glanced down at it even though I knew it was her favorite and a special treat she'd only gotten when Christian snuck her some. "What do you mean watching me?" she asked, holding perfectly still as I raised the half of a ball to her lips.

She didn't part for me, letting it rest just beneath her nose where I knew she could smell the cheese and mint. "Christian's weren't the only eyes I planted inside your father's home at the first opportunity. I hacked into his cameras, and had Christian place a few of my own in your bedroom."

"You watched me in my bedroom?" she asked, her voice muffled as I placed the bite of fried cheese ball in her mouth. She chewed, but it was clear she mostly wanted it out of her mouth.

"You shouldn't waste it. We both know it's delicious," I said, popping the other half into my mouth and smiling as I chewed.

"You watched me in my bedroom," she repeated, the question disappearing from her voice as she studied me and my lack of shame.

"What's wrong, λουλούδι μου? Are you thinking of all the times I watched you play with yourself while you read in your bed?" I asked, watching as shame made her cheeks heat.

"You watched me touch myself?" she asked, her voice sputtering. All her thoughts of food forgotten, she crossed her arms over her chest as that feeling of violation settled over her. Thalia would quickly realize that she had no secrets from me, and there was nothing to feel shame about, because I'd known every inch of her body before I'd ever gotten my hands on her. I knew exactly what she liked from the male leads in the books she favored. I knew the way her fingers danced over her clit when she wanted a fast release.

I fed her another bite even though she didn't seem at all interested in it any longer, because I would always do what was in Thalia's best interest. For the moment, making sure she had enough to eat for the first time in her life and went to bed full and satisfied was high on my priority list.

"I watched you and I stroked my cock to the sight of you with your legs spread and your fingers pumping into your sweet, little cunt. I imagined your fingers were my cock, wondering just how tight and warm you'd be when I finally sank inside of you," I admitted, grasping her chair by the arms and turning it to face me fully. I leaned my weight on the arms, pressing into my hands as I crowded her.

"Why would you do that? Why was that necessary for what you wanted?" she asked, reaching over my arm to grab a tomato fritter and tear off a piece. She raised it to my lips and let me accept the bite, using it as a way to create a modicum of distance between us with distraction.

"Why don't you tell me what it is you think I want, Little One?" I asked, tilting my head to the side as I studied her. "Because I promise you, watching you was entirely about what I wanted."

"You married me for power. You married me because it makes you the head of two of the six families. You married me because it was the easiest way to take back the control they stripped from you," she said, leaning back once again. Her stare hardened, as if the words she spoke reminded her that it had never been about her in the first place.

But she couldn't have been more wrong.

I scoffed, chuckling beneath my breath as I dropped my hand to the top of her thigh. "I could have any city I wanted. My allies outside of Philadelphia are remaking the world as we speak, preparing to shift it under a singular power who happens to be the man who taught me everything I know. I didn't need to marry you for power," I said, taking another bite and chewing thoughtfully as I allowed her time to process my words.

"Then you did it for revenge," she said.

I pointed a finger at her, as if ringing a bell. "I took back the city for *your* revenge. I could have just plucked you out of it and taken you somewhere else. No one would dare to risk Rafael's wrath over a woman," I said. I touched my hands to her bare thighs gently, letting my fingertips dig in ever-so-slightly until her skin compressed beneath my grip. "I married you because I want you. Because I want you in my bed. Because I want to look at your swollen belly and wonder if the baby will have your eyes. Because I want to fuck you until your legs tremble so much you can't stand up when I'm done with you."

She swallowed, staring at me as I backed away and gathered another bite of food to feed to her.

"Calix—"

I stood, holding out a hand for her. Apprehension flitted across her features, but she placed her hand in mine and allowed me to guide her toward the house. "I married you because you're mine, Thalia. Nothing matters beyond that. Nothing."

28

THALIA

He held my fingers tightly grasped within his, interlacing them in a way that felt far too comfortable for me. I wanted to hate it. Wanted to despise the stain of his blood-soaked hands on my skin. He led me into the bedroom, ignoring the way I dragged my feet, and headed straight for the bathroom.

I tried to find solace in his promise not to touch me unless I begged him to. My body was drawn tight, every muscle locked as I prepared myself for the fight that would come if he went back on his word. In the end, I had no reason to trust him, no reason to believe that anything he'd told me was true. He was a murderer, and he'd stolen me from the man who was meant to be my husband.

It was fortunate I hadn't loved Damianos or felt anything when I'd watched him crumple to the floor in front of me, the hole in his head allowing me to see inside to what made him. It was an odd sort of reminder of our mortality, and how we were all just sacks of meat to be destroyed and manipulated however necessary.

But I couldn't say that my hypothetical love for my potential husband would have stopped Calix from killing him. I suspected it was the opposite, in fact, and that frightened me more than anything. How much loyalty and honor could I expect from him if he would have killed the man I loved to take me as his?

I swallowed as he released me, wishing I'd had the time to grab the towel from my seat on the patio. As my bravado fled, I felt far too exposed by the skimpy bikini I'd donned just to irritate Calix. It hadn't worked out the way I'd wanted, and I highly doubted I would make the same mistake again.

More clothing was better where Calix was concerned. I needed less skin for him to touch with his strong, calloused hands that reminded me of how they felt roaming over my body.

He plugged the drain in the enormous claw foot tub that sat in front of floor to ceiling bay windows. I stood back by the vanity on one side of the bathroom, hiding myself behind the seat in the center of the room as if it could protect me if he tried to bathe with me. The sound of running water filled the room as he started the tub, and I swallowed as I dropped a single hand to the top of the marble counter.

He approached me slowly, that distinctive, arrogant pace of his doing nothing to settle my nerves. To think that this man had watched me touch myself in the privacy of my bedroom; to think that he'd been privy to the most private of my moments in a life that had been controlled in every other aspect...

I didn't know what to do with that. I didn't know what to make of a husband who didn't expect me to pretend to be naive. Lydia had taught me how to please my husband in theory. She'd spoken of all the games women played, from being coy and sweet to submitting to every one of their husbands' desires—no matter how frightening they may seem at first.

But I didn't want to submit to Calix. I didn't want to bow to him out of fear the way I would have with Damianos.

I wanted him to fucking earn it, because he damn well had a lot of years to make up for.

Calix stepped up behind me, using the pressure of his hips at my ass to twist my body until I faced the bathroom counter straight on. He wrapped his arms around me, running his fingers down my bare arms until I shivered and goosebumps raised on my flesh. The sight of his strong hands on my skin made something inside of me clench tight, feeling empty of everything I knew he could offer me.

His hands continued to slide down until they covered each of mine, pressing my palms into the countertop and leaning his weight into my back. His mouth rested against the side of my head and he murmured into my hair with a groan that he punctuated with a shallow thrust of his hips against me. "Gray," he said simply, pushing harder at my hands to make his meaning clear.

"The counter?" I asked, my voice sounding far too breathy to be natural. It betrayed every amount of desire building within me, and every bit of all the things I couldn't want from him.

"The house," he corrected, sliding his hands back up my arms once again as he lowered his head to my shoulder. My head shifted to the side to give him better access, defying me and the logical response to his touch.

My body was a fucking traitor for him, leaning into him and craving even the simplest deception of affection. For so long, all I'd known was pain. I just wanted to be touched in ways that didn't hurt.

"The entire house is gray?" I asked, chuckling as I tried to process those words. What an absurd concept, to think that an entire house could be one color. One note. One shade.

He rubbed his lips over my skin, pressing a kiss to the spot where my neck met my shoulder and smiling into the hollow when I shuddered. "Gray, black, and white. This is your home, λουλούδι μου. You deserve to be able to see it," he murmured against me. Everything in me stilled as he continued to rub his mouth against me, and I watched my reflection in the mirror as I blinked.

Tears burned my eyes. It was such a stupid thing to care about. What did it matter if a house was in full color? It would always be shades of gray to me. But there was something about knowing that I saw the same thing as everyone else that made me feel less broken.

It went against everything my father had been determined to make me believe about myself.

He had said time and time again that my color-blindness was a deformity, a mutation that he would have rid himself of when I'd been born if he'd known. But by the time I'd revealed I couldn't see colors, the rest of the families knew of my existence.

To kill me would have raised more questions, so I'd been trained to hide my secret. To hide my deformity. To never let anyone know the daughter of Origen Karras was ruined from birth. But Calix didn't make me feel broken. He didn't make me feel like I was damaged. He made me feel unique, like my perspective was beautiful.

"Why would you do such a thing? How can you want to live in a world without color?" I asked, swallowing back the surging emotions as I turned away from the mirror. I spun in his arms, placing my hands on the fabric of his white button-up shirt at his shoulders.

Calix stared down at me, all traces of arrogance fleeing his face as he studied me. He seemed to realize that the confession, this moment, meant something to me. It had sunk inside of me and threatened to claw away at my reserve. "Maybe I want to see the world through your eyes," he said softly, reaching up to tuck my hair behind my ear. His fingers lingered at the slight tip at the tops of my ears, at the oddity Lydia had insisted I hide at all times.

My breath caught.

"The world through my eyes is boring," I said, tilting my chin down to look at the floor and trying to swallow past the tightness in my throat. They were too much, the sudden fullness in my chest and the warmth trying to fill the cold recesses of my soul.

"Somehow I doubt that's true," he said, sliding his finger along my jaw until he could grasp my chin in his hand. He lifted it, raising it until I met his stare. "Come with me."

He took my hand once more, guiding me away from the bathroom and the tub that was still filling with hot water. "Where are we going?" I asked as he led me through the bathroom and to the hallway outside.

Guiding me a few doors down, he brought me to the closed French doors I'd seen earlier in the day and resisted the urge to go snooping behind. I'd assumed it would be his office, but as he placed his hands on the handles, I realized how wrong I'd been. "You may have been sheltered and a prisoner in your own life, but you still found a way to live a thousand other lives."

He pushed the doors open, stepping out of the way so that I could move into the ornate, bright space. Windows lined the outer walls, illuminating the room in the fading light of the evening. The other walls were covered with shelves that extended to the ceiling, a rolling ladder on a rail making it possible to reach what was on the top. Some of the shelves were empty, but most of them...

Most of them were filled with books. More books than I could have ever imagined in my lifetime.

"What is this?" I asked, spinning to look at him as he stepped into the library.

"Yours," he said, moving to a shelf on the left. He plucked out a book I recognized, a story about a clan of witches who were dedicated to the stars in the sky. "The books over here are ones you've already read. The ones everywhere else are ones I thought you may like, given your reading tastes."

"How do you know what I've read?" I asked, thinking back to all the times I'd read on my e-reader. I'd longed to hold the physical books in my hand, but my father and Lydia would have been furious to discover what I read. As it was, it seemed they hadn't bothered to look at my download history.

"Christian connected your device to an account I owned, not your father's, so all your purchases came to me," Calix said, shrugging his shoulders as I walked over to the books he claimed I'd read.

"This isn't all of them," I said, running my fingers over the spines.

"I didn't purchase any you didn't particularly enjoy," he answered, coming up behind me. He swept my hair up, wrapping it around his fist and tugging my head to the side with gentle pressure. He used his grip to tip my head back, twisting my neck so that I craned to look at him as he stood behind me. "I most *definitely* purchased any of the books you liked enough to touch yourself while you read them. I have watched your fingers dance over your pussy so many times, thinking of how you must have longed to have a man drive inside of you. I pictured you clenching down on me as you came, taking the cum from my balls. Now I have to wonder if you'll turn to me to ease the ache reading gives you."

He pulled away, releasing my hair as I fought to catch my breath. My protest hung between us, wordless as I couldn't force myself to tell him that I would *never* ask him to touch me. The moment he got his hands on me, I melted, and the sweet little oddities he'd gone out of his way to give me didn't help me resist him.

He was far more charming than he had any right to be.

Calix reached above my head, grasping one of the books and flipping through the pages. He earmarked a chapter when he came to what he was searching for, tucking the book under his arm and taking my hand in his. He guided me to the bathroom once more, leaning down in the doorway to press a kiss against my lips as he handed me the book. "Have a nice bath, Little One."

He retreated quickly, leaving me to close the door and lean my weight into it as I eyed the nearly-filled tub with apprehension.

Calix Regas would be the death of me.

I flipped the page, enjoying the way the warm water surrounded me and soothed the aches I had no business even having. It wasn't as if I'd done anything remotely strenuous the day before, lounging in and out of the pool most of the day.

I'd found it difficult to relax when I first lowered myself into the bath, eyeing the locked door as if it would open at any moment. It wasn't as if Calix hadn't already seen everything I had to offer. He'd helped me wash myself in the shower the night before.

But, having since admitted that I was incapable of resisting his touch, I had a feeling locked doors would become my new best friends.

I carefully avoided the scene Calix had earmarked for me after my curiosity had driven me to open it and skim the scene. The words on the page had told the story of a witch running through the woods, trying to escape the hunter chasing her. It wasn't written in a way that was meant to be terrifying, and the witch knew it was all a game, but her blood pumped regardless. Adrenalin flooded her veins, even knowing that the male who chased her wouldn't hurt her.

He'd just fuck her into the forest floor, taking the prize he'd won in their game.

I'd gone back to the beginning, wanting to start the story all over. I loved the harsh world of fantasy, relating to the beaten down but not broken women far more than the ones I tended to find in contemporary romance. I'd never gone to a normal high school where girls could interact with boys. I'd never gone to college and had a carefree life.

The mafia life was far more similar to the somewhat archaic worlds of fantasy, and I didn't care to think about what that said about my life. "Are you reading a good part?" Calix asked, and I glanced over to find the door open and him leaning into the doorway.

His arms were crossed over his bare chest, his ankles crossed as his shoulder rested against it. The picture of casual, he watched a flush stain my cheeks as if he hadn't ignored the locked door and let himself in anyway. "It's all a good part," I said, swallowing back my nerves at having him nearby. He was too far away to see into the tub and my nakedness beneath the surface, but that didn't stop me from trying not to notice the way his crossed arms highlighted the rippling muscles of his abs and all his olive skin on display.

He moved into the room, coming closer until he erased the comfort I'd tried to convince myself of. He'd stripped out of his suit in the time I'd spent in the bath, the rippling muscles of his abdomen shifting as he walked toward me. Only a pair of dark boxer briefs covered any part of his body, leaving the lean, well-defined tone to every inch of his body open to my view.

"What are you doing?" I asked, snapping the book closed. Calix took it from my hands as he approached, tossing it onto the seat in the center of the too-large bathroom.

"What do you want me to be doing?" he asked, lowering himself to his knees beside the tub. Only above his sculpted chest stayed visible, and I winced for the harsh tile under his kneecaps.

"Getting out," I said, the lie coming instinctively from my parted lips.

"Tsk tsk," Calix said with a teasing lilt to his voice as his brow furrowed mockingly. He grabbed the bottle of shampoo I'd set on the floor beside the tub before getting in, squirting some into his hands and lathering them together a bit. "And here I was hoping you'd ride my face."

"Calix!" I protested, the incredulous tone of my voice amusing even me. Nothing about this man should come as a surprise any longer.

"Lean forward," he said as he laughed. I did as he instructed, trying not to moan when his gentle fingers massaged the shampoo into my scalp. It was foolish to take so much joy in the little things he did to take care of me, but I couldn't help but lean into his touch.

"You don't have to do this; you know?" I said, a breathy sigh escaping.

"You're my wife. I take care of what's mine," he said, guiding me back to lower my head into the water. I had a brief moment of panic with his hand on my shoulder pressing me into the water.

It would be so easy for him to kill me, and if he truly had married me for my family name and the connections it would give him, then perhaps it would be the wise thing to do. Take my fortune through marriage, and then get rid of me so he would never have to worry about me stabbing him in his sleep.

I gripped the edge of the bathtub with both hands, shaking my head slightly as I fought back the fear for a moment.

Calix held my eyes from his place beside the tub, his features gentle with an understanding he shouldn't have had. He shouldn't have known me well enough to know what I feared in that moment.

Drowning seemed like a terrible way to go. I'd have rather he suffocated me while I slept so I didn't see it coming.

"Trust me, λουλούδι μου. Close your eyes," he said, pressing slightly harder at my shoulders. I heaved in a deep breath, slowly letting him lower me into the water. My face stayed above the surface as my hair splayed out around me, and I arched my neck back so that Calix could cup handfuls of water to rinse over the very tip of my forehead and wash away the shampoo.

When he was finished, he allowed me to sit up in the tub once more. My breathing was deep and unsteady as he caught my cheek in his palm. Turning my head to face him, he leaned his nude upper body over the edge of the tub and captured my mouth with his.

Gentle. Soothing. He teased my lips with the barest whisper of a caress, as if he thought the slightest pressure might break me. "I married you. Not your name," he murmured, the words spoken against my mouth. He kissed me once more, keeping his silver eyes open and intent on mine. "Not even death could save you from me now."

His lips touched mine once again, the pressure of his mouth growing more insistent as I opened for him. His tongue swept inside cautiously, as if he feared I may be luring him into a trap so I could bite it off.

It was tempting in a way, but the gentle way he touched me chased away the thoughts of violence. The thoughts of retribution that demanded I make him pay for the way he'd used me.

I just couldn't bring myself to care in that moment, and I definitely couldn't bring myself to care when he pulled back and proceeded to work conditioner through the ends of my hair.

I was so fucking screwed.

29

CALIX

Thalia sat out in the lounge chair on the patio the next day, soaking up the sun. She'd refrained from wearing a swimsuit, favoring a lacey white sundress that made her look like an avenging angel. The darkest parts of me loved seeing her in white; loved the reminder of our wedding when the colorless fabric had been stained with the blood of the men who'd tried to keep me from her.

"Rafael and Ryker are here to see you," Christian said, walking into the kitchen where I sat slicing fresh mango and pineapple for Thalia. I was determined to make sure there was always something she liked to eat readily available for her, because I suspected she wouldn't think of it on her own. Old habits died hard.

I sighed, laying the knife on the island counter. Turning to the sink at my back, I rinsed my hands of the fruit juice and shifted my attention back to the entryway to the kitchen. Rafael and Ryker sauntered into the space that they'd become well acquainted with after we'd arrived in the city. Both men had stayed with me for nearly a week, carefully laying preparations for our attack.

Failure was not an option.

"Did you come to deliver more bad news?" I asked, moving around the island to greet them.

"Good to see you too, dick," Ryker said, chuckling as he looked out the door to the patio. He couldn't see Thalia with the way she'd curled up in a lounge chair with her back to the house, but he was far too nosey for his own good.

"Did you need to see me? Or did you just come to peek at my wife?" I asked, crossing my arms over my chest as I quirked a brow up.

The hatchet-wielding madman shrugged as if it mattered very little to him. "Mostly to peek at your wife, yeah. I have to get back to Calla and the kids. Figure I should at least get to see what all the fuss is about before I leave. Is she outside?" he asked, gesturing toward the patio as he took a step forward.

I didn't need to worry about Ryker in a way I might about other men. He'd been hopelessly devoted to his wife since the moment he'd seen her strolling through the park with her son, years before they ever got together. That didn't mean I had to like his bullshit when it came to my wife, especially knowing he was doing it for the precise purpose of getting under my skin.

Thalia stood from her lounge chair, dropping her book onto it as she strode toward the open door and stepped into the house. She held Ryker's stare as she walked, not bothering to back down as she crossed over the threshold. She approached me, reaching beyond me to grab a slice of mango off the wood cutting board and taking a bite out of the fruit before she chewed thoughtfully. "Could we at least pretend I am more than a zoo animal to come *peek* at?" she asked, tearing another bite off the mango pointedly.

I was far too aware of the knife at my back, resting on the counter, as Thalia took a step away from it and made me breathe a sigh of relief. The last thing I needed was for her to convince Ryker and Rafe that she'd enjoy throwing weapons at them.

They tended to throw them back and laugh about it.

"But you're the prettiest zoo animal I've ever seen," I said, wincing from the glare she threw at me with a swift turn of her head.

"I can't decide if that was supposed to be a compliment and you really are that stupid, or if you're mocking me," Thalia said, shoving the last bit of mango into her mouth.

"Definitely a compliment, and he most definitely is that stupid," Rafael inserted, moving to the island and snatching up a piece of pineapple. He popped it into his mouth and retreated with economical steps.

"And you are?" Thalia asked, folding her arms across her chest.

"The man who made him what he is today," Rafe said, returning the gesture.

"I find it slightly disturbing that you're so proud of turning him into a murderer," Thalia said, scoffing as she sank her teeth into her bottom lip.

"Oh, don't worry, Mrs. Regas. He was already a murderer when he came to me in Ibiza. I just made him *enjoy* it," Rafe said, his lips spreading into a cruel grin.

Thalia swallowed, shifting on her feet as she turned her stare to Ryker, as if she couldn't quite wrap her head around someone enjoying death. One day, I'd show her the beauty that came with it and the similarities between blood and paint.

"Little One," I said, reaching out to touch her arm. She swatted me away, curling her hand to slap at my skin in warning.

"Don't touch me," she hissed, the soft woman from the

night before fading before my eyes, as if she hadn't already known I was a murderer. I'd certainly enjoyed killing her father, and my only regret was that it was too fast for my taste. "Every time I think just maybe you're different, something reminds me that you're not. You're just like the rest of them, aren't you?" she asked.

"Yes," Rafael answered for me, shrugging his shoulders. It was totally inconsequential to him if my wife was happy with me, and his bitterness over not yet having his own woman was apparent.

I glared at him before I turned my full attention to Thalia. "No. I'm not like the rest. Do you know why?" I asked, taking her hand in mine. She allowed it, glaring down at where my ring glimmered on her finger. "Because my obsession with you knows no boundaries. I would do anything for you. Any of the others would have owned you, but it is you who owns me, λουλούδι μου."

My flower froze, staring at me for a moment as if I'd grown a second head. "You hardly know me," she whispered, glancing at the two other men, who were now witnessing our intimate moment. It was clear she expected me to care; she expected me to be mortified by the admission that she was my everything, but I would never be anything less than proud to have her standing at my side.

"Just because you hardly know me doesn't mean the same can be said in the reverse. I know you better than anyone, I suspect, after all the hours I've spent watching you in the privacy of your bedroom. I know you enough to love you and everything you will grow to be outside of that prison," I murmured, watching as her eyes widened.

"You love me?" she asked, tearing her hand out of my grip.

"I've always loved you," I admitted. Even if that love had

been something different when we'd been younger, it had been just as present.

"What am I supposed to do with that exactly?" she asked, tilting her head to the side as her face twisted with pain.

"You could say it back," Ryker observed, ever the helpful bystander.

"I don't even know him," Thalia said, taking a step back. She'd been raised to expect certain aspects of her marriage. Rape, coercion, but not love. What would she do with the knowledge that I was wrapped around her finger? "I don't know what's worse—that you genuinely seem to believe you love me or that you left me in that house if it's true."

"Thalia—" I said, wincing when her brow furrowed and tears pooled in her eyes.

"You left me there!" she screamed, the shrill sound filling the kitchen. "You don't leave someone behind if you love them. I never would have left you. *Never.*"

"λουλούδι μου," I murmured, my heart breaking at the sound of pure betrayal in her voice. "I tried to come back for you. I swear to you, I tried more times than I can count."

"My father had him beaten every time he tried to leave our island," Rafael interjected, stepping toward her as I stripped my shirt over my head. Thalia watched me, only shifting her attention back to Rafe when he stopped directly in front of her. He touched her cheek with a gentleness I hadn't known he possessed, staring at the touch as if it unnerved him greatly. I wondered for a moment at the oddity of my tolerance of him touching my wife, and realized Rafael was the closest thing I had to a brother. If I could trust anyone in this world, it was him. "He tried, Thalia. I swear it on my mother's grave." He swept his thumb through the tears on Thalia's cheek, wiping the moisture away as I grabbed her hand and touched it to one of the scars on my abdomen.

Her thumb swept over the puckered flesh that had faded some in the years since the injury. "Eventually, Rafael's father and mine allowed me to leave. They said if I got myself killed over a stupid girl then I didn't deserve to live, anyway. I was only a few blocks from your father's house when I was ambushed," I explained, guiding her other hand to the second scar on my abdomen. "Damianos Hasapis had the honor of shooting me, then they left me to crawl my way out of the city before I could bleed to death. Christian got me out. I would have died otherwise," I said, nodding my head toward the front door where I knew the other man waited, guarding us while giving us privacy.

"Damianos shot you?" Thalia asked, turning a shocked, teary-eyed stare up to me as Rafael stepped away. He and Ryker made their way out to the patio, leaving me with my heartbroken wife who didn't understand anything of the events that had led us here.

"He knew even then that he was going to fight for your hand, Little One. Your betrothal to Damianos was no surprise, and he wanted me out of the way because he knew I would protect you," I said, carefully avoiding mention of the marriage contract that had marked Thalia as mine. It had been the very thing that had brought us together, but it had become irrelevant just as quickly.

I'd come to care for her as a girl in her own right, her sweetness and innocence something I wanted to protect at all costs. In the years since they'd separated us, she'd grown into a fierce woman I wanted to possess, but neither of those things existed because of our marriage contract. They existed because of who Thalia was and who she'd become.

"You tried..." She trailed off, her bottom lip trembling as she leaned forward and her forehead rested against my chest.

"Of course I tried, λουλούδι μου. You don't leave someone

you love behind," I said, raising a palm to the back of her head. I cradled it as her body shook with the force of her sobs, holding her tight to my chest.

She raised her arms, wrapping them around my waist as she pulled me in tighter. Her nails dug into my back on either side of my spine, as if she couldn't pull me close enough.

I wished I could do more to soothe her. "Shh, Little One. I'm here now," I whispered, holding her tight as I grabbed her by the backs of her thighs and lifted her into my arms.

"I hated you. I hated you because you didn't come back for me," she cried, snuggling into my neck. "And they shot you for trying to get to me." I cradled her, letting her wrap her legs around my waist as I carried her toward the stairs. She clung to me, wrapping me up in an embrace with all of her limbs as if she couldn't quite bear to let me go.

And my flower broke.

I emerged into the kitchen, heading straight for the bottle of Ouzo and taking a swig of it. I grimaced against the potent flavor of black licorice as it burned its way down my throat, turning to grab a bigger glass from the cupboard. I poured some into the tumbler, diluting it with ice water and a lemon wedge out of the fridge before I took another sip.

"Is she okay?" Ryker asked, stepping forward.

"She's sleeping," I said, nodding gently. Even if part of me wanted to throttle the two of them for the heartbreak they'd caused her and the realization that she'd never been abandoned in the city determined to destroy her, it was a conversation we'd needed to have.

Maybe with the truth out in the open, Thalia could move

past her bitterness. She could move past the anger toward me that clouded her judgment.

"That could have gone better," Ryker said, nodding in time with his words.

"It was necessary. She was furious with you because of old hurts. Now she can move on," Rafe answered, standing from the counter stool where he'd sat while they waited for me to emerge from the bedroom.

I didn't think Thalia would sleep for long, but she would probably sleep hard while she did. "I presume you came for some other reason than to antagonize my wife."

"Jeno's body is still missing. You need to deal with him quickly. You know better than anyone that revenge makes men do desperate things. Thalia and her sister won't be safe until he's dead," Rafe said, raising a brow at me.

"My men are already searching the city for him. I can't exactly kill him until they find him. Unless Ryker would like to stay in the city and hunt him down, I fail to see what else I can do at this time," I said, my irritation with Rafael coming through.

"You need allies within the city," another male voice said from the entrance to the kitchen. Christian lingered at his back, his gun already drawn and pointed at the one who'd intruded on our conversation.

"He refused to wait," Christian said, answering the unspoken question lingering between us. "As he is an heir to one of the six families, it seemed wise to let you make the choice whether he should live or die."

"And who are you?" Ryker asked, his fingers twitching at his side.

"Elias Lykaios. The son of councilman Nico Lykaios," the man said, and I vaguely recognized his words to be true. Elias had been only a few years older than me when we were in school, attending alongside Jeno and me.

"Do you mean to pledge your father to an alliance with me?" I asked, not bothering to beat around the bush. This conversation and business needed to be over with before Thalia could wander down. The last thing she needed was to be worried about her safety.

"Fuck no. My father will never waiver from his loyalty to Karras and Hasapis," Elias said, a bitter chuckle escaping him.

"They're dead," I said.

"Not all of them, seemingly," Elias said, raising a brow. I glared at Christian for allowing him entrance without consulting me first, and the other man shuffled his feet but held my gaze. "There are those of us who no longer agree with the antiquated ways that our elders conduct business. We didn't agree with the choices that were made and led to your banishment. We could be persuaded to assist you if you were to help us with our own shifts in power."

"You'll separate from your father?" I asked, wondering what an heir would expect in return for that kind of loyalty.

"Of course not. I'll kill him and take his seat on the council. I just may require a few men to make sure I survive the transition. After that, we can agree to cooperate with one another on the council. The Hasapis, Karras, and Galanis families have had far too much power for too many years."

"What of Atticus Ariti? Will he vote with us or against us?" I asked, knowing damn well Elias and Atticus had been the best of friends in school. The younger man had taken his father's place after the elder was killed in a drug raid years ago.

"He votes with me," Elias said, tipping his head to the side. "But we do have one condition."

"And what's that?" I asked, staring him down.

"Eugene Regas cannot be the head of your family if we are to move forward in this. You must deal with your father; whether you kill him or simply keep him under control is your choice, but he is just as bad as Origen was, if not worse. I'll not be complicit in his return to power," Elias said.

"I wouldn't have respected you if you would have. My father knows his place, and it has required him to do as he's told for years now. He won't be a problem. I'll be the Regas family member to assume the council seat," I answered, nodding toward Christian to see him out. "Give me the night to consider it. I'll contact you with my answer in the morning."

Elias nodded, allowing Christian to guide him out of the room and out the front door of the house.

"You'd be a fool not to take his bargain, but equally foolish to trust him," Rafael instructed, heading for the door.

"I am quite aware, and despite what you may think I am no fool. Now get out so I can see to my wife. Find Jeno before he ruins everything."

30

THALIA

Crying was the worst.

I woke up wrapped in Calix's arms. His silver eyes gleamed down at me, filled with a gentleness that made my heart ache. Undiluted hatred for him was far easier than acknowledging the something else that thrummed between us. He'd been my savior.

He'd evidently almost died trying to live up to that, and while the bitter part of me wanted to question it, and cling to the possibility that it was nothing more than a poetic lie, the heartbroken dreamer inside of me wanted it to be true. More than anything, I wanted the boy I'd loved as my protector to have been there through it all.

Clinging to that childish dream felt like slow dancing with a grenade, or trying to hug a porcupine and expecting not to get hurt in the end. But I hadn't pushed him away when he'd curled me tighter to his chest, settling himself against my back until I woke up. We'd spent nearly an hour like that, curled up in a bed I didn't belong in but couldn't seem to force myself to leave.

It was only hunger that had finally driven me up, forcing

us to go down to the kitchen so that Calix could feed me until I felt like I might burst. When I finally retreated to the library for some privacy, he'd admitted that there was some business he needed to tend to out of the house, but he didn't want to leave me when I needed him.

I didn't want to tell him that I would always need him, or that I'd needed him at my side for the years that had separated us, but somehow survived without him. I'd told him to go, instead, burying my face in the pages of a new book and trying to get lost in it.

Christian kept me company as I curled up in the chaise lounge, watching over me as I failed to distract myself. My mind was a mess, a complete disaster as I read the same sentence over and over again. His frustrated sigh made me glance up as he stood from the armchair he sat in, moving toward the shelves of books I hadn't read. He grabbed an older-looking book, running his fingers over the surface gently, almost reverently. If it hadn't been for my desire not to be alone, I might have been angry that Christian watched over me like a child. But I'd spent far too many years of my life locked away in my bedroom alone.

Even just the presence of another person felt like a blessing.

Stepping up beside me, he held it out until I reached out to accept it from him. "What is this?" I asked, looking over the surface. There was no title on the cover or the spine, just a simple, leather binding that was entirely unembellished.

"I found it in your father's office after I killed everyone in the house, the day of your wedding," Christian admitted, his words coming without any inflection, as if killing a household of people was a casual affair, without leaving a stain on his soul. "From what I can tell, it belonged to your mother."

"My mother?" I asked, opening the book to the first page

with delicate motions. It had been so long since I'd seen her perfect script on a page that tears stung my eyes. All my memories of her were tainted by the feeling of blood splashing against my legs when my father had swung the axe down and severed her head from her body.

My throat closed as I stared at a name and Pennsylvania address I didn't recognize written on the inside of the front cover. "I stopped reading as soon as I realized what it was. Her secrets were hers to keep, but I have to imagine she would've wanted to share them with you when you were old enough. Now she can," Christian said, backing away and going to the chair he'd occupied before. He sat down, thumbing through the book he'd been reading and pretending to pay attention to the pages as he watched me turn to the first full page of my mother's handwriting.

She was as much a stranger to me as Calix was, but maybe now I could get to know both the people they'd stolen from me.

The front door opening snapped me out of my reading, forcing me to close my mother's journal. I'd spent the afternoon buried within the pages, reading about the life she'd had before her marriage to my father.

If I'd hoped to find a glimmer of positivity, a few years of joy before the abusive, loveless marriage she'd shared with my father, that quickly vanished. Her childhood had been far too similar to mine, as if women within the families were trapped in a time loop without change. I tucked the journal back into the shelf where Christian had found it, hoping he wouldn't mention it to Calix if he hadn't yet.

The journal felt like something to be shared solely

between my mother and me. As her last surviving child, I had to hope she would have wanted to share her deepest thoughts and confessions with me, but they shouldn't have to be shared with a man she didn't know, and Calix wouldn't hesitate to read in the way Christian had.

Nothing was private from my husband.

Calix's form strode straight past the library on his way to the bedroom, and I peeked my head out of the open door to watch as he disappeared with swift, economical steps. His urgency drove me forward, my curiosity getting the best of me.

I'd have thought he'd check on me immediately after returning from his business, with how hesitant he'd been to leave me in the first place. But he'd ignored me entirely in favor of something held within that bedroom.

I wanted to know what was so fucking important, and it bothered me that I'd so quickly come to *expect* his gentle care and attention. I didn't like being ignored, as if it hadn't been the norm for most of my life.

If he wanted to claim he loved me, then I had damn well better be the center of his entire universe. I wouldn't be a favored toy to play with when it was convenient and cast aside when a better prospect came along.

I wouldn't be my mother.

The bedroom was empty as I stepped inside, but the sound of running water came from the adjacent bathroom. Steam had already started to form, fogging the mirror as I glanced into the room and moved toward it against my own will. My feet led me there, my heart as heavy as lead in my chest.

What had he been doing that he needed to wash away?

If his business had involved another woman and he needed to clean himself of the evidence, I would survive. I would keep my distance and accept that this marriage was just as fake as the one I might have shared with Damianos. I would accept that Calix's pretty words had been nothing but poetry meant to lure me into his bed.

They had almost worked.

I stepped into the bathroom, my bare feet moving across the marble tile floor carefully so I didn't make a sound. The shower doors were fogged with steam, disguising some of my view as Calix tipped his head back and let the water from the showerhead cascade down over his face. He swept his hands over his features, thrusting out an arm suddenly. His palm cracked against the shower wall as he hung his head forward, letting the water drip down the back of his neck once again.

The muscles of his shoulders twitched, his abs clenching as he pulled his hand back from the shower wall. He grabbed his bottle of body wash off the shelf, squirting some into his palm and lathering it quickly before he ran the soap over his body. He started at the tops of his shoulders, the water turning gray as it leaked off his skin.

I took another step closer, drawn to that odd gray tone that seemed too dark to be water but too thin to be mud. Spots dotted his skin, patches of darkness on his cheeks and neck as he ran his hands over the flesh and washed them away.

There was no shape to them, no rhyme or reason to the pattern work of the darkness upon the canvas of his flesh. It was like the splatter of paint...

Oh.

Realization struck me at the same moment that Calix twisted his body suddenly. His open palm slapped against the glass of the shower door, his fingers splaying as he leaned into his hand. His eyes gleamed from behind the fogged glass, his head tilting to the side as he studied me. My heart pounded in my chest, fear of the man who *enjoyed* killing coursing through my veins. My adrenaline froze me in place, leaving me with nothing to do but stare back at him. "Are you enjoying the show, Little One?" he asked, using those splayed fingers to grip the glass. He pushed it to the side, opening the shower door and revealing the nudity the steam had hidden before.

"I just wanted to know what you were so anxious to wash away," I said, my voice quiet in the bathroom. It was a miracle he heard it over the sound of running water and the adrenaline surging through me, paralyzing me entirely. I couldn't seem to move away; couldn't seem to tear my eyes off the rippling muscles of his abdomen. I swallowed as my gaze trailed lower, following the definition of his abs to the deep lines that led me straight to temptation.

His cock twitched as my gaze settled on it, as if it could feel the weight of my stare. Even without looking at Calix's face, I could practically feel his arrogance as he wrapped his fingers around the base of his shaft and stroked slowly toward the tip. He was already hard, his cock swollen and curving up slightly, stretching toward his belly button as he continued to stroke it.

"Were you worried that I left you here to go seek the company of another woman?" he asked, drawing my eyes back to his face. His lips were twisted into a cruel smirk, but he said nothing of my outright staring at his cock. The muscles in his arm shifted as he stroked it again, but I refused to look down to watch his palm pump up and down over himself. "I haven't washed my cock yet if you'd like to see if you can smell another woman's pussy on me, my jealous little flower. I promise you I have nothing to hide."

"I hate you," I seethed, turning to exit the bathroom in my humiliation. He still hadn't answered my question, choosing to mock me instead.

Our marriage wasn't a love match where I knew what to expect from him, but neither was it the typical arranged marriage where I knew my place was to keep quiet and spread my legs. Could he really blame me for trying to understand the rules in such an uncertain situation?

"I didn't say you could leave," Calix said, the command dropping his voice low. My feet stopped moving, even though I knew I should keep walking. I knew I should put as much distance between us as possible. "I'm washing blood spatter from my skin if you must know. Look at my suit if you question it."

I glanced down at the white shirt of his suit near the shower door. Dark stains spotted the fabric randomly, the sheer amount of it making my breath catch. "It isn't a secret you're a killer. Why would you rush to wash it off?" I asked, swallowing as I turned back to face him.

"It appears to make you uncomfortable. I didn't think you would want to see just how much I enjoyed sending a message today," Calix explained, cocking his head as he lifted his free hand to run over the side of his neck. He arched into the touch, the corded muscles of his shoulder flexing as he turned to the side. He twisted around, dumping more body wash into that hand and giving me a perfect, unobstructed view of his ass without shame. His muscles shifted as he kept stroking himself as he rubbed soapy hands over his abs, making me secretly wish I could see it.

"Who were you sending a message to?" I asked, trying to consider why I cared. There was only one person outside this house who mattered to me, and I would gut him myself if he'd hurt her. He damn well knew she was his only leverage over me, and I highly doubted he would so easily expend it.

"A few of Damianos's men who weren't at the wedding were left behind to guard the house during the ceremony so they survived the carnage. I needed to remedy that," Calix explained, continuing to rub the soap along his skin. Water sprayed on the bathroom floor with the door open, but he didn't seem to care as he leisurely cleaned himself while on display. "I sent their dismembered bodies in a crate to Damianos's brother, Tobias, to make sure he knows what I'll do to any men he sends into the city without my permission. Is that what you wanted to hear, Little One?"

"How many bodies did you need to fill a crate?" I asked. Calix chuckled at the question, confirming my immediate thought that it was an odd sort of thing to fixate on.

Who the fuck cared about the shipping logistics?

"Only four today, λουλούδι μου," he said, rinsing the soap from his hands. "But it wasn't the volume that required such a large container. Bodies don't take up much room once you chop them into pieces."

"Then what took up so much room?" I asked, grimacing as I considered if I really wanted to know.

"Do you really want to know?" he asked, studying me as I decided if my curiosity was morbid enough to hear the gory details of what he'd done. These men had almost been responsible for my pretty cage, but so was the man who stood in front of me. Damianos never would have spoken to me about such matters, and I couldn't decide if I loved or hated that Calix didn't treat me as if I was a sheltered princess in need of protection.

"Yes," I said, watching as his head jerked back in surprise.

A morbid grin claimed his face as his eyes narrowed in challenge. "Then take off your clothes and come into the shower with me, my flower. I'll tell you all about my latest artwork."

He placed a hand on the wall beside him, leaning forward as he pushed me to do as he said with a smile that threatened to unravel me.

I was nothing but a flower beneath his feet that he could

play with and torment until he stepped on me and crushed me into nothing.

Still, I reached up to ease the embroidered straps over my shoulders. The tag when I'd gotten dressed that morning had said it was a white dress, but the delicacy of the lace was far too appealing for me to avoid it.

The fabric fell to my feet in a small puddle, leaving me standing before Calix in nothing but a pair of pale, lacy underwear. Calix's gaze fell to my breasts immediately, his silver stare turning molten as his jaw clenched.

I slid a finger beneath the strap on each side of my hip, shimmying them down my thighs until I was naked in front of him. He grinned as he held out a hand to help me over the wet floor. Once I was safely over the puddle, he stepped back from the shower door, moving farther in and giving me room to stand beneath the water without him touching me. The water poured down onto my chest, the warmth sinking into my breasts as it trickled down over the smooth expanse of my stomach. Calix's gaze followed it, landing on the apex of my thighs as he sank his teeth into his bottom lip.

"Fuck, you're beautiful," he grunted. I wasn't sure if he wanted to fuck me or eat me alive with the way he stared at me, and I was left with the distinct reminder that curiosity killed the cat.

"I'm in the shower, Calix. What took up so much room in the crate?" I asked, leaning my back into the wall opposite of him as I stepped out from beneath the spray.

He stalked closer, his cock hard and looking as much like a weapon as it did something that brought me a great deal of pleasure. I still remembered the way it had felt to have him tear me in two. The way his hand felt wrapped around my throat as he fucked me.

Stopping just in front of me, Calix placed a hand on the

wall behind my head and stared down into my eyes as he reached the other hand lower. Grasping me around the back of my thigh, he lifted my leg until he could rest my foot on the angled bottom shelf meant for shaving.

He backed away slowly, staring at my spread legs and the way he'd put my pussy on display. "Are you wet?" he asked instead of answering my question. A predator toying with his meal before he devoured it whole.

"I am in the shower," I pointed out with a roll of my eyes, holding my head high in spite of the way my cheeks heated with his pointed stare.

"Are. You. Wet?" He didn't clarify, because he knew damn well he didn't need to. "Will I find you slick when I drop to my knees and put my mouth on you?"

My hips shifted as I squirmed. "Yes," I said, not bothering to deny it. The physical reactions of my body meant nothing. They weren't acceptance of who he was and what he'd done.

It was all a biological reaction to the perfection of a sculpted Greek God standing in front of me. "Touch yourself," he growled, standing far enough away that he'd have a perfect view of it. "You want something from me? This is my price."

"You want me to play with my pussy so you can watch?" I asked, placing my palm against my stomach. I slid it lower, ghosting my fingertips over the flesh I'd explored so many times. When my nerves tried to take hold of me, I reminded myself that he'd seen it all before. He'd watched while I'd been entirely unaware.

At least this time I could control the narrative. I could determine what he saw or didn't see.

"This better be one hell of a story," I said, using two fingers to circle my clit as he watched.

"You can pretend all you want, but you're wet while we talk of blood and death. I told you I *dismembered* four men, and you asked for details while your pretty little pussy wept for me. I may be a villain in this story," he said, coming closer until he stopped in front of me. He slowly lowered himself to his knees, his face just above the place where I touched myself. His gaze stayed planted on my face as I teased my clit, my breath coming much more quickly with his proximity and the scent of him filling my lungs. He placed a hand on top of each of my thighs, drawing a deep breath in as he leaned closer to murmur softly between us. "But so are you, Little One."

"I've never been a villain in anyone's story," I sighed deeply as my fingers worked faster. Calix raised a hand to grasp my wrist, stilling my motions as I squirmed for more touch.

"Of course you have," he murmured, guiding my hand away so that he could stare at the swollen pink flesh between my legs. He leaned forward until his mouth was only a breath from my skin. "Even a villain has to be made before she can rise."

He closed the distance, dragging his tongue through my flesh from entrance to clit. My back arched, straining toward him as I sought out more. He'd manipulated me right where he wanted me, but as he hoisted my leg higher and buried his face between my legs, I couldn't find it in me to care.

"Calix," I whimpered, dropping my hands to the dark hair on top of his head. The wet strands slid through my fingers as he fucked me with his tongue, sliding his other hand up and over my stomach. He gripped my breast, using the touch to force me back into the shower wall and pin me there. He devoured me like a man starved, abandoning my entrance to torment my clit with slow, firm circles that threatened to make me come undone. "Oh God."

He shoved me into the wall, his mouth becoming more frenzied on my flesh as my legs trembled. The orgasm blinded me momentarily, flooding my world with white as it washed over me. I gasped, gripping the back of his head and holding him still as I rocked my hips against his face.

"That wasn't exactly the plan when I got in the shower," I said, my breathing ragged and my voice strained. I couldn't quite seem to find the ability to function, and I stumbled when Calix lowered my leg to the shower floor and stood in front of me.

His face glistened with my arousal as he leaned forward, laying a kiss to the side of my neck. "Maybe not yours," he murmured, a chuckle making his voice quake. He ran his lips over me, teasing me as I settled and remembered what it was to breathe. "I arranged their body parts into the shape of a flower, Little One. Let's hope it serves as the proper incentive for them to stay away from you."

λουλούδι μου.

His flower.

Oh my God.

The breath returned to my lungs in a rush, filling my chest as he touched his lips to mine. The meaning of his words lingered between us. The meaning of his message that wouldn't mean anything to anyone else.

It did mean something to me.

He slowly backed away, leaving me floundering as he stared at me. "This is the part where you go to bed if you don't want me to fuck you into the shower wall, Thalia," he said, giving me the distance to flee the bathroom if I chose.

I pursed my lips, dropping my gaze to the hardness of his cock.

"What if I don't want to?"

31

CALIX

"In that case," I said, prowling toward her. Thalia lifted her chin high, refusing to show any sign of embarrassment over her near confession. I left her with just enough distance that she could slip out of my arms and escape if she needed to. "I just need one word from you, Little One, and then I'll make you mine the way those pretty amber eyes are begging me to. But there's something you should understand before you say it," I said, cutting off her reply when her lips parted. I touched a finger to her mouth, groaning when she shifted and took the tip of it inside. She wrapped her full lips around it, dragging them over the surface and tormenting me like the little tease she was.

"And what's that?" she asked when she finally released it, nipping at the tip with a playful grin.

"As soon as you give yourself to me, knowing fully well who I am," I said, reaching between us. I cupped her pussy, sliding a finger through her lips until it sank inside of her. She whimpered, her hips moving of their own volition as the heel of my palm ground against her sensitive clit. "*This* becomes mine. I will feast on it when I want, fuck it whenever I demand. Except for rare circumstances, you will give me complete control of your body."

I worked my finger deeper, burrowing it inside of her as I pressed a second against her entrance and pushed it inside. She stretched around me as I began to pump them slowly. "If I say no?" she asked, her breathy voice igniting a fire inside of me.

"Then you're free to go," I said, quirking a brow up at her. It might kill me to allow her to walk away when I had her pussy wrapped around my fingers and her taste on my tongue, when I was so close to sinking my cock inside her, but I would. I'd do whatever it took to show her that I wanted her willing submission, not to take her by force.

She twisted her lips, biting the corner of her mouth as she covered my hand with hers. "Just this?" she said, guiding my hand away from her pussy. She brought it to her mouth, touching my fingertips to her lips. She smeared her wetness over herself, making me want nothing more than to lean forward and lick it off her mouth. "Or does that include my mouth, too?"

Gripping her by the hips, I spun her to face the shower wall. Taking each of her ass cheeks in a hand, I spread her as she arched her back with a gasp. "It includes all of you, λουλούδι μου. Your pussy, your mouth, and your ass are mine to use as I see fit," I said, gathering her long, dark hair and wrapping it around my fist. I guided her head to the side, dropping my mouth to the top of her shoulder as I sank my teeth into her flesh. She groaned as I slid my cock between her thighs, rubbing against her pussy and kicking her legs apart so that nothing was in my way. Her legs spread, letting the warm air of the shower kiss her swollen cunt as my cock glided through her silken flesh.

"I'm fairly certain that's not how this is supposed to work," she said, dropping her head forward until the top of it touched the wall.

I laughed, the sound rumbling up my throat as I stared at the line of her spine and squeezed my fingers into her ass. I thrust my hips again, gliding through her and tormenting the both of us. "This is your chance to give consent. This is your chance to tell me you trust me with your body, and if you can't do that then it all stops until you can. It's all or nothing with me, Little One. The choice is yours."

She groaned, thrusting her ass back at me and nearly impaling herself on my cock. The devious thing was determined to take what she wanted and not give me the chance to require more from her.

But I wanted her submission, and I wanted it to be something she gave me knowingly.

"I need the word, λουλούδι μου," I said, angling my hips down so that she couldn't take what she wanted.

"*Yes.* Just fuck me already," she ordered, the admission lighting something inside of me. It might not have seemed like much to someone else, but I knew exactly what is had cost her.

"Thank fuck," I groaned, lining myself up and driving forward. I slid into her tightness, slowly working through her greedy flesh as she clenched around me. It hadn't been long since I'd last been inside her, not in the grand scheme of things, but that didn't stop it from feeling like the first time.

There was no condom between us, no barrier to separate us, as I slid into her a little further with each shallow thrust of my hips. She whimpered, spreading her legs farther and tipping her ass up for me. With my hand in her hair, I held her in place the best I could until my balls touched her pussy.

Pulling back and sliding through her again, I gave her the

chance to protest, or give me any sign that I might be hurting her. There were none, just her desperate, frantic breaths as she shoved back into me and tried to meet me stroke for stroke.

"Calix," she moaned as I increased my pace. Only the sounds of running water and my hips slapping against her ass accompanied her little whimpers as I took what I wanted.

"Fucking hell," I groaned, sliding my free hand upward between her breasts. I grabbed her by the throat, holding her still as I leaned forward and inhaled her scent. She filled my lungs, feeling like the first breath of fresh air in weeks.

I restricted her breathing lightly, applying just enough pressure that she gasped under my hold. I turned her head to the side so I could watch her eyes roll back, her lids drifting closed as her pussy tightened around me. Her orgasm slammed into her with the force of a freight train, and only my arm kept her from collapsing in front of me as I pounded into her through it. I held her in place, treating her like my personal fuck toy as she tried to get her footing underneath her again.

Her whimpers came out all as one, the first fading into the next and into the next until there was no separation between them.

Sinking my teeth into her flesh hard enough to bruise, I groaned into her shoulder as I came. Filling her with me in the way that she had always been meant to be, I swore I saw stars as I pumped through the slick aftermath of our lovemaking.

She winced when I pulled out while slowly releasing her throat and releasing my grip on her hair when I was certain she would be able to stand on her own.

I hadn't fucked her quite hard enough. I'd remedy that later in the night.

She turned her gaze downward to stare at where my release trickled down her thighs and shift to press her legs together. "We forgot a condom," she said, squeezing her eyes shut as if she couldn't believe we'd been so stupid.

"There won't be any condoms for us, λουλούδι μου. You are my wife, and there will be nothing between us, ever," I explained, watching her as she turned to face me. Defiance crossed over her features, and she folded her arms in front of herself.

Breeding her had always been the point of her eventual marriage, and I was certain it wasn't a welcome reminder of what she'd once expected of her wedding night. But I didn't want to breed her to cement an alliance, not when I'd already killed off all of her family.

I wanted to because I wanted her to have my children, and I wanted the element of protection it would enable me to give her. No one could force her to suffer the consequences of my actions or her father's empty promises when she carried the future of two families within her womb.

That would go against the very code of the six families.

"Our world is no place for a child," she scolded, and the reminder of her harsh life made me cup her cheek in my hand.

"Our children will have a very different life from ours. Our children will have two parents who love them more than anything and will protect them at all costs. They'll have the life we never dared to dream of, Little One. I promise you that," I said, touching my lips to hers briefly.

She turned away when I pulled back, stepping toward the shower door and reaching out to grab a towel. It was all I could do not to grab her and force her to lie down on the bed with her ass elevated to make sure my cum stayed planted within her pussy.

Baby steps. We'd get there in time.

For now, I'd be grateful that she'd taken my cock and my cum, and that she hadn't cut off my dick in the process.

It was the small victories that won the war.

32

THALIA

Calix's father's house loomed as he drove the *Koenigsegg* up the driveway. I couldn't imagine the elder Regas man had been pleased to be forced out of the home that had once been his and to have his son prevent him from reclaiming it.

I didn't know much about the way Calix had gone about reclaiming the city, but it was not lost on me that he never mentioned discussing things with the older man.

Eugene Regas had not been in charge of the Regas family since their return; of that I had no doubt.

"What's your father's place in all of this?" I asked. Even if he hadn't been the one to swing the axe that killed my mother, I would never forget the fact that he'd played a very vital role in her death.

Without his actions, I'd have grown up with Calix to look out for me.

I didn't think I could ever forgive the man who had become my father-in-law for what he'd done and all that he'd taken from me. Even worse, I didn't think I wanted to bother to try.

Maybe Calix was right about me becoming the villain of my own story, because I felt anything but heroic since I'd beaten my father with the very cane he'd used to torment me and keep me obedient.

I wanted to revel in watching the world burn.

"Wherever I tell him to be," Calix answered, confirming my thoughts that his father wasn't in charge.

"Will you be the one to claim the seat on the council, then?" I asked, cocking my head to the side as he slid the shifter into park. I wanted nothing more than to leap out of the car and race to see Malva where I knew she waited inside the house, but I waited for his answer anyway.

"I will, and you will take the Karras seat," he said, shocking me into silence. My eyes widened as my mouth dropped open. I didn't think I'd *ever* heard of a time when a woman was allowed to sit on the council of the six governing families.

"That isn't possible," I whispered.

"Every family must have a representative on the council so long as they are within the city. I have no intention of taking you away from here, and that means that the seat belongs to you as the eldest remaining Karras," Calix said, reaching across the car to unbuckle my seatbelt as I stared at him in stunned silence.

"They won't be pleased," I said, thinking of the harsh men I'd had rare interactions with throughout my life. Most of them had been there the day they'd killed my mother, allowing her to suffer for an affair, as if they weren't all guilty of the same crime themselves.

Made men weren't known for their fidelity.

I shuddered as I thought of the day Lydia and my father had brought me to one of the stables in the city, forcing me to watch so I would know the kinds of things a man "would get from a whore if his wife wasn't to his satisfaction."

"I imagine there are a great many things about the circumstances that won't please them," Calix said with a chuckle, opening his door and sliding out of the seat. He came around to my side, pulling it up and open for me and holding out a hand.

I accepted it, staring up at him as he closed his fingers around mine gently and guided me out of the car.

"But you don't care," I observed, falling into step beside him as he led me up the front steps to the manor. The house was nothing to sneeze at, but it wasn't the elaborate fortress that Calix and I now called home, either.

"Hello, son," Eugene said, stepping out of the front door and crossing his arms over his chest. "The girls are inside. You and I have things to discuss."

"They can wait until I get Thalia settled with my mother," Calix snapped, ushering me through the front door and ignoring the heated glare his father aimed at his back.

"There are far more important matters to deal with than holding your wife's hand to walk her through the house! We need to plan for taking back my seat and the way the families will try to prevent that," Eugene said, the urgency in his voice shocking me. It was so unusual for a man to discuss such matters in front of a woman, I'd thought it unique to Calix.

But perhaps it was simply a matter of his upbringing.

"I've already begun making arrangements. I will not stand alone when they summon me to face the council," Calix answered, leading me through the foyer and toward the door to the back patio. He stopped just before we reached it, pausing to speak to his father. I watched through the glass door as Malva ran screaming around the yard.

There was a soccer ball clutched in her hands, cradled to her chest as an older woman chased her. The smile that lit my sister's face was entirely carefree, nothing like what I'd expected to find in the girl who'd just seen the beginning of her parents' murder.

"You did this without consulting me?" Eugene asked his son. I squeezed Calix's hand, catching his attention as I stepped forward. He released me, understanding the silent plea. I wanted no part in the coming argument with his father. I wanted to watch my sister play as she always should have been allowed.

I pushed the glass door open, stepping onto the back patio as the male security guards sitting on the furniture gave me firm nods. Moving as if in a trance, I walked past them all and didn't stop until the grass at the edge of the lawn tickled my toes.

I knew the moment Malva noticed my presence, spinning to face me with that broad smile on her beautiful features. She broke free of the woman's grip, screaming happily as she barreled toward me.

I braced myself on the grass as she collided with my chest, flinging her arms around my neck as I sniffled back the tears that sprung to my eyes. "Thalia!" she shrieked, pulling back and smiling at me.

I cupped her cheeks in my hands, turning her head from side to side as I looked her over and searched for injuries. "Have they hurt you?" I asked, glancing at the woman over her shoulder briefly before turning my attention back to the little sister who was my entire world.

"No! Of course not. Evangeline is the best! Did he hurt you?" she asked, looking down and finding me in one piece.

"No, he hasn't hurt me. Calix is my husband now," I said tentatively, not knowing how much she knew about the situation or how much she might have been deceived about.

"I know! Isn't it great?" she asked, looking over my shoulder. Calix stepped out of the house and onto the patio, looking casual in a pair of jeans that were slung low on his hips and a simple black t-shirt.

"Great?" I asked, tilting my head to the side as I studied her.

"Evangeline says he loves you. That he's *always* loved you. He won't let anything bad happen to you. Not like Damianos," she whispered, leaning in as if it was a secret that she wasn't meant to tell me.

"Malva, you know he killed your parents. Your mother is gone, too," I said, keeping my voice gentle. As much as I'd hated Lydia, she was at least mostly tolerant of Malva. She'd indulged her and spoiled her as much as she possibly could, leaving me to suffer as a sacrifice for her child's happiness. I couldn't even blame her completely.

I'd been nothing to her.

Malva shrugged, her lips twisting to the side. "I know I should miss her, but I don't. Does that make me a horrible daughter?" she asked, looking over her shoulder. I caught Evangeline's eyes, feeling immensely grateful that she'd given my sister someone safe to confide in and seek out comfort in my absence.

Even if it did also fill me with a jealous longing, wishing I could have been that for her.

"I think that means she was a horrible mother. If you can move on from her loss so easily, then she wasn't doing her job very well. You are the sweetest, kindest girl I have ever met," I said, blinking back the sting of tears. I'd worked so hard to protect her from the harsh realities of our lives, and now...

Now it was out of my hands for the time being.

"I'm the only little girl you spend time with," she said, raising a brow at me playfully. Dismissing the emotion clogging my throat, I huffed a sharp laugh and grabbed her around the back of the head. Pulling her into my chest, I clung to her for a few moments.

"I've known plenty of little girls in my lifetime. They liked to torment me when I was young," I explained, pulling back and tucking her hair behind her ear.

Her brow furrowed, a moment of concern touching her blissful face. "What made them stop?" she asked.

I twisted, glancing over my shoulder at the man who watched our interaction with an intense stare. He made no attempt to hide his blatant observation; didn't bother to disguise the way he watched me. "He did," I said, letting my lips curl into a smile.

Even after they'd banished him from the city, the girls at school had never bothered me again. They'd ignored me, pretended I didn't exist like the ugly duckling among them, but it was better that way.

I hadn't wanted to be friends with kids who were capable of making fun of me for looking a little different, anyway. Malva was fortunate enough that she didn't have my color-blindness or pointed ears, that her eyes weren't as big and her lips didn't stick out too far. I'd always been teased for my features being too big for my face.

Until my face had grown into them.

"Of course he did," Malva said, grinning and waving at Calix from around me. He gave her a little smile and waved back with a slight flick of his hand.

The last time I'd seen Malva, she'd been staring down the barrel of his gun and terrified of the man she now waved at as if he was our savior from the brutal reality of our world. I turned back to my sister as Calix took the first step toward us, slowly closing the distance between us.

"It's good to see you, Τζάνεμ," Calix said, reaching past me to rub the hair on top of Malva's head. She giggled as she looked up at him, leaning forward to wrap her arms around his waist quickly.

"I'm so confused," I mumbled, not wanting to remind Malva of the terror of my wedding day but not wanting to be clearly missing information.

"I've checked in on Malva every time I leave the house to tend to business," Calix answered as Malva retreated from his grip and walked back toward his mother. We watched as they resumed their play, twirling through the yard as Malva tried to keep the ball away from the older woman. "I couldn't bring you yet. Not when you were so upset. You can see how happy she is here. I needed you to be in a place where you can understand first."

"That wasn't your choice to make," I snapped, but I couldn't deny the truth. I'd have frightened her with my own uncertainty about the turn of events, whereas Calix and his mother had done a fabulous job convincing her she was safe.

I just had to hope it was true.

"I've instructed my mother that Malva is to always feel loved. She is to be the center of her world, and my mother never had any other children outside of me. She wasn't able to dote on me the way she wanted, not with my father raising me to be the heir to the Regas family. I promise you this is just as much a gift for my mother as it is for your sister and you," he said, wrapping an arm around my waist and pulling me into his side.

"For me?" I asked, turning my head so that I could look up at the side of his face as he watched Malva.

"You've been taking care of her for too long. Doing everything you're told because you have to set a good example of what the family will expect from her," he answered, turning his attention down to my face. "Now you can just be."

"I can just be what?" I asked, turning my stare back to where Malva waved me on.

"Come on, Thalia!" she squealed, laughing when Calix's mother wrapped her arms around my sister's waist and lifted her off her feet.

His answer shocked me still for a moment. "Be whoever you want to be, λουλούδι μου. As long as you do it with me."

33

CALIX

I groaned in my half-sleep, settling closer to Thalia's back and pressing my cock into the flesh of her naked ass. She moaned, the deep, throaty sound torn from her sleeping form.

I paused for a moment, carefully waiting to see if she would wake up or continue to dream. Releasing the grip I kept at the base of her throat while we slept, I trailed my fingers down along the valley between her small, pert breasts. She arched her back, leaning into me, but her breathing remained in the rhythm that I'd come to expect of her sleep.

"Are you awake, Little One?" I asked, continuing to slide my hand lower. My fingertips trailed over her hip, curving around to reach between our bodies. I lifted her thigh slightly, spreading her legs just enough to slide my cock against her pussy.

She was wet, the aftermath of our lovemaking the night before clinging to her skin as I waited for a response that never came. Tilting my hips, I guided my cock to her entrance and slowly pushed inside.

I'd meant it when I said her pussy was mine. I'd meant it

when I said I would use it when and how I saw fit. If that meant she dreamt of me fucking her while I moved inside her, so be it. Thalia gasped as I released her, letting her legs close together and trap my cock in the haven of her thighs as I shifted to get a better angle and pressed myself closer into her back.

"If there is a heaven, this is what I imagine it must feel like," I murmured, pressing my lips to the side of her neck. She arched into the touch as my hand slid up her front, ghosting over her skin until I could grip her by the base of her throat.

My thrusts inside her were slow, leisurely, waiting for her to wake up but enjoying the knowledge that she was comfortable enough with me to sleep this deeply. I'd exhausted her so much the night before, she didn't wake as I moved inside of her.

I would spend my entire day inside of her if it were up to me. She would sit on my cock as she read a book so she could take her pleasure from my body whenever she needed it.

"Calix," she whispered, her throat moving under my hand. I would never tire of hearing my name on her lips and her acknowledgement of exactly who it was who fucked her.

Knowing she'd given herself to a stranger and hadn't even known my name the first time felt wrong in a way I didn't want to accept. She had to have known, deep down.

"Good morning, λουλούδι μου. How did you sleep?" I asked, wedging one of my legs between hers. I tilted her forward, shifting her until half her stomach pressed into the bed. Laying some of my weight onto her, I covered her with my body and ground my cock deeper.

She parted her legs for me more, opening herself up so that I could get deeper inside of her.

"You really want to ask that right now?" she grumbled, her

voice filled with disbelief. I chuckled, pulling back and then thrusting back into her in a slow, deep glide. She moaned for me, and it brought me great satisfaction that she didn't pretend to be disturbed that I'd slid inside her while she slept.

Thalia knew as well as I did that she wanted to give me control. She just hadn't quite accepted it yet.

"I want to know what you dreamt about—"

The door to our bedroom burst open, and I rolled Thalia fully beneath me. She gasped and tried to roll to look at whatever had interrupted us, but I shielded her with my body and reached under the edge of the mattress.

Snatching the gun from beneath it, I spun to face the doorway as I kept Thalia protected beneath my weight. "Calix!" she protested, struggling against my hold as I leveled my aim on the intruder.

He wasn't bothered in the slightest by the gun pointing at him, straightening the jacket of his suit as if it inconvenienced him greatly that he had to be there at all. Every helpful, Christian hurried up behind the man.

"The council has sent a messenger," Christian said, looking between the man and where I pinned my naked wife to the bed beneath me. My cock was still planted between her legs, though only half inside her with all the commotion. He looked at our position, swallowing and averting his eyes. "I told him he had to wait."

"That went well, I take it," I said, less than impressed with the fact that he'd allowed the messenger to come up to my bedroom when he suspected I was sleeping.

We'd have words.

"The council requires both of you to present yourself for Calix Regas' judgment. Tobias Hasapis has demanded payment for the blood debt you owe him after killing his family. Should the majority of the council vote for him, you will not leave ο λάκκος alive," the messenger said, waiting in the doorway.

"They couldn't have waited until normal calling hours to summon me to my potential death?" I asked, earning a gasp from Thalia where she lay beneath me. I shifted my hips forward, burying myself to the hilt in her pussy, and felt the moment she tensed.

Her horror only drove me to want to push her further.

I pulled back, moving slowly and trying not to draw too much attention to the parts of us that were joined.

"The council is waiting," the stranger said, crossing his arms over his chest. He was clearly not pleased with the fact that I hadn't moved to get out of the bed, instead staying firmly planted in the haven of my wife's cunt.

"They can wait another twenty minutes. If I'm going to my death, I want to do it having fucked my wife one more time first," I said, chuckling when Thalia shrieked beneath me, swinging her hand around her back to try to hit me.

I caught it, pinning it to her back and holding her there.

"I really must insist—"

"This will go much quicker if you get out so I can make her come already," I said, stuffing my gun beneath the mattress once more and trusting Christian to keep his gun trained on the intruder.

The man grunted, his frustration evident in the sound as he turned and left the room. *Finally.* The door closed behind him, and I glanced over my shoulder briefly to see if Christian had been foolish enough to stay in the bedroom.

He hadn't.

"Let me go!" Thalia shrieked, struggling against my grip on her arm as I shifted and spread her legs farther. Pinning her into the mattress, I fucked her in slow thrusts that gave her time for the heat to build once again.

For the adrenaline and fear to give way to the pleasure that could come afterwards.

"I meant what I said. I want to finish fucking my wife," I murmured, touching my lips to the side of her neck. Her pussy fluttered around me, betraying her fight for what it was. She was far more concerned with the way she thought she should have reacted to the interruption than she was about the actuality of my cock inside of her.

"There are *people* here," she protested, letting out a tiny whimper as her free hand gripped the pillow beside her head.

"There will always be people here, Little One," I reminded her, thinking of the security staff who could always overhear when she screamed my name. She'd have to get used to knowing that other men heard her cry out her pleasure and knew *exactly* what was happening. "The sooner you come for me, the sooner I'll allow you to get dressed."

I released her arm when she finally stopped struggling, reaching my hand beneath her body to toy with her clit. She whimpered in response, stretching her arm behind her to grasp me around the back of the head and pull me closer. "I'm going to gut you," she whispered, but she arched into my touch as I slid my hand lower and felt the place where I plunged inside her.

Spreading my fingers to surround my cock, I felt the smooth glide of my cock within her. Felt the way she stretched to take me.

"No, you're not. You like my cock too much," I groaned, slipping a finger inside her alongside my cock. She cried out, shattering in my arms.

I fucked her through it, quickening my pace and being mindful of the hellfire she'd rain down on me when she came to her senses.

I wanted to come before she found something to throw at me.

I shoved deep, groaning out my release as Thalia stilled beneath me when I flooded her with cum. My cock twitched inside of her with the force of my orgasm, leaving me with only a moment to catch my breath before she bucked back against me and tried to dislodge me from her body.

"You asshole!"

"An asshole wouldn't have cared if you came." I shrugged, moving back off her body and getting to my knees on the bed. She grabbed her favorite moisturizer off the nightstand, hefting it into her hand as I dove forward and took it out of her grasp.

That shit would make a mess when she missed.

"What is wrong with you?!" she asked, swinging her legs over the edge of the bed and standing in a hurry. She went for the closet, only glancing over her shoulder at me when I followed. She reached for her robe, but stopped when I placed a hand on top of hers and guided her toward the dresses. Snatching a black dress off the rack, I laid it out on the ottoman in the center of the room.

I'd hand-picked it for the first time Thalia would sit on the Karras seat at o λάκκος, the boning in the bodice reminding me of armor. I'd just thought to have a bit more time before she wore it.

"I can't go back there," she said, crossing her arms over her breasts and staring at me as vulnerability leaked into her features.

I had no way to know if Thalia had been dragged back to the scene of her mother's murder in the years since it had happened, but I had to imagine she hadn't. Women weren't often permitted in the pits, only for grand exceptions like her mother's infidelity.

"I promise nothing bad will happen to you," I said, reassuring her softly as I approached.

"You heard him! They're going to vote on whether or not you have to *die*, Calix. Don't make me promises you can't keep," she hissed, turning her back on me. She gathered up a lacy black bra and panty set in spite of her protests, already knowing there was no avoiding going with me.

If the council demanded her presence, they would have it.

She pulled the underwear up her thighs, pausing before she settled them into place. She hurried for the bathroom to clean up, and I allowed it even though my instinct was to require her to go to the meeting with my cum coating her thighs.

I dressed in my favorite suit in her absence, waiting for her to return. The underwear hid her pussy from view when she finally did, and she shrugged her bra on before allowing me to pull her dress off the hanger and tug it over her head.

"Do you really believe I would allow you to come if I thought I wouldn't be able to protect you?" I asked, zipping up the back of her dress as she pulled her hair out of the way. I walked around her, grabbing her brush off the vanity in the closet and carefully running it through her long waves.

"I don't know."

"I wouldn't, λουλούδι μου. Trust that I have everything covered, but there is something I need from you," I murmured, guiding her out the door of the closet and back to our bedroom. She grabbed the pair of black, strapped heels I'd set out, perching on the edge of the bed to fasten them on her feet.

"What could you possibly need from me? You clearly don't require my advice on how to manage the council," she said, the note of bitterness in her voice surprising me. I didn't think she would want to be involved in such business more than necessary, but perhaps, like everyone else in her life, I had made the mistake of underestimating her.

I crouched at her feet, settling my hands on top of her thighs. "I know we still have a great deal to figure out between us as to the nature of our relationship. But in there? We have to be united. If we do not project the image of strength and appear resolute in our goals, we won't make it out alive. Do you understand me?"

She swallowed, saying, "I understand," then she squared her shoulders and stood in front of me. She crossed the room to the bathroom door, yanking it open and pausing to look over her shoulder. "Never let them see you bleed."

34

THALIA

The windows of the back seat of the car seemed far too oppressive as we approached the industrial district I remembered very clearly. The ramshackle buildings had haunted my vivid nightmares for years after the loss of my mother, reminding me of what waited for me if I dared to defy my father's rules.

A blade just waiting to swing, a neck just waiting to be severed.

The town car pulled up in front of the abandoned warehouse with heavily armed security standing around the back of it. The families made no attempt to disguise their treachery or the crimes they committed here, and there was no reason to.

The police worked alongside the guards each family provided, securing the location from all manner of people who would grow curious.

I lifted my chin as one of the suited men stepped forward, opening my door for me as Calix climbed out the other side. I placed my hand in the stranger's, pivoting until my heels touched the ground outside the car.

Allowing him to pull me free, I focused on the feeling of my silken dress settling around my thighs. It gathered on one side, draping asymmetrically and leaving one leg revealed, while the boning of the bodice pushed my breasts high. I waved the man out of my way so that I could walk toward the warehouse. Calix fell into step with me without a word and settled his hand on the small of my back as he leaned in and pressed his mouth to my hair.

I practically felt the glare he aimed toward the man who'd dared to touch my hand, the look a firm reminder of just who I belonged to in the games we would play today. One day, I might risk his wrath to test his limits and toy with another man just to irritate him.

Instead, with my anxiety over the pits rushing through me, I leaned into his touch more than I cared to admit. The back doors of the warehouse swung open as we approached, and Calix led me through them.

The last time I'd been here, I'd been far more concerned with what was happening than finding my way around on any future visit. Back then, I'd have sworn I would never willingly return.

Calix led me to a set of stairs that curved around the pit itself. We ascended the steps as I stared down over the metal railing into the sand below. There was no stain of blood to show the spot where my mother had died. As if her very being had been washed away.

I turned away, forcing back the threat of tears that burned my throat. I couldn't show any emotion to the men who would use it against me and deem me too feminine and emotional to claim my seat on the council.

Calix rounded the top, guiding me at his side to a room encased in glass. It hung above the pit itself, stray grains of sand crunching beneath my feet and haunting me as my heels clacked against the wood floors. I couldn't have said if the room or stairs had existed the last time or if they were new, but I got the general impression that Calix had been in that room before.

He halted before the glass door, wrapping his fingers around the olive branches crafted out of metal. Six of them extended from the center toward the edges, representing the six families.

Calix pulled the door open, holding it for me as I led the way into the room. Four other men sat within, holding court in chairs arranged in a circle at the center.

"Welcome back to ο λάκκος, Thalia Karras," one of them said. I recognized him from his dealings with my father.

Alexander Galanis.

He was also the father of one of the girls who had tormented me before Calix stepped in.

"Regas," Calix corrected with a smirk, snagging my eye with his. He studied me as he took a few steps to the side, lowering himself into what I could only presume was the Regas seat.

"That won't be the case for long. She'll have no need of your name when you're dead," Damianos's brother Tobias said. He glared at Calix before turning his dead-eyed stare to me, letting his gaze travel from my feet to my head.

"Let us not get ahead of ourselves," one of the others said. He buttoned the jacket of his suit as he stood, holding out a hand to gesture me toward the only remaining seat. "While it is admittedly unorthodox, with no other surviving Karras to claim their seat, Thalia will have equal rights in all decisions made by this council."

"Thank you, Lykaios," Calix said, smiling slightly as the other man gestured me on. I walked past two of the other council members, pausing in front of the shining metallic seat that remained. I ran my fingers over the back of it, touching the symbol of my family that was etched into it.

The fish emerged from the water, surrounded by anemone as I turned my back to it and faced the circle at the center. Two spikes pointed toward the ceiling in the very center of the back of the chair, looking menacing. I lowered myself into the seat, touching the arms and running manicured nails over the metal.

Calix cleared his throat, raising a brow at me as he drew my attention to him at last. "Should we begin?"

35

CALIX

I slid my hand into the mouth of the serpent at the end of the left arm of my chair. Its body wrapped around the leg, etched into fine detail. The others followed suit as Thalia watched, and I nodded her on, even though I wished there'd been more time to prepare her for what was to come.

Power came at a cost. There could be no dominion over the city without pain.

I pressed my middle finger down against the button formed from the serpent's tongue, the needle at the center puncturing my skin until blood dripped down around the button and into the locking mechanism beneath it.

I kept my eyes on Thalia's as she inserted her finger into the serpent the same way I had. Her eyes widened as the tip brushed over the needle, but she swallowed back her apprehension. The eyes of the other five families rested on her shoulders as she squared them, turning her gaze away from mine and looking straight forward.

Tobias sat across from her, his head cocked to the side as he watched her the same way I did. She didn't so much as flinch when she pressed her finger into the needle, bleeding herself for the right to claim her place on the council.

Once the vial below her button had filled with blood, all of the needles retracted into the locking mechanisms within the chairs. Blood slid down the bodies of the serpents, draining into channels as the slight decline in the circular floor pulled it toward the center. Thalia leaned forward in her seat as the blood mixed and surrounded the six points at the center circle, the six tails where they extended from our chairs to intertwine into one body.

Six families. Six heads of the serpent.

The gear at the center of the circle between us turned, the metal groaning as it spread apart and the panels of the floor retracted back into their hidden pockets beneath our seats. My feet dangled as the ground beneath them disappeared, leaving me with no way to stand from my chair until our business was concluded.

Thalia stared down into the hole in the floor in horror, getting a bird's eye view of the pit below and of the sandy enclosure where her mother had died for a crime that was far from worthy of death.

It was rare that I'd been permitted within the council chamber as a boy, only often enough to have some idea of what would happen should I assume my place as head of the Regas family one day. More often than not, I'd sat in the sandy pit below, playing with the axes and knives and shields while I looked up at the dangling feet of the men above.

Never had a woman sat there, delicate heels pointing down like daggers.

Thalia tore her gaze off the pits below, pursing her lips as she pulled her hand free from the serpent's mouth. She shifted in her seat, crossing her legs carefully and revealing a long line of bare thigh in the asymmetrical hem of her dress.

Leaning back in her seat, she donned the mask she'd worn for most of her life.

An indifferent Queen upon her throne.

She drew her finger into her mouth, sucking away the drop of blood that remained while the men in the room watched her, waiting for a reaction. "I presume there is a point to your dragging me from my bed so early in the morning. Might I request you make it?"

"Origen should have killed you along with your whore of a mother. A slut can only breed a slut," Alexander Galanis said, his voice lacking vehemence. He spoke as if it was common knowledge that all the men in the room thought similar.

To kill a child for the crimes of her mother....

I hated it here.

"A pity for you, I suppose," Thalia said, seemingly unruffled by his wish for her death as a girl. I couldn't imagine it was an entirely strange concept to her, with a father who didn't care whether she lived or died outside of what he could gain from marrying her off.

"Enough," Elias ordered, rolling his eyes. "We have a genuine conflict that has been brought forward by a member of the Hasapis family. Surely that is more important than petty squabbles amongst ourselves."

"How convenient for you to find yourself sitting on the council during such a time of turmoil, Elias. Your father's heart must have been simply unable to handle all the stress that Regas caused with his attack on two of our most dear families," Alexander said, glaring at Elias from across the open chasm between them.

"It would have been difficult for any man to possess a functioning heart when it was cut from his chest," Elias answered, leaning forward. "We all know my father did not die of natural causes. I won't pretend he did."

"You killed him to take his place on this council," Alexander accused, and I sat back in my seat. Thalia mirrored the posture, draping her forearms on the golden arms of her chair and watching the show. Listening for any bits of information the others were foolish enough to provide, not fully grasping that they had not one, but two enemies in their midst. "I have to ask myself, why now?"

Elias leaned forward, gripping the edge of one arm of his chair as a single one of his hands came down upon the head of the snake. "Because it is time for a new generation to control the six families. I am as much an opportunist as my father was before I killed him at our family dinner."

"You may be within your right to usurp your father's throne, but Regas's involvement goes against the treaty between our families. We are not to interfere in the hierarchy of the others. Not only did he nearly eradicate two family lines, but he involved himself in the politics of the Lykaios family as well for his own benefit. Such things are forbidden, and he will be punished for them," Alexander said, glaring over at me.

He clearly thought he'd trapped me within the confines of the treaties we were all required to submit to, but I smirked. "I swear on the life of my wife and the potential child growing in her womb, I did not leave her side yesterday. I'm not sure how I could have been involved in this coup when we were nowhere near the Lykaios estate."

Alexander turned to Thalia, his nostrils flaring in irritation. "And what was it that you did all day, Ms. Karras?"

"My husband and I visited his parents. His mother is looking after my sister as we adjust to our new marriage. *Newlyweds,* I'm sure you understand," she said, scrunching up her nose playfully, but disgust followed in its wake as she turned her attention away from him.

Aleksander's fingers tightened on the chair as he leaned toward her, her blatant dismissal of him grating on his last nerve. "All night long?" he asked her, leaving her with no choice but to lean away as he got closer to her space than he should have.

I'd have the chairs rearranged once I had better control of the city and the council, putting her beside me so that no one could come between us. "Of course not. We went home, where he bent me over the sofa and fucked me until I couldn't walk. Is that what you wanted to hear, Councilor Galanis?"

"Listen here, you little—" Alexander snapped.

"Whore?" Thalia finished, scoffing. "I find it difficult to believe you would have called me a whore if Damianos had fucked me until I cried on our wedding night. So am I a whore for having sex with my husband, or am I a whore because I enjoyed it? If it's the latter, you might consider asking yourself why your wife doesn't enjoy sex with you. It says far more about you and the shriveled piece of meat dangling between your legs than it does about your wife."

Elias and Atticus chuckled, raising fists to cover their mouths and disguise it. "λουλούδι μου," I murmured, leaning forward with a smile and cocking my head to the side. "Play nice."

She met my smile with a sly grin of her own, picking at her nails absently. "Anything for you, η ψυχή μου," she said, making my cock throb in my pants. The devious tormenter would be the end of me.

My soul.

Fuck.

"My brother would have enjoyed breaking you," Tobias said, leaning forward until I almost worried he might fall out of his chair. I supposed plummeting to his death would have been too convenient.

Pity.

"He would have tried, but it will take a far greater man than Damianos Hasapis to break what has already learned to bend," Thalia said, glaring at Tobias intently. The other man didn't back down, the muscle in his jaw flexing before he finally turned his attention away and allowed Thalia to be the victor of that skirmish.

"Enough games. I've called the council to order to demand payment for the blood debt owed to me by Calix Regas for the cold-blooded murder of my family. When he is dead, I will take Thalia Karras as my wife to unite our families as my brother wanted," Tobias proposed, looking toward me and waiting for me to squirm.

"Over my dead body," Thalia seethed, showing far too much emotion. It was something they could use against her in the long run, but perhaps it would let them underestimate her.

"But Thalia, you said yourself; you do not break. Let me see how far you can bend," Tobias growled, gripping the arms of his chair.

"You can theorize all you want, but it is a moot point. You see, I've been banished from this council. I am no longer held to the treaties that bind it together. Your father thought he was clever to get rid of us, but he made it so that I do not need to obey your laws. I can do as I please, and there is nothing you can do about it," I said, watching as Tobias's nostrils flared in fury.

"Then what is to stop me from killing you here and now?"

"You could, but we both know I have allies in very high places. I have spent a great many years making it effectively impossible for you to kill me without signing your own death warrant. So as I see it, you have three choices. One, you can kill me and take your chances with the wrath of Rafael Ibarra and Matteo Bellandi. Two, you can banish me *and* my wife from this city, knowing we will not be held to your laws and may come back for vengeance yet again. Or three, and this is my personal favorite, you can reinstate the Regas family to the council and make me the head of my line. I will once again need to obey the treaty and the governance of the council going forward, and I promise you; that is your only hope of ever controlling me."

"I move to reinstate Calix Regas as the head of his family, and give him the seat he is owed upon this very council," Elias said, pressing his hand back into the open mouth of the snake. He pricked his finger, pressing down the button to collect his blood while he waited.

"Second," Atticus murmured, following suit.

"Thalia, my flower, would you care to third the motion?" I asked, watching as she raised her chin in understanding.

United we could have our vengeance.

"Third," she murmured softly, pressing her poor, abused finger back onto the needle. Blood ran down, swinging the mechanisms as the panels closed in the floor. With a majority reached, business had concluded.

"And just like that, you've taken back power in the city you haven't even been a part of for over a decade," Alexander scoffed, rising to his feet.

"I assure you; while it may have seemed quick to you, this is the result of years of careful planning. I meant it when I asked if we should begin. I am nowhere near finished enacting my revenge," I warned, pointing a finger at his seat. "Now sit down. There is still one final matter to be discussed today."

"I move to reassess the hierarchy of the council itself. The Hasapis family is no longer strong enough to lead us. I call for the trial by combat in ο λάκκος in one month's time. Let our battle decide who is worthy, as has always been done," Atticus said, holding to the conversation we'd had in the dead of night.

"You realize all families must be present in such a battle? What hope do I have against four men decades younger than I am? More importantly, what hope does *she* have?" Alexander said, turning toward Thalia.

"She's a woman. She won't be expected to fight. She will merely have to forfeit her chance to govern the council," I said.

"The treaty says all must be present in ο λάκκος. I promise you, I will make sure she fights. If she wants to play like a big girl, then she'll need to learn to fight like one."

"Don't you worry about me, Councilor Galanis. I am strong enough to beat an old man with one foot in the grave. I will see you in ο λάκκος. Try not to be too embarrassed when I win," Thalia said, standing from her chair smoothly. She pinned Alexander Galanis with one last smug grin and turned on her heel.

I rose, following after her to leave the others to discuss the battle in one month. They knew as well as I did that there was no way around it.

There was no voting on a challenge to the power.

There was only war.

36

THALIA

Christian waited outside the warehouse building as Calix and I exited, leaning his weight into the passenger side door with his ankles casually crossed.

As if he wasn't surrounded by armed guards who would kill him without hesitation, he barely paid them any attention. They weren't worth his worry and weren't worth his notice. He stared at the ground, scuffing his shoes through the dirt at his feet. Dust floated into the air as I took my first step off the concrete surrounding the building, walking on my toes so my heels didn't dig into the gravel and dry earth.

Christian looked up from beneath his lashes, his face remaining angled down as Calix and I made our way toward him. His stare settled on my face briefly before trailing down my body and checking for injury.

He moved fluidly when he found none, pushing off the car and tugging the door open for me. I strode toward it with quick steps, my urgency to get away from the armed men around me taking over. With the adrenaline of the meeting fading, I realized how foolish I'd been.

I'd baited the council of the six. I'd used my words against them when I'd been taught all my life that I was to remain silent.

I bent forward slightly, lowering myself into the backseat and moving over so that Calix could follow, while he kept his body firmly planted between me and the guns at his back. My gaze snagged on Christian's once more, the intensity of his stare making me bristle.

"Are we going to have a problem, Christian?" Calix asked, leaning his weight into the arm he'd placed on top of the car. With his body filling the open door, his voice dropped low as he spoke. I stopped in the middle of the seat, watching the exchange between them in confusion.

Christian cleared his throat, meeting Calix's stare. "Of course not," he said, pursing his lips as if he was biting his tongue.

"Good," Calix said, reaching forward to clap a hand down on Christian's shoulder. "Because I'd really hate to have to kill you." He lowered himself into the seat beside me, crowding me when I didn't shift over but just stared at him.

He never bothered to look away, holding my challenging gaze with a quiet stoicism that kept my mouth firmly clamped shut. I couldn't decide if his irritation with Christian was because he was pissed at me for my behavior or if it was something else that drove it.

Either way, his face remained as hard as stone—chiseled in his indifference as Christian closed the door and made his way to the front.

"When we get home," Calix murmured in response to my questioning gaze, leaning in to touch his lips to my temple. I swallowed, letting myself feel the affection in his tone.

Whatever had pissed him off, he didn't seem angry with me. That had to be enough for the moment, because I wasn't certain my frazzled nerves could take another conflict.

"Out," Calix ordered simply the moment we stepped into the house. The security within, including Christian, made themselves scarce and disappeared out the front door.

"Who peed in your Cheerios?" I asked, crossing my arms over my chest. Calix's gaze fell to my breasts, and the way the position of my arms pushed them up higher. It felt as if they might burst free from the armor of a dress he'd put me in, and I watched as he parted his lips and ran his tongue over his bottom teeth slowly with a smirk that was twisted with depravity.

"I have to be able to trust my team implicitly, especially when it comes to you. They'll be responsible for your safety when I can't be, and that inherently means they'll be spending time alone with you. If there is something I need to know about your relationship with Christian, now would be the time to disclose that so we can avoid a bloody spectacle," Calix said, moving around the kitchen island. He fussed with grabbing fresh fruit from the fridge, and the motivation wasn't lost on me.

I often said no to the more complicated foods he prepared, or didn't eat enough to satisfy his desire to see me properly fed, but I'd never met a fruit I didn't like. He grinned, turning to deposit the fresh strawberries back in the fridge and emerging with whole berries covered in chocolate. My mouth watered, because although I'd never tasted the combination of two of my favorites, I could just imagine how marvelous they must be together.

"You think I have feelings for Christian?" I asked, resisting the urge to step up and take one of the berries. This was a trap, and he was using chocolate to bait me into a conversation I had no desire to have because of how absolutely ridiculous it was.

"I think he's attracted to you," Calix said, grabbing a knife from the block and stabbing one of the strawberries. He used the knife to guide it to his mouth, taking a bite out of the fruit casually, as if he wasn't intending to torment me. "He's a straight man so that's unsurprising. I can excuse that as long as he keeps his fucking hands and greedy little eyeballs to himself. It'd be a shame if I had to cut them out of his skull and feed them to him."

"His greedy little eyeballs?" I asked, rolling my own eyes at how ridiculous he was. "You think if I did have feelings for Christian, I'd have asked him to arrange for me to have a one-night stand with a stranger? Not to mention, if you're going to make threats, they should be achievable. Christian would be dead long before you could actually feed him his eyeballs."

"You'd be amazed what the human body can survive if the person knows what they're doing, Little One. Taking out a man's eyeballs isn't particularly difficult," Calix answered, taking another bite of the strawberry.

As appetizing as that sounded...

I gulped.

"I'm going to go take a shower while you work out your mood," I sighed, shaking my head and intending to turn my back on the volatile man who didn't seem to realize how alarming it was that removing a man's eyeballs was an easy task for him. I didn't want to think about all the other things he'd done.

"You handled yourself well with the council," Calix said, taking a step around the island. I froze in place, watching him with wary eyes as he moved slowly toward me. He behaved as if I were a feral animal, ready to bolt at the first sign of aggression.

A wiser woman probably would.

"I behaved foolishly, and I will pay the consequences for that when I have to fight for a position at the head of the council, even though I do not want it. I'm under no illusion that I'm capable of taking on Tobias or any of the council members who do not have one foot in the grave. I'm far too small to inflict any major damage," I said, shaking my head.

"You were brave in the face of a group of men most of the city fears, with good reason. It takes an Θεά to choose strength over life, to choose death over being broken," he said, taking a few more steps toward me. He stopped before me, a fresh strawberry impaled on his knife as it hung by his side.

"Some would argue that I have spent all of my life cowering and broken down," I said, quirking a brow at him. Even when he'd known me as a child, I'd done everything I could to remain quiet and out of sight. I'd hidden my flaws and my oddities, trying to be the perfect girl that my father would mold into a biddable woman.

In this city, alliance through marriage was far more important than money.

"You were never even close to broken, λουλούδι μου. You were simply waiting for your time to strike," he murmured, reaching up with his hand that held the knife. He brushed the back of his knuckles over my cheekbone, the knife pointing away from my face but filling my vision. He drew it back far enough to take a bite, chewing thoughtfully as he touched the rest of the berry to my lips and stained them with juice. "You voted with me. You took my side. Why?"

I parted my lips to speak, and he used the opportunity to slide the berry between them. I sank my teeth into it carefully, all too aware of the sharp blade that was so close to my mouth and the man who wielded it. I didn't *think* Calix would harm me, but he was far from the most stable man I'd ever met.

That should have been terrifying, but I couldn't seem to stop leaning into his presence the more I learned about him. I couldn't seem to stop taking comfort in his instability, or the unpredictability of who he was. Would I wake one morning and see the unhinged side of him that had motivated him to massacre two families? Or would I continue to experience the side of Calix that fed me incessantly and fussed over the luxuries he'd surrounded me with?

I chewed thoughtfully, considering the answers I could give him. It would have been true to say that I stood a far greater chance of escaping all of this unscathed with him by my side rather than Tobias, but even still....

"Because now you owe me a debt," I said, swallowing the berry and staring up at Calix. He cocked his head to the side, his lips parting into a bright grin.

"Is that so?" he asked, lifting his empty hand between us. He pressed his open palm against the front of my throat and squeezed lightly as he tossed the stabbed strawberry stem into the farmhouse sink. "And how would λουλούδι μου like me to repay such a debt?"

"I want Malva to come and live with us," I said, my throat moving against his palm.

"No," Calix said, his voice lacking any inflection.

"You owe me—"

"When this conversation finishes, I fully intend to put you on your hands and knees on the kitchen island so I can lick your fucking cunt until you scream, Little One. Is that something you would like your little sister to walk in on?" he asked, smirking when my mouth dropped open.

"I didn't agree to—"

"What did I tell you the first time you let me inside of you? I own your body now. I will do what I want to it—when and where I please. I've waited far too long to have you. I will not limit myself so soon," he said, taking a step back. He kept his grip on my throat as he moved, giving me no choice but to follow as his fingers squeezed tighter.

I swallowed, knowing there was no way around that. As much as I could have negotiated with any normal man to be more willing to save sex for the bedroom, the dark gleam in Calix's eyes made it clear that he would *not* be making that concession.

He brushed his fingers against my shoulder, pushing the strap over the edge until it draped along my bicep. Spinning me so suddenly that I grabbed the island to steady myself, he wrapped himself around my back. Holding my throat to keep me arched back, he reached around to pluck one of the remaining strawberries off the island. He pressed it to my lips, the flavor of chocolate melting against the heat of my mouth as my breath came in ragged gasps.

"Eat," he ordered, and I parted my lips, letting him slide a chunk of the berry in and force my jaw wide open. Sinking my teeth into the flesh, I winced when the chocolate cracked and crumbled, falling to the top of the island.

I chewed as he pulled what remained of the berry away from my mouth, trailing it over the side of my neck and down to the back of the shoulder he'd bared. A cool line of juice slid over my skin, and I looked over my shoulder at him to find his silver eyes gleaming as he watched my face. He lowered his mouth to the trail he'd created, dragging his tongue over my skin and licking the strawberry juice off me.

"What else is it that you want from me, Little One? How can I repay the debt I owe to my wife?" he murmured, his mouth hovering at the sensitive spot just behind my ear. He kissed the skin there, then shifted slightly lower and sank his teeth into my flesh hard enough that I suspected I might bruise.

I whimpered, trying to form a coherent thought that wasn't drowned out in the sinful acts of Calix's mouth and the filthy promise of what his mouth would do if I allowed it.

He released my throat, trailing calloused fingertips over my collarbone and brushing the strap off my other shoulder. "I want to be able to see her whenever I want," I said, swallowing as his fingers went to the zipper at the back of my dress.

He guided it down slowly. "I won't have you around my father without me present. I don't trust him with you."

"But you trust him with my sister?" I snapped, spinning on my heels to glare at him.

"He won't harm either of you unless he wants to find his way into an early grave, but we both know that words have a far greater capacity to hurt you than any physical abuse he could inflict. He stands to gain nothing by spewing his nonsense at Malva, but if he believes he can drive a wedge between you and I, he will torment you. I won't subject you to the verbal warfare he will use to harm you. I'll have my mother bring her here when you want to see her if I cannot accompany you. Is that acceptable, λουλούδι μου?" he asked, grasping my chin and holding it as he leaned down to press his lips to mine.

He lingered just a breath away, giving me time to respond before he took from me. I knew what would happen the moment he viewed our negotiations to be over. I glanced back at the kitchen island, swallowing and sighing. "Yes. That's acceptable to me, η ψυχή μου."

His mouth spread into a closed smile, pressing into mine as he dropped his hands to the top of the boned bodice of the dress and pressed it down. I shimmied my hips to help him get the structured top down over them, closing my eyes when he touched a hand to the small of my back and drew me against his chest.

Something about the fabric of his suit touching me felt like sin. It felt like being his plaything, with him perfectly composed. He draped my hair over one shoulder, spinning me to face the island again. His fingers grasped the waistband of my underwear, tugging them slowly over my ass until they slid down my thighs and fell to my feet. "Up on the counter, Little One," he ordered, laying a sharp slap on my ass. The swat echoed through the kitchen, making me turn a shocked look at him as I climbed up onto the stool beside me.

Using that to get up onto the counter, I hesitated as the hard marble dug into my shins and knees. "I'm not sure—"

"Bend," Calix said, holding my questioning gaze as I glanced at him over my shoulder. I swallowed, leaning my body forward and touching my hands to the countertop. Calix spread my knees slightly, and the coolness of the air conditioning kissed my bare pussy as my thighs opened.

He didn't touch me, leaving me in that position while I waited in the silence for his touch. But there was nothing, just the sound of my breathing. I turned to glance over my shoulder, earning a sharp slap of his palm against my ass cheek again.

"Ow!" I screeched, turning forward again.

"Did I say you could move?" he growled.

"I was seeing if you're still there! What the hell are you doing?" I asked, a flush heating my cheeks when I thought of him behind me, doing God knows what with my pussy and ass bared to him.

"I'm enjoying the view. There is more to savoring a meal than simply eating it, Little One," he said. His hands finally touched the top of my ass, sliding over the oversensitive skin that must have been pink from his harsh treatment.

He lifted my cheeks, spreading them wide as everything inside of me clenched. "I don't think—"

"There is no corner of your body that will be hidden from me. No part of you I will not know intimately. I may not take your ass today, but I will when I decide you're ready. There's no point in hiding it from me," he said, and the warmth of his breath brushed over that part of me.

I whimpered, squirming and trying to force my hips to still. I was under no disillusion of what he might do if I moved against his instructions.

He'd made that much very clear.

His breath dipped lower, caressing the heat of me. I waited for the first brush of his tongue against my folds.

I was wholly unprepared for the way he sprang on me, because the first brush of his tongue was *not* soft or tentative. It was the kiss of a man who knew what he wanted, the firm pass of a tongue through my flesh a reminder of whose pussy it was. He devoured it from the first touch, getting to know every inch of me before sliding his tongue inside and fucking me with it.

"Fuck," I groaned, hanging my head forward as he licked me like his life depended on it.

His mouth disappeared as quickly as it had touched me, his fingers replacing his tongue as he slid two inside of me and curved them. Pumping them ruthlessly, he stroked over my g-spot with expert precision. "Calix," I murmured.

"That's right, wife," he said in return, pressing a kiss to my lower back. He dropped his mouth lower, kissing over the curve of my rear and biting the flesh harshly. I squealed, knowing that the bite itself would leave a mark. "This is where you belong. Whimpering and needy for my cock, your pussy dripping wet and practically begging me to fuck it."

He pulled his fingers free, grasping me around the hips

and tugging me down from the island. I scrambled to grab hold of the far edge as my legs dangled until my toes could barely brush against the ground. I'd only just found my purchase when he unzipped his pants, lined his cock up with my entrance, and shoved inside.

I grunted, arching my back into him as he filled me. Wrapping his hands around my throat, he pulled my head back and held it against his chest, pinning me still. Pressing me between his cock and his hands on my throat, he pounded with ruthless thrusts that struck the end of me. The pinch of pain entwined with my pleasure as I saw stars and my eyes rolled back in my head.

Calix's dark chuckle made his chest shake. "You're so fucking perfect for me, aren't you, my flower?" he asked, something dark tinting his voice deeper. "Here I was thinking I'd have to work you up to taking me the way I've wanted to fuck you, but you'll just keep begging me to fuck you harder."

He dropped a hand to my clit, stroking it as he moved inside of me with furious strokes. "You're not a girl who was broken by her life. You handle yourself like a queen, and you're going to make me into a fucking king," he grunted, shoving deep.

My orgasm crashed over me as I cried out, turning my legs to jelly as they trembled and struggled to hold me up. Only Calix's hold on me kept me standing; only the place where I was impaled on his cock kept me from collapsing to the floor.

He kept fucking me as I went limp, chasing after his own release until he grunted, his cock twitching deep inside as he filled me with his release.

It wasn't until he released my throat and let me straighten my neck that I realized how battered my body felt. How exhausted I was. When he pulled his cock free from my pussy, the rush of fluid that followed made me spin to glare at him.

Every time he finished inside of me was another shock, as if it was the first time. I couldn't seem to remind myself enough that he wanted me pregnant, while I just wanted to discover myself as a person first.

I glanced down at where it dripped down my thighs, drawing Calix's attention to it. He used two fingers to gather up the evidence of his orgasm, slipping them back up to my pussy and pressing those fingers inside of me once more. A brutal smirk twisted his lips and his eyes gleamed in victory as I swallowed. "A good girl doesn't waste what she's given, λουλούδι μου."

37

CALIX

I tossed back my ouzo, grimacing when I looked toward the entryway to the kitchen. Thalia slept soundly after a long day of relaxing in a hot bath with a book and letting me feed her far more than she would have eaten on her own.

"What was so urgent, compañero?" Rafael asked as he walked into the room. I glared at Christian as he retreated from the kitchen, moving away from the stairs that led to the bedroom upstairs. The man was on thin ice after the way he'd ogled my wife earlier, and as much as Thalia might believe there was nothing between them, I understood men far better than she did.

"Tobias Hasapis is going to be a problem," I said, grabbing a tumbler from the cupboard above the sink. I placed it on the kitchen island, trying not to imagine the way Thalia had looked with her entire body on display for me earlier in the day.

Rafael stopped not far from the spot where she'd rested her knees, leaning a single hand against the counter as I poured him an *ouzo* of his own. He glared at it,—he'd never developed a taste for the odd liquor with the licorice flavor—before pulling the glass toward himself. "And why is that?"

"He wants me dead so that he can marry Thalia himself," I explained, pouring myself an additional drink. I hoped Thalia would sleep through the worst of this conversation, because as much as she was required to be involved in our business with her seat on the council, I would spare her whatever I could.

She didn't need to know all the details of what we must do to secure our power in the city.

"That surprises me," Rafael murmured, sipping at his *ouzo* as he glanced toward the French doors to the backyard.

"It did me too. Before her father was dead, sure, I could see marrying her as a power move to secure an alliance in the city. But with him and most of his men dead, marrying her is mostly nostalgic. While Tobias could believe her to be the eldest of what remains of the Karras family, the family will never have any sort of power to offer outside of money," I said, expanding on the thoughts that had already taken root inside of me through the course of the day.

"And I presume you cleaned out all of the accounts and transferred the money into your own name? Transferred ownership of the properties?"

"Of course. The paperwork was complete and just waiting for her signature once Thalia and I were officially married. She isn't aware of what she signed by any means, but everything that once belonged to Origen Karras is now mine. Tobias has nothing to gain financially from marrying her and all he would need to do is look at the public record for the properties to know it," I answered.

"There must be something we do not know. Some reason the Hasapis family has for believing Thalia to be important enough to attempt twice to marry her, in spite of her lack of assets now. Tell me about her mother," Rafael said, coming back and taking a seat on the counter stool.

"Neri was from New York as far as I knew. The daughter of a distant cousin of the Lykaios family. They arranged her marriage to Origen when she was visiting her family in the city, and she never left again," I said, shrugging. I hadn't looked too much into her mother's history, as it seemed irrelevant. As brutal as it was, the lives of women within the families weren't typically interesting. They were controlled by the men who were their elders, their lives written from the moment they were born.

"And Origen? Did he have any skeletons in the closet that we weren't aware of?" Rafe asked. He crossed his legs at the ankles, kicking back and looking far too comfortable in my kitchen.

"Perhaps you could try asking me instead of discussing me as if I am not right upstairs," Thalia said, entering the kitchen with a scowl for the man sitting at the counter. Her black satin nightgown draped over her delicate curves, looking far too sexy for her to be in the sight of another man. The slit in the hem went to the top of her thigh, parting to reveal the long entirety of her leg as she walked toward me.

"You're supposed to be sleeping," I murmured, dropping my mouth to hers gently as she stepped into my arms. "And you need more clothes on if you're going to be walking around."

"Then you should have bought me more covering nightclothes," she said, reaching over to take my glass from my hand. She took a delicate sip of the liquor, swallowing it down without a single sign of distaste on her face.

"Go back to bed, λουλούδι μου," I ordered, ignoring the

way Rafael sipped his liquor. His lips tipped up in amusement as I wrapped my arms around my wife, trying to shield her from view. It wasn't that I didn't trust him; he was perhaps the only man in the world that I trusted implicitly with Thalia.

But he didn't have to torment me all the same.

"Tell me what you're talking about," she ordered, crossing her arms over her chest.

I sighed, thinking about a way to get out of admitting just how quickly I'd taken over the finances that would have otherwise been hers. It wasn't to take anything from her, and I'd easily give her access to the accounts I'd created.

But I doubted she'd understand I'd done it to protect her.

"We were discussing what other reasons there may be for Tobias's interest in marrying you. By all traditional family standards, you're damaged goods now. No offense," Rafael said, smiling slightly.

"Did you really just say no offense to calling me damaged goods? How is that not offensive?" Thalia asked, twisting in my arms. I was far too aware of the way her nipples pressed against the silk of her nightgown, straining in the chill air conditioning of the kitchen.

Fuck's sake.

I wrapped my arms around her front, covering her breasts with my arms as she leveled me with a glare over her shoulder. She wasn't oblivious and damn well knew what I was doing.

I grinned at her.

"Never said I agreed with the assessment, only that Tobias would be likely to," Rafe clarified.

"Fair enough," Thalia said, finally giving in as some of the tension left her body.

"I doubt you know too many details about your father's business. He wasn't the type to include you in it, so I didn't think we should bother you with this kind of thing," I said, leaning forward to smell her hair.

"Well, I may not know much about my father's business, but from the sound of things, I know more about him than you do," Thalia said, dropping her voice lower as she spun out of my grip.

"And why is that, Little One?" I asked, chuckling beneath my breath.

Thalia grinned, her lips tipping up with the kind of smile that told me I had clearly underestimated her deviousness. She touched a finger to the t-shirt covering my chest.

"At least I know that Origen Karras is not my real father."

38

THALIA

"What are you talking about?" Calix asked, his brow furrowing as he stared at me. I was certain it was difficult to imagine Origen Karras raising a child who wasn't his, and I'd never made sense of it myself. But I hadn't exactly been able to ask him, on the off-chance that he hadn't connected the dots or there had been something I'd missed.

I suspected, in the end, he simply didn't know. He wouldn't have cared so much about where my *mutation* came from, only that it was an abomination for it to exist in the first place.

Unless I'd been valuable in some other way.

"I'm colorblind," I said, looking between the two men. "He isn't."

"Children inherit traits from one parent all the time. I have my mother's eyes," Rafael said, speaking of his multicolored gaze that had to have been a recessive trait compared to the typical Spanish eye color.

"That's not how colorblindness works," I said, stepping forward to snag the pad of paper off the fridge. It had a few items on it for a shopping list, but I flipped to the back side and grabbed the pencil. "Monochromacy is determined by the X-chromosome. Women have two of them—one from each parent. If either of mine didn't contain the trait associated with colorblindness, I would be able to see color."

"So your mother was colorblind too?" Calix asked, twisting his lips as he considered it.

"No. She could see color, but women can be carriers of colorblindness without actually being colorblind. She probably had one affected X-chromosome, but the other functioned normally so her sight wasn't affected. I just happened to inherit the wrong chromosome from her. Men only *have* one X-chromosome so they cannot be asymptomatic carriers. So for me to be colorblind..."

"Your father would have needed to be colorblind," Calix agreed, nodding his head in thought. "Are you certain Origen wasn't colorblind and just well versed in hiding it? He always wanted you to disguise it, and it would make sense why he was so disgusted by it in you. We hate reflections of what we perceive as our own weaknesses."

"He was not. He could pick a color out easily. I've seen it more times than I can count," I said, thinking of all the times he'd thrown his *normalcy* in my face. Once I'd learned about the mechanics of it, I'd spent the rest of my life looking at every man in Philadelphia who was around the right age, assessing the way they reacted to colors and wondering if they might have been my real father.

My only hope was that my mother's journal would contain some evidence of who he might have been.

"What are the odds that Hasapis knows she isn't a Karras at all?" Rafe asked, and Calix shook his head. There was no way to know, or even begin to speculate.

"I never even asked if my father knew. I don't know that

anyone else knows, but it seemed worth mentioning," I explained.

"What if he's harboring Jeno? Would your brother know?" Calix asked, his shocked stare meeting mine.

"Harboring Jeno? You killed him at the wedding," I whispered, feeling my face twist with my confusion. I grasped the tumbler, tossing back a massive gulp. I was *not* drunk enough for this conversation. Clearly they'd been drinking for longer than I'd thought if Calix forgot killing my brother.

"We can't find his body," Calix admitted, pursing his lips to the side as he considered the information and what it might mean.

If my mother had intended for me to go to the address in her journal, had she also trusted Jeno with a secret?

"You didn't think to mention that?" I asked, crossing my arms over my chest. The world was crashing down around me, the reality of what my lineage might mean. Of what that address could mean.

"I didn't want to worry you," Calix said, reaching out to touch my cheek with a gentle finger. I clamped my mouth shut, keeping the journal and the address to myself. It didn't appear that Christian had mentioned it, or that he'd mentioned allowing me to google the address on his phone.

Calix clearly had his secrets. He wasn't going to have mine, too.

The sun beat down on me as I collapsed to my knees, the thud of Calix's wooden spear making mine vibrate against my palms. "Ugh," I groaned, forcing myself to my feet and taking a step back from him. He watched me, his face unbothered as he twisted the spear in his hand. It spun at his side, the dull point digging into the grass beneath our feet as he shoved it deep. "This is fucking archaic."

"No question there," he said with a chuckle. "The spear is one of the best weapons you'll find in ο λάκκος. Swords, shields, axes, and a morning star are all intended for closer combat. You'll want the spear because it will enable you to keep a greater distance between you and your opponent." Calix stepped behind me, wrapping his fingers around my grip on the spear. "The spear is lightweight compared to all those weapons. We don't have time to build up enough muscle in you, so we have to work with what you have. That means focusing on your endurance and the way your body moves, not the strength within it."

"This is impossible. They're going to fucking kill me in the same spot as my mother," I groaned, hanging my head forward. The thought of suffering through all those years under my father's roof for it all to end in the worst place imaginable was too much.

I wanted to go back to bed.

"First of all, the battle is *not* to the death. Anyone who kills owes a blood debt to the family, so if they were to kill you they would be forfeiting their life to *me*. You aren't going to die, Little One."

"Okay, I'll just be bloodied so severely that I'll *wish* I was dead. That's very comforting, thank you." I said, smiling at him from over my shoulder.

He kicked a foot between my legs, nudging until I stood with them shoulder-width apart. "I will bleed long before I ever let them touch you," he murmured, pressing his jaw into my temple. He guided my hand to the front of my body, using his other hand that he'd placed at my waist to move my hips in tandem with the movement of my arm. "It's an extension of your arm. Just another part of you. You're acting as if you are holding a spear in your hand and you're afraid it will bite you."

"How am I supposed to act like I'm not holding a spear when I'm looking at a spear?"

"Don't be so literal," he snapped, breathing slowly at my back. "Close your eyes."

"I would like to maybe not stab myself in the face. How am I supposed to see with my eyes closed?" I asked.

"You're not, but you don't need to worry about poking yourself in the eye when your eyes are closed. If the spear is a part of you, you should always know where it is even without seeing it," he said, guiding my free hand to touch the spear as he moved it from one hand to the other. I let my eyes drift closed, sinking deep into the feel of his hands on mine.

"This is ridiculous," I said, allowing him to guide me through the movements.

"Just get to know the fucking spear, Thalia," he warned, but there was the slightest chuckle in his voice.

"If I'll have you to protect me, can't I just sit and watch the show? I'd really hate to miss any of it," I murmured, letting my voice drop lower.

"Be careful, λουλούδι μου. You're at risk of distracting me from the task at hand. Besides, the only way I'll allow you to watch the show is if you're sitting on a throne where you belong. Not trapped in the sands of ο λάκκος," he said, stepping back. He left me to keep taking my hands through the motions, curving the spear back and forth as I got to know the way I needed to shift my balance to make up for the slightly heavier extension of my arm.

I listened to his steps, heard the way his wooden spear dragged against the roots beneath the grass when he plucked it from the ground.

I stood, waiting for him to tell me to do something. The

sound of his wooden spear cutting through the air sent me into a flurry of motion, reacting without thought. I spread my hands along the spear, raising it above my head just in time to block the blow as my eyes sprang open to watch his spear crash toward me.

Mine dug into my hands, making my palms ache with the force of the blow he dealt. With the force that had been aimed for my head. "You could have killed me!" I shrieked, yanking my spear away and taking a step back.

The bastard shrugged, spinning the offending weapon at his side with a smug grin. "But I didn't."

"I fucking loathe you," I snapped, shoving my spear into the ground at my side. I was supposed to trust him to protect me, to put my safety first, when he was willing to risk my life for a sparring session.

"I would never have tried it if I hadn't known you would stop me. You're thinking too much, but when you just let go and follow your instinct, you're a warrior, λουλούδι μου," he said, his voice softening as he realized how much his outward carelessness had upset me.

"I'm nothing close to a warrior. I'm just a girl that's never been allowed to be *anything*," I said, hanging my head in shame. I couldn't be a warrior. I couldn't be an artist. I couldn't write stories that made people escape from the misery of their lives.

I was just nothing in the shell they'd created.

"Is that who you are?" Calix asked, taking a single step toward me as he dropped the spear to his side. "Or are you the woman who very nearly killed her father with the same cane he used to abuse her? I thought you were the woman who would paint this city black with the stain of blood—the only woman I've ever known to face down the council of the six and not so much as flinch when they tried to put you in your place. You are either a queen or a pawn, Little One. Only you can decide your future. Would you like to be the pretty trophy tucked safely in my home, or will you kill them all for what they did to you?"

"I thought you already did that," I whispered, staring up into the unhinged darkness gleaming in his silver gaze.

"Jeno is alive. Tobias is alive. The entire Galanis family was complicit in the murder of your mother and my banishment. They allowed a *child* to be dragged onto the sands of ο λάκκος and subjected to horrors she had no business witnessing. I won't rest until they know the kind of fear you felt in the moments before your father took your mother's head. Until they scream the way you did as I fell upon the sand. I want you to be a part of that. I want you to hold the knife to their throats and show them what happens to men who underestimate you, but I will not force you, and I won't think less of you if that is not the path you choose."

He dropped his forehead to mine, staring down at me as I blinked up at him. "I don't think I'm capable of that."

"λουλούδι μου, you are capable of bringing this city to its knees. All you have to do is pick up the spear and accept the challenge," he said, taking a step back. He wrapped his fingers around my weapon, yanking it from the ground and placing it upon his open palm so that it balanced.

I stared at it for a moment, contemplating the kind of life I wanted for myself. I could live in comfort, reading and drawing and doing whatever made my heart happy, or I could become something far more sinister.

I picked up the spear.

39

THALIA

The next day, Christian ran by my side as my lungs heaved. He wasn't the slightest bit winded as we made our way around the perimeter of the yard, all too aware of the watchful gazes of two other members of Calix's security. One of them stood on the balcony outside the guest bedroom, his eyes bearing down on me as I came to a sudden halt and gasped for breath. Placing my hands on my knees and leaning forward at the back end of the yard, I tried to fight back the pain that erupted through my side.

I was not made for running.

"Keep moving, Monster," Christian said, his voice gentling as he stopped advancing a few feet in front of me. He ran in place, his motions assured. "Even if you can't run anymore, you need to cool down with a walk."

"Fairly sure drowning myself in the pool would be faster," I wheezed.

"Drowning would be accurate. Your muscles could cramp and then what? You'd be dead weight at the bottom of the pool. Move your ass," he said, forcing me to stand straight with his harsh words. Calix had run off with Rafael to search for Jeno, and as much as I wanted to go and be a part of finding evidence of my *still-living* brother, preparing for the coming battle was more important at the moment.

"Your bedside manner is shit," I argued, forcing my legs to move.

"I'll work on it when you're actually in your sickbed and not just complaining for the sake of it. You've always hated cardio." He laughed, as if he found it very entertaining that the part of training my husband had chosen to fixate on was by far my least favorite.

My feet moved slowly, but they moved, and at this point in the day I was just grateful they functioned at all. Christian had made me do two painfully slow miles around the yard, *after* doing one hundred squats just because he was a cruel bastard.

"It won't be long with the way you and Calix are determined to kill me," I said, breathing deeply and rhythmically to try to bring my heart rate back down to a more sustainable throb.

"You'll manage. Adapting and surviving are what you do best," he said, dropping from his run and walking at my side. He glanced toward the man standing on the back patio and watching us, his eyes then drifting up to the man on the balcony, as his fists clenched at his sides.

"He thinks I'll maul you if I'm left alone with you. I've watched over you for years, but all of a sudden, I can't be trusted to be alone with you," he muttered, keeping a careful distance between us.

"You didn't tell him about my mother's journal," I said, contemplating the question I had to ask him. If I couldn't trust him with my secret, Calix would be furious, but I couldn't just not try.

"It should be up to you whether you share that with him. The last words you'll ever read from your mother are deeply personal, and I refuse to take that and taint it by having him rummage through it for crumbs of information that might be useful to him."

"I appreciate that more than you could possibly know," I said. As much as I hated the way Christian had deceived me, he was the only hope I had of getting what I needed without having someone run right to Calix.

He was my only hope of delaying the inevitable, and our moments without prying ears nearby or the risk of cameras were few and far between now.

"I hate to ask this of you, Christian. Really, I do, but I can't have a baby right now," I said, letting my voice drop low. I smiled as I said the words, trying not to give away the seriousness of the conversation to any of the men who watched us from a distance.

Christian tensed at my side, then he swallowed uncomfortably. "Then you should speak to Calix about that. I'm sure he will understand."

"I don't think he would. He's made his intentions clear, but it isn't his choice to make. I will not go into ο λάκκος with a life growing inside of me. It's far too dangerous right now," I explained, pausing to grab my ankle and pull my leg behind me to stretch it out. "I just need to buy some time."

"A child provides stability to your marriage. I don't mean between you and Calix," he said, interrupting me when I started to interject that children were not known to be a quiet, peaceful influence on married life. "But to all those looking on and searching for weaknesses. A marriage can be dissolved with the snap of a finger in this life, but a child is far more difficult to erase. It goes against everything the six families hold dear to kill a child, when this life is driven by legacy."

"A child should not be used as glue to hold together a business arrangement," I said, wincing back from my own words. No matter what I felt for Calix, no matter what he claimed to feel for me, nothing would ever erase the fact that marriage was nothing but a tool. It was the contract that bonded families together, forcing them to be allies when they otherwise might have murdered one another in cold blood.

"What exactly is it you're asking me to do, Thalia?" Christian asked, shaking his head. "I cannot keep him from having sex with you. He would kill the man who tried. *You* had that power, but it seems as if you didn't think the consequences through."

"He never made his intention to impregnate me clear until we'd already been together," I growled in warning.

"So stop having sex with him now that he has. That's the easiest solution," Christian noted.

"I'm not sure that's an option." I didn't want to admit that I'd given Calix open permission to fuck me when he wanted, that in my moment of desperation to get off, I'd agreed that he would have the final say in something like that.

The lines of consent were always fuzzy in this life, blurred to the point of nonexistence. Any other husband would have raped me on my wedding night, whether I screamed and cried or acted like I wanted it.

I'd been happy to have some semblance of a choice, for even just a little while. I hadn't been thinking about the long-term ramifications. What was so wrong with settling into married life before bringing a child into the picture?

"I need birth control," I said suddenly, the words erupting from me far more abruptly than I'd intended. "I need to have control over this one thing, at least until the battle is over and done with."

"You cannot seriously be asking that of me. No." He shook his head, hanging his face forward so that he didn't have to meet my stare. "Calix will *kill* me for that. Do you understand what you're asking me to do?"

"He wouldn't, and I would never tell him where I got it," I explained. If he ever found out I had it at all. I wouldn't use it for long, and it would be entirely feasible for it to take two months for me to become pregnant. It happened all the time.

"It wouldn't take a rocket scientist to know exactly who you would turn to for this, Thalia. Are you fucking kidding me right now? You know *nothing* about the man you married, so let me make something very clear. Do you know what he likes to do to the men who betray him?"

I shook my head, confident in the assumption that I did not want to know. Christian reached out to grab my arm, and I froze as he realized he'd touched me. "He likes to turn them into human candles. He'll tie or nail them to the very top of a stake, wrap them in kindling, douse them in gasoline, and light them on fire to burn while all of his men watch and are reminded of the price for their betrayal."

"Nero was a Roman Emperor."

"*That* is what you choose to fixate on? I just told you that your husband will burn me alive if I do what you're asking of me. Who the fuck cares if Nero was a Roman Emperor? The Romans stole everything from the Greeks. Why shouldn't we do the same now?" he asked, scoffing as he turned his irritated gaze toward the house.

Calix stood there, glaring at the place where Christian's hand wrapped around my forearm. Christian released me suddenly, piercing me with a glare before he shook his head and stalked to meet Calix. From his reaction, there was no doubt in my mind that he'd tell Calix exactly what I'd asked. He'd do it to save his own skin, because there had to be an explanation for his hand on me.

The cruel malice in Calix's face made sure of that.

"Christian, wait," I pleaded, following after him. My mind raced as I tried to come up with a solution, with something I could offer as a reasonable explanation for the moment Calix had witnessed. The only thing that came to mind was my mother's journal, but I couldn't.

I couldn't share that with him, not yet at the very least.

I hurried to catch up, my steps quicker than Christian's despite the ache in my muscles. He moved like he was walking to his death, when the reality was I would be the one to face the consequences if he revealed my request.

"Would you like to explain to me why you put your hand on my wife?" Calix asked, his voice deadly calm. I'd never heard it so absent of all inflection, so flat and toneless. His face was colder than it had been on the day he'd slaughtered a church full of people.

"I wanted her to listen to my answer when I told her I couldn't get her what she asked for," Christian said, glancing at me from the side of his eye. His face fell, his head bowing forward as he hesitated to continue.

"And what is it that my wife asked you for, Christian?" Calix said, turning that cold, cruel face toward me.

He held my gaze as Christian continued, his focus never wavering from my stare. "Birth control."

Calix raised his brows, his jaw flexing silent warning. "Is that true?" he asked, the question clearly meant for me. I could try to backtrack; I could imply that Christian was lying and hope Calix believed me.

But at what cost?

"Yes," I agreed, steeling my shoulders against the intensity of his glare. "It's true."

Calix sighed finally, nodding as he pursed his lips in thought.

"Get in the fucking house, Thalia," he ordered, that flatness settling over me. Something wasn't right in it, like the calm before the storm.

"Calix—" I started, cringing back when his face twisted brutally.

"I said get in the fucking house," he said more firmly, his voice remaining quiet. I swallowed, glancing toward Christian and wondering if he cared that I was about to walk to my death.

It certainly felt like it, anyway.

I moved forward, stepping just past Calix on my way to the French doors that led into the kitchen. Calix stopped me with a hand on my bicep, his fingers squeezing as he dipped his head to the side to brush his lips against my ear. "I expect you to be naked and on the bed when I get there. Do *not* test me right now, Little One."

I nodded, wincing away from him when he finally released me and making my way up to the bedroom.

Fuck.

40

THALIA

I paced in the bedroom, wrapping my arms around my torso that was covered in the silk of my robe. I'd risked Calix's wrath to shower, unable to stomach the thought of facing him with my body covered in the evidence of my run.

With every moment I spent in that lightning-fast shower, and with every moment I'd spent pacing in the bedroom and wondering what was taking him so long before he could make his way to me, my fear bled to rage.

How fucking dare he send me to my bedroom like an errant child?

If I didn't want to be a mother, then I damn well wouldn't be a fucking mother. Whether that came with an end date was *my* decision.

I stormed to the window that looked out over the backyard, throwing it open so that I could lean closer to the screen and peer down at where I saw my husband. He stood beside the chiminea on the patio, his suit jacket draped over one of the patio chairs. He slowly rolled the white fabric of his sleeves up each forearm, watching as two of his other men brought a struggling Christian to the outdoor kitchen.

They pinned the back of Christian's arm against the counter, holding him still as Calix moved to the chiminea and grabbed hold of the handle of what looked to be a fire poker. I winced when it glowed, the light radiating off the end conveying a heat I didn't want to imagine.

He took a step toward Christian as one of the two men holding him spread his fingers open, laying the back of his hand flat until the palm that had grasped my arm faced the sky. "Calix!" I screamed, slapping a palm against the screen. There was a moment where I thought it might fall from the window, clatter to the patio down below, and cause enough distraction to snap him out of whatever trance the devil had caught him in.

Calix turned a dark stare my way, his eyes narrowing as they trailed down to where the robe covered my chest. "Quiet." I couldn't even hear his words over the pounding of my heart; only saw the way his lips moved.

I pressed my lips into a line, my jaw clenching as I fought to follow his order. Whatever move I made would only make it worse and punish Christian for my stupidity even more.

Calix moved toward him, staring down at the other man as he muttered something to him. He didn't hesitate before he touched the white-hot metal of the poker to Christian's palm.

Smoke rose off of Christian's ruined hand, and I could swear I heard the way his skin sizzled beneath it. I gagged as the scent of burning flesh reached the screen, flinging myself back and raising a hand to cover my mouth.

Who the hell had Calix become?

"Nobody touches my wife. Is that understood?" Calix's voice came from the patio as I took more steps back, trying to shut out the words of agreement that came from his men. Calix disappeared from sight as I looked over at the bed beside me, my fingers dropping to the silken belt tied around my waist. I couldn't bring myself to untie it, to be so naked and vulnerable when he came up.

Not knowing what he was capable of.

"Fuck," I whispered. My lungs heaved as I squeezed my eyes shut, slowly unknotting the tie at my waist. I clutched the two sides of the fabric together, holding them closed as slow, calculated footsteps came up the stairs.

My eyelids flung open when the doorknob turned and the door opened slowly, the tiniest of creaks confirming it as Calix appeared on the other side. He stood in the hallway, a hand pressed against the molding as he leaned forward. "What did I tell you to do?" he asked, making me swallow as I glanced over at the bed.

"You *branded* him," I said, my voice trembling as I stared at him in shock. "How could you do that?"

"After they took me away from you," he said, taking a step closer to me. He lifted a hand to run the backs of his fingers over my cheekbone, drawing a shuddering breath from my lungs. "I spent the next decade in *El Infierno*. I learned about *penitencia* from the devil himself. Christian made the mistake of touching what is mine. Now he will never be able to look at that hand and not be reminded of what I will do should he repeat that mistake. Next time, it will not be his hand that I maim, but his cock that I'll sever from his body."

"All he did was touch my arm, Calix. It wasn't—"

"And he would do far more if he thought I would allow it. Today I made certain he knows that path is very, *very* unwise if he likes his limbs attached to his body," Calix answered, shaking his head. "There are parts of this life that I don't imagine you will ever want to be part of. Enforcing men, no matter how much they might have been friends, is one of those things. But you will shut your mouth and not question me on it."

"Excuse me?" I asked, cocking my head to the side.

"Unless you are willing to be the one to face the consequences of a betrayal, and make no mistake, Little One, they will come for you first. You are my only weakness and all here know it. So unless you want to be the one they take and they rape and they hurt because of my inability to do what needs to be done, then I suggest you shut up and accept that this is something you know *nothing* of."

"You could inspire loyalty in your men by treating them well," I snapped, crossing my arms tighter over my stomach.

Calix dropped a hand to my shoulder, brushing the silk of my robe off to reveal bare skin. "This is not the land of unicorns and rainbows where no one betrays the people they love. This is the land of bloodshed and vengeance, where even a man's wife can go to another man behind his back. I have treated you well. Most would say far better than you could have hoped with any other husband at your side, and still you went to him before me."

"I knew you'd say no," I whispered, hanging my head in shame. I hadn't wanted to ruin it all. I hadn't wanted to make Christian suffer the consequences for what I'd done.

I'd just wanted a choice.

"And you did it anyway, without ever taking a single fucking second to wonder if there was a goddamn reason I would say no. I would give you the entire world, but I would not give you that. Everything I do is for you. *Everything.* They would not make you fight if you were pregnant, Thalia. I'm trying to keep you from having to fight on the same sands where your mother died. The least you could do is ask me about it," he snapped, his rage twisting his lips as he stared down at me.

"I didn't know—" I started.

"Because you didn't fucking ask."

"Calix—" I protested, wincing when he stepped back from me.

"If you don't do as I tell you right now, I am going to bend you over the edge of this bed and fuck your ass while I'm far too angry to be as gentle as you need me to be. It will hurt and you will bleed. So for the love of God, get on the fucking bed, Thalia," he snapped, making me step back in fear. I pried open my robe with trembling fingers, scrambling to get up on top of the bed as he'd instructed. "On your back."

I moved to obey, placing my head on the pillow in the center of the bed. My damp hair clung to the side of my head as I settled into place, staring down my body at where Calix allowed his heated gaze to trail over me.

"What are you going to do?" I asked, swallowing around the words. He remained silent as he unbuttoned his shirt, shrugging it off his shoulders and tossing it to the side. He stripped his pants down his legs as soon as that was done, kicking his socks and shoes off as well.

"I'm going to fuck my wife," he said, grabbing my ankles and shoving them apart until my legs were spread obscenely. He placed a hand in between them, crawling up onto the edge of the bed and prowling until his weight hovered over me. His skin never touched mine, the warmth of his body kissing my skin as I fought to control my ragged breaths.

Calix wouldn't hurt me. I had to believe that, or what else did I have?

He reached over my head, sliding his hand between the headboard and the mattress. Something clanked as I twisted my neck to try to see what he was doing, his free hand grasping my right wrist and wrenching it over my head. A cuff wrapped around my wrist, the fabric soft but tight as he secured it.

"What are you doing?" I asked, tugging against the hand that wouldn't come any lower.

He ignored me, grabbing my other wrist and repeating the process until both arms were trapped above my head, spread just far enough apart that I couldn't reach one with the other to unclasp the cuffs.

"I already told you; I'm going to fuck my wife, and you are going to lie there like a good girl and let me fill you with so much cum, it drips out of you for a week," he said, staring down at me as I shifted my legs against the bed. Trying to get higher on the mattress, trying to maneuver to get more control over my arms.

"Calix, please," I begged, staring up at him as my bottom lip trembled. Something about being tied up, about having no control over how and when he touched me, erased all the trust I'd thought I had in his inability to hurt me.

"Shh," he murmured, touching a finger to my lips. He trailed it down over the front of my throat, continuing through the valley between my breasts and over my belly button, until he touched it to my pussy and slid it through me. With his eyes holding mine captive, he slid that finger inside of me and chuckled as he pressed it deep. "Are you frightened, Little One?" he asked, the scent of burnt flesh lingering in the room to punctuate his words.

I nodded carefully, wondering what the right answer was as he slowly moved his finger inside me, adding a second one while I fought back the moan trying to escape.

"Your pussy seems to disagree with that assessment. Either that or you like the fear far more than you want to admit. Will it turn you on when I chase you through the house one day, knowing that when I catch you I'll hold you down and fuck you until you scream?" he asked, and my body reacted to the words that should have sent a ripple of terror through my body. My stomach clenched, my hips moving toward the contact of his fingers as he prepared me to take his cock. "I think that's a yes," he added, that cruel chuckle tinting his voice as he pulled his fingers free and brought them to his mouth. He sucked them clean as he stared down at me, studying me for a reaction before he shifted his hips between my legs and lined his cock up. There was no preamble as he drove inside, filling me completely on that first thrust.

He pounded so deep that my entire body jolted with the force of it, my hips jerking back into the mattress. He grunted, setting a furious pace that echoed the anger on his face. There was no rhythm or concern to his fucking.

Only the drive for his own orgasm and taking the edge off his rage.

My pussy clenched around him, seeking out what it needed to find my own pleasure, but his movements were too erratic, almost as if he intentionally kept me from an orgasm. If it hadn't been for his eyes on mine, and the way he seemed to still crave that connection that thrummed between us, I might have felt as if I could have been anyone.

But I was still his wife; I was still the girl he sought out and claimed to love.

He was just punishing me with his cock, depriving me of the one thing that would make sex between us feel less one-sided. "Calix, please," I begged, lifting my legs higher and trying to get a better angle for him to stroke over that spot inside of me.

"You can come when I believe you regret what you did, and not a moment before," he snapped, shoving deep as he dropped a palm against the front of my throat. He leaned down, touching his nose to mine as his ragged breathing mixed with my own. He grunted as he came, driving deeper and restricting my breathing as he held my gaze.

I whimpered as my air returned, watching with exhausted eyes as he pulled his face away from mine. His cock slid free, his mouth trailing down over the front of my throat until he could wrap his lips around my nipple and bite down harshly.

The feeling shot straight to the abused space between my legs where I'd been deprived of my orgasm. He rose to his knees, staring down at my pussy before he grabbed one of the spare pillows and shoved it beneath me. Lifting my ass off the bed and forcing my back to arch at an uncomfortable angle, he collected what little of his cum had dripped free and shoved it back inside of me.

"Untie me," I said, my voice trailing off as a sneaking suspicion rose within me. Surely he couldn't mean to....

He stood from the bed.

"Calix!"

"I'll be back when I'm ready to fuck you again, λουλούδι μου. Until then, be a good girl and hold still. I won't be pleased if I come back to find you've wiggled your ass off that pillow. If you waste my cum, I might as well pour the next load down your throat."

The fucking prick pulled on his boxer briefs and left.

41

CALIX

Thalia whimpered as I slid through her slick, cum-filled pussy. “Are you sorry yet, λουλούδι μου?” I asked, reaching a hand around her to grasp her breast in my palm. She moaned, arching her back, having long since become desperate for the orgasm I wouldn’t let her have.

I’d left her tied up for the entirety of the day, only coming to see her when I wanted to fuck her or feed her. She wanted to use the bathroom, but I wouldn’t allow her to clean my cum from her swollen, used pussy. Not until she came and could go to sleep for the night.

Not until I knew part of me was so deep inside of her that there was no chance I wouldn’t find my way to her womb. Her body would take from me, and then it would give me the greatest gift imaginable in return.

“I’m sorry,” she sighed finally, her body limp in my arms as I curled my chest tighter against her back. With her laying on her side, she tried to shift her arms that I’d pulled tight when I’d maneuvered her into the new position. I slid my hand down from her breast, grasping her around the thigh and lifting her leg high into the air.

The shift enabled me to get deeper, burying myself balls deep inside of her drenched cunt. I'd already filled her with cum four times throughout the day, keeping her trapped like she was my personal toy to use whenever I wanted a break from work. Feeling the aftermath of that—feeling her the way she was meant to be—drove something within me to the brink of instability.

I never wanted to leave the haven of her body.

"You're sorry for what, exactly?" I asked, moving slowly and drawing strained whimpers from her. I hadn't let her use the bathroom, the added pressure of a full bladder making her need to come even more intense. I wanted her desperate. I wanted her writhing with my name on her lips.

I wanted her *mine.*

"I'm sorry I didn't come to you first. I should have asked you," she said, her voice barely a breath. There was almost no life left in her body, only the driving need to come keeping her from the depths of sleep.

"Even if I had said no, you do not go to another man when I tell you that you cannot have something. Is that clear? I treat you well, and I will always do so because I love you," I said, pausing to let my words really sink in. Her body spasmed at my words, the physical response to the statement, which she hadn't yet accepted, giving everything away for her. "But never forget who owns you. In this life, you are mine to do with as I please. If I want you to spend the rest of your days tied up with every hole stuffed full of my cum, then that is how you will be, and there is not a person in this world who can stop me."

"Calix—" she said, her breathy sigh settling the beast rattling at the cage. I was still so furious with her, even hours later. I couldn't imagine untying her and letting her roam free when she'd tried to betray me in such a way.

I could feel the way her arms trembled, see the way her

face twisted every time she tried to move her shoulders. The position had long since made its point, the pain of it causing no permanent harm but distinctly uncomfortable. On a different day, I'd have drawn a bath and tended to the injuries I'd caused.

But today I wouldn't wash away the gift I'd given her.

"Tell me you understand, Little One. Your life will be much easier if we're on the same page about this. You will be my equal in the eyes of everyone else, but in here, you're just fucking mine," I growled, dropping a hand to her clit.

I nudged it with a single fingertip, her entire body jolting like a live wire in response. She was strung so tight, her orgasm so close to the surface that I knew it would be blinding when I finally sent her over the edge. "I understand," she whispered, the dejected tone almost making me question if I'd gone too far.

But she came with the next stroke of my finger over her clit, her body going taut and pussy squeezing my cock so tightly I thought it might take it off. I groaned, following her over the edge with the tightness of an iron fist wrapped around me. She was so slick as I filled her once again, thrusting through her until her body finally relaxed.

There was no life to her form, just the exhausted woman who now understood the kinds of consequences she would face with me. I would push her; I would take from her and always demand more.

Where my men would face the threat of torture, of being branded or burned alive or dismembered, Thalia would only ever face punishment in my bed.

I reached over her head, finally uncuffing her from the headboard and helping her stand. Her legs were limp as I helped her to the bathroom, against my better instincts, leaving so that she could have a few moments of privacy.

She was half-asleep by the time I settled her back into the bed, but that didn't stop me from grabbing the necklace I'd placed on the nightstand when I'd returned to the room to fuck her one last time before allowing her to sleep.

Lifting the silver chain, I draped it across the front of her throat. The deceptively delicate-looking, titanium links covered the hollow of her throat just below the spot where I liked to hold her. I wrapped my hands around the back of her neck, twisting the tiny lock on the back as I connected the two ends of the necklace.

Thalia blinked up at me sleepily, confusion lacing her face and I knew the argument would come when she tried to take it off the next morning and found she couldn't. The only way to take it off would be to cut the chain or have a key.

Something in me settled the moment the tracker was locked around her neck, hidden discreetly by the single onyx gem that rested at the top of her chest. "Sweet dreams, Thalia," I murmured, kissing her gently before grabbing a pair of shorts and tugging them on.

I left her sleeping, making my way to my cell phone downstairs. Rafael sat with it, watching the screen with interest. "Her heart rate is slowing to a normal pace," he said, the observation something that might have seemed odd to anyone else.

Taking my phone from his hand, I stared down at the numbers as my wife's heart settled from the exertion of getting fucked. I'd never need to wonder if she was still breathing if she tried to run from me. Never need to wonder where she was.

I held all the information I needed to track her back down at my fingertips, and Thalia had no idea.

"Any regrets?" Rafael asked, quirking a brow. He studied me as if I were a science experiment, and I supposed maybe I was. It wouldn't be too much longer before he was coping with the same sorts of feelings with his Isa.

"No. I've done what's necessary to protect her from her own foolish stubbornness. I can't protect her if she can't be honest with me, so now I'll let technology tell me what it can," I admitted.

"You still think she's keeping something from you?" Rafael asked, pouring a drink for me to toss back.

"Definitely. I just don't know what yet."

"Give Christian some time. He may come around after you made yourself very clear today. If he knows something, and he doesn't tell you after today, then you'll know you need to dispose of him at the very least," he said.

"Thalia will hate me if I do."

"Bah," Rafael said, waving a hand. "Just don't kill him in front of her and she never needs to know."

I snorted. I couldn't wait until Rafael had to deal with having his woman with him instead of protected in another city.

He had a reality check coming his way.

42

THALIA

Three days passed before Calix allowed me to leave the house again, his fury fading in small increments. Calix's mom helped Malva stir chocolate chips into the cookie dough as I sat at the island of his parents' kitchen, watching the two of them as they went through the motions of an activity that Malva should already know how to do. I couldn't even work up the motivation to try to help, knowing I would only get in the way.

I'd never even eaten a cookie, let alone made them.

Calix was occupied speaking with the security staff he'd placed around the house, and it comforted me to know that Malva was well-protected. Even if it was by the man I wasn't entirely certain I could trust. The necklace I couldn't seem to get off my neck was confirmation of that inability to trust, because I could have sworn that if I looked hard enough I could see the tiniest of locks at the back of the clasp.

"That's a beautiful necklace," Evangeline murmured, her eyes twinkling as she held my gaze. She helped Malva start shaping the balls of cookie dough. "Did Calix give it to you?"

"I woke up wearing it one morning," I said, chuckling

beneath my breath. I only had the vaguest memory of him putting it on me, but I didn't think his mother wanted to hear the story of how her son had fucked me so hard I'd slept for twelve hours straight.

"That sounds like Calix. He's always had good taste," she said, glancing over the back of my shoulder as Eugene stepped into the room. Calix's father gave me the ickies; something about his presence was so different from his son's that I immediately tensed and pushed my shoulders up higher.

As if I was waiting for the cane to crack against them, expecting him to demand the very same standards my father had.

"You're going to spoil her rotten if you keep it up," Eugene snapped at his wife. Malva kept her head down, and I suspected that she'd been told to avoid interacting with the older man any chance she got.

Evangeline patted the top of Malva's hand comfortingly, encouraging her to continue with her task. "You just let me and Calix worry about that," she said, her face carefully blank as she turned it back down to the cookies.

"You think it doesn't concern me? This is my house, no matter what that boy would lead you to believe. I never agreed to taking on the girl when he told me we were coming back here, and I definitely never agreed to allow him to be the poster boy for this fucking family."

"I cannot imagine what it must be like to live to be your age, and still have absolutely no concept that you are not wanted somewhere," I said, turning to glare at him. My stool swiveled with me, my fingers clutching the light fabric beneath me. "Now if you don't mind, we were having a conversation before you inserted yourself into something that is frankly, none of your fucking business."

"What did you just say to me?" Eugene asked, his jaw clenching as he stared down at me.

"Malva, why don't we go and play in the other room? We'll finish the cookies in just a minute," Evangeline said, taking a towel and wiping Malva's hands clean. Evangeline hustled Malva out of the room and my respect for her immediately grew. Whatever she thought of her husband and what might come, she would do what she needed to protect Malva from witnessing it.

The same way my mother had tried to protect me before they took her away.

"I said what everyone who has the misfortune of being near you thinks. Nobody wants you here. You are a useless waste of energy, a detriment to the Regas name, and if it hadn't been for you—" I cut off, holding perfectly still as Eugene raised his hand. The back of it cracked against my face, the signet ring on his finger catching my lip as my head snapped to the side.

"Eugene!" Evangeline scolded as she stepped back into the kitchen.

I raised a hand, touching a finger to the cut on my lip as I turned my stare back to him. "Are you finished with your tantrum?" I asked, wiping the blood away. It stained the bottom of the white sleeve of my blouse, the darkness of it looking like a smear of ink.

"He never should have been allowed to marry you. He always was a little bitch for you. You've taken him from what could have been a great man and made him weak. I raised him to be more than your plaything," Eugene said, shaking his head in disgust as he fidgeted with his ring.

"I find it quite ironic to have you criticize anyone for weakness, when you hit like a ten-year-old girl relying on her jewelry to cause pain," I snapped, rolling my eyes and turning my stool back to face the island counter, dismissing the man I wanted nothing to do with, who was not worth my time.

"You little fucking—"

"What exactly is going on here?" Calix said, stepping into the room. I couldn't see him with the entrance to the kitchen behind me, but I could feel his presence like a heavy weight. I could just imagine the way his eyes were shifting from me to his mother to his father, his stare inquisitive as he tried to piece together the puzzle.

I glanced at Eugene from the corner of my eye, my cut lip curving into a smirk at the subtle notes of fear on his face. Having spent most of my life with fear as my closest companion, and the driving motivation for anything and everything I did, I knew it well.

Looking at Eugene's face was a victory, like returning home to put the abuser in his place.

"Does it bother you? To know that your son will choose me over you if you force his hand?" I asked.

"Whores are common. He only has one father," Eugene said, making the energy in the room shift even more. Evangeline raised a hand to cover her mouth, but her eyes were not surprised. I couldn't imagine it was even close to the first time Eugene had said something along those lines, but it was probably the first time he'd been stupid enough to say it in front of Calix.

"I am ready for my judgment," I said, pausing to run my tongue over the blood welling on my lip. I pursed them together, the swelling in the bottom one already making my mouth feel distorted. "Are you?"

I swiveled my seat to face Calix, watching as his silver gaze trailed over my face. It stopped when it snagged on my lip and the beginning of swelling there. He stepped forward slowly, placing two gentle fingers beneath my chin and lifting my face so that he could inspect it more thoroughly. "Are you alright?" he asked, his voice soft.

His stare penetrated mine, searching for any sign of the sort of injury he wouldn't be able to see. He looked for any wounds caused by his father's barbed words, the kind that could wrap around my heart and do far more damage than a signet ring.

"I'm fine," I murmured, leaning into his touch.

"Good," Calix murmured, tapping the fingers of his free hand against the counter before he turned to face his father. His posture was straight, shoulders held back as he stepped up to his father. "Which hand?" he asked, turning to face me.

"The one with the ring," I said, glancing down at Eugene's right hand.

Calix nodded, moving to the counter and pulling open one of the drawers. He reached in, hefting the stainless steel meat mallet and tossing it twice before he turned his attention back to his father. "Move the cookies, Mom," he said, glancing at her from the corner of his eye. Evangeline hurried to gather up the bowl of cookie dough and the cookie sheet, retreating into the dining room with them.

Calix watched her go, and I hoped that she would take Malva far enough away that she wouldn't need to hear what was about to happen. I was tempted to follow, to see to my sister, but I realized with a shock that I trusted Evangeline to be there for her.

I wanted to watch Eugene suffer.

Calix reached down, grabbing his father's hand and pressing it against the counter. "Calix!" Eugene protested, pulling against his son's hold.

"Would you like to break it, or should I, Little One?" my husband asked, looking at me over the kitchen island.

As tempting as it was... "You're stronger. You can break it

better than I can," I said, planting my elbows on the counter. I leaned forward, watching as Eugene clenched his fingers into a fist.

Calix didn't care. Holding his father's wrist pinned to the counter, he swung the tenderizer and brought it down on Eugene's fingertips where they dug into his palm. Eugene screamed in pain as they crushed, the crack of bones resounding beneath the shrill sound. Calix did it again, pounding the mallet down until Eugene's fingers were a twisted, gnarled mess. Blood splattered from where the bone shards protruded from his skin, the hand ruined in a way that I knew even surgery wouldn't be able to fix.

When Calix was satisfied that the hand was completely and totally broken beyond repair, he tossed the bloody mallet into the sink and pried open his father's broken fingers while his father cried. Eugene whimpered in pain, clutching at his forearm as if it could stop Calix from snapping them backward and grinding the bones against one another.

He pulled the signet ring off Eugene's finger, the black stain of blood covering the band. Finally releasing his father's hand, he held the ring out to me. "A token of his apology, λουλούδι μου."

I smiled as I took it, enjoying the horror on Eugene's face far more than was normal as I pushed the ring onto my finger. It was far too large for me, but I held it up to let the light streaming in through the windows make the metal gleam. Blood dripped down onto my skin.

"If you don't mind going to spend some time with your sister, I would like to have a few words with my father. Is that alright with you?" Calix asked, staring down at where the blood touched me.

"Of course, η ψυχή μου," I said, standing from the stool. I walked around the counter, around Eugene's form where he clutched his crushed hand to his chest, and kissed my husband softly. I raised a hand, using a thumb to wipe the spatter of blood off his cheek as I pulled away.

And I left him to deal with the errant father who needed to be put down like the rabid beast he was.

43

CALIX

I rolled up the sleeves of my shirt, glaring at the drops of blood that stained it with red. Just the knowledge that my wife couldn't see the color made me furious.

She couldn't appreciate how stunning the brightness was against a pure background. She'd never know the shock of it against the snow in the winter. It had made it harder to appreciate my favorite color, to revel in the way it looked as it poured from my victims' wounds.

My father glared at me in silence, cradling that broken hand to his chest as if he could save it. He was fortunate I hadn't broken the other one preemptively, because the thought had crossed my mind. "You do not lay a hand on my wife, her sister, or my mother, ever again. Is that clear?" I asked, brushing at a perfect spot of blood on my sleeve.

"I am your father—"

"That doesn't make a damn bit of difference to me. I know you come from bygone times when it was important to respect our elders, but considering my elder was an abusive piece of shit who let his own foolishness get us banished from this city in the first place? Hard pass." I rolled my eyes at his stupidity. He'd always had the brain of a goldfish; his lack of planning making him act far too impulsively for a man with the kind of power he'd been born into.

He would have seen our name burned to the ground if I hadn't raised it from the ashes.

"You'd do anything for that stupid piece of ass. She's got you so pussy-whipped you'd even turn on your own father, and you're too stupid to see it for what it is. She will be your destruction, Calix. The council will not be pleased to have a woman sitting among them, and she'll drag you down with her," my father said, slapping his unbroken palm down on top of the counter. If I'd had the meat mallet in my hand, I might have broken it too.

"The council has determined that I will be the head of the Regas line going forward and sit in the council seat due to your incompetency. I suggest you find something to keep you occupied, because I can promise you there is no room for you in my business," I said, tapping the top of his hand condescendingly.

I turned on my heel, making my way in the direction I'd seen Thalia go. I'd spent far too much time with a man who wasn't worth my time, when I could have been watching Thalia flourish and love the only family member who loved her.

"Her mother was the same way, you know?" he asked, something dark in his voice making me pause. I turned to look back at him, and the cruel sneer that rode his face as he spoke about a woman who had died because of his stupidity. "Thought all men should fucking worship her like she was some saint, never letting anyone play with her when Origen wasn't looking. You should teach Thalia a lesson the same way I taught her mother one. No woman is too good for a Regas cock, no matter what she seems to think about it."

Everything in me froze, the confession hanging between us as I turned around the rest of the way to face him. To face the *Ηλίθιος* who had murdered a woman for his own pleasure. "Neri is dead because you raped her?" I asked, my fists clenching at my sides.

Fury for the girl who had lost the only real parent she'd ever known, in the most traumatic of ways, surged through me. As if Neri hadn't already suffered enough, she'd been forced to kneel there before her husband and be punished for something that had been taken from her.

"Oh, don't act so offended. If the stupid bitch had just done her part and kept her mouth shut and hidden the evidence, nobody would have needed to know anything at all. She got what she deserved for acting like I'd brutalized her," Eugene grumbled, grimacing as he tried to move his fingers. "I need to see a doctor, thanks to you."

"Make sure you see one outside of the city," I said, my fury overriding my satisfaction that the shock was wearing off, allowing the pain of his hand to really settle in. The thought of telling Thalia what he'd done, that her mother had been a victim and never made a choice that led to her loss...

Fuck.

All of this could have been avoided. I would have never been taken away from Thalia in the first place and I could have remained in the city to protect her, if only my own father hadn't raped her mother.

FUCK.

"Why? Too ashamed for anyone to know what you've done?" my father asked, as if he truly expected me to feel regret for hurting him.

"Because the moment you step foot back in my city is the

moment I will kill you. I will lay you down on this very counter and carve out your organs one by one and feed them to you until you die. Get the fuck out of my city and don't ever come back, unless you want to taste your own spleen." My fury laced my voice as I glared at him, having never meant anything in the way I meant that.

"Are you out of your fucking mind? Where am I supposed to go?"

"GET OUT!" I shouted, and for once, Eugene Regas did the smart thing.

He fucking left like the coward he was.

I grabbed the vase of flowers off the island counter, throwing it into the dining room with a roar. The glass shattered across the table, the flowers Thalia could never see the colors of spreading across the surface as the water flowed. I immediately regretted it when I thought of my mother having to clean up the mess or of Malva's bare feet when she walked into the room.

But that didn't stop me from picking up one of the counter stools and hurling it at the table. The wood cracked on the legs, buckling as the heavy table rocked from the assault.

"Calix?" Thalia asked, stepping into the room. Her face was the picture of shock, her mouth hanging open as she took a tentative move toward me. "What's wrong?"

I pinched my brow between two fingers, squeezing as I tried to find a way around admitting this truth to her, but it always had a way of coming out. This was one secret she would never forgive.

"My father just admitted that he raped your mother all those years ago. She never wanted him, so he took what he wanted without any thought of the consequences for any of us. You were left without anyone to protect you, and your mother was *killed* for something she didn't even do. He stood by and watched Origen slaughter her and never said a fucking word." I knew why he hadn't; he would have been executed. Banishment would have been the least of his concerns in the face of raping another man's wife, even if it meant his entire family suffered for his actions.

"I never could make sense of it," Thalia admitted, shaking her head slowly. "I was too young to understand back then, but whenever I look back; my mother was far too afraid of my father to risk something like that. It all makes sense now."

"You aren't angry?" I asked. This was one thing I would understand if she couldn't forgive. It didn't mean I would let her go, but I would get it all the same.

"Of course I am. I'm fucking furious, but not at you," she said, stepping toward me. She pressed her chest against my stomach, wrapping her arms around my waist and laying her head against my torso. I folded her into my embrace, sighing in relief the moment I felt her tucked safely in my arms where she belonged.

She turned a rage-filled stare up to me, and I knew her next words would be just as bloodthirsty as any man's. "But I want his fucking head for what he did to her."

I stared down into my wife's amber eyes, searching for any hint of doubt. There was none to be found, only the promise of vengeance—of death and the wickedness that she was learning to embrace.

I said the only thing I could while looking down at the woman I loved more than anything in this world. "Anything for you, Little One."

44

THALIA

I swallowed down my nerves as Calix led me into ο λάκκος the next day. True to his word the night before, he'd sent his men to track down his father after banishing him from Philadelphia under the threat of death. To live his life, finding a new place to settle and wait out the rest of his days, wasn't a fair fate after what he'd done to my mother.

"Are you sure you want this?" Calix murmured as we ascended the stairs. "I'll give you anything you ask. I just hope you can live with it on your conscience, Little One."

"I will never be able to live with myself knowing he roams free while my mother rots in the Νεκροταφείο below us as we speak. She deserves the peace that will come from knowing every last one of her abusers has also entered the afterlife," I said, striding toward the doors of the council chamber. "They cut off my mother's head because of what *he* did to her. I want his put on a stake to show what happens to men who take what is not theirs to touch."

"Then that is what you will have, my bloodthirsty flower," Calix murmured, grasping the handle of the door and pulling it open for me. The rest of the council waited in their chairs around the circle in the room, staring at us expectantly as we moved into the room.

"You called this meeting, Regas. The least you could do was be on time," Councilor Galanis muttered, watching as Calix guided me to my seat. I lowered myself into the metallic chair.

Calix gestured to the man waiting at the entrance as he moved toward his seat, sitting down slowly as two men dragged his father's filthy, beaten form into the council chamber. He'd been gagged with a cloth wrapped around the back of his head and knotted, his broken hand swollen and purple where it was tied to his good one behind his back.

"What is the meaning of this, Regas?" Elias Lykaios asked as the two men dragged Calix's father to the center of the room. They left him kneeling at the center of the circle between us all, his head hanging forward as I glared at him.

"Eugene Regas, you stand accused of raping the wife of a former council member of the six families. How do you plead?" I asked, watching as one of the men unknotted the gag from the back of his head. Eugene spit the rag from his mouth onto the circular mechanism at the center of the room.

"I do not respond to bitches who never learned their place," he said finally, running his tongue over his teeth that were darkened by blood.

"Then allow me to pose the question as well, Regas. Did you rape the wife of a former council member?" Elias asked, leaning forward in his seat.

"No. I did not *rape* Neri Karras. Rape would imply she didn't want my cock, and we all know that the Karras women practically beg for it," Eugene said.

"I put it to the council to decide the fate of my father, given the new turn of events," Calix said, standing from his seat. He stepped onto the outer ring of the circle, tapping his foot twice against a spot in the wood. The center circle where his father knelt rose from the mechanism, spinning as it approached the ceiling while Calix returned to his seat.

He placed his hand within the snake's mouth, signaling the beginning of the formal meeting. I followed suit, carefully controlling my face as the pin pressed into my finger and blood swirled down into the floor. The remainder of the floor surrounding that center circle retracted, parting to reveal the sands of the pit beneath the council chamber.

"I nominate Elias Lykaios to stand in as an impartial party to lead the proceedings," I said, following the guidance Calix had given me in the car on the way to the pit.

"Seconded," Calix agreed, raising a hand. "Do we have a third?"

Tobias and Alexander kept their hands down, but it came as no surprise that Atticus raised his hand, stating "third" proudly.

"What evidence do you have of these allegations?" Elias said, turning to look at me.

"He confessed to Calix in a fit of rage when trying to convince him that I should be taught a lesson in the same way he taught my mother one. I have no physical evidence, as it has been over a decade since the incident in question. But I think it is fairly obvious to anyone who spent any amount of time with my parents that my mother was not likely to risk my father's wrath on a worthless affair," I said, turning my head up to glare at the man who had helped my father take everything from me.

"Calix, do you corroborate her statement that your father confessed to you?" Elias asked.

"Yes. What she says is true," Calix answered, studying the man who served as head of the proceedings.

"That isn't enough," Galanis barked, practically spitting with his rage. "We cannot kill a member of one of the six families without any actual evidence beyond the words of a married couple. They could purely want to eliminate Eugene to eradicate his ability to take the Regas seat on this council."

"I do not need the council to kill my father, Galanis. Remember that when you consider your next words. I brought him here to make sure that this council knows that what was done here all those years ago was wrong, and an innocent woman was put to death because the people who sat in these seats did not do their due diligence. She never should have been killed for what was done to her; in fact, it should have been my father who bled on the sands of o λάκκος. Instead, my family line was banished for the criminal acts of one member, because of the corrupt assholes we allowed to remain in power," Calix said, looking about the room before settling his gaze on Galanis once again. "Most of us here are new to the council. We are not the ones who made the choice that has had a ripple effect across this city for decades. But let this serve as a warning for us—of what can come if we become negligent in our duty."

"What is it you hope to achieve here? You must know we cannot convict him off your word alone, or else we would be just as guilty of corruption as the generation you criticize," Elias said, tapping the fingers of his freehand against the chair.

"I ask that we go back to the old ways, to the tradition that has served us through countless disagreements," Calix said, lifting his chin and meeting my stare. "I ask that we let o λάκκος decide his fate."

"And who would we nominate as the champion of the council in this case? Who would we nominate to risk his life for the reputation of a woman who is already dead?" Galanis asked, staring about the room. He had to know that nobody would choose to nominate him, unless the goal was for Eugene to live.

"There's no need to put it to a vote," Calix said, standing from his chair. "I volunteer to represent ο λάκκος and take his head for my wife, and for the mother we wronged."

"All those in favor?" Elias asked, and I raised my hand immediately. As much as it should have frightened me to see Calix on the sand below, there was a twisted sense of vindication in watching him destroy the man who had ruined everything, and in the same place my mother had died.

It had all come full circle, righting the wrongs that had been committed before I was old enough to understand any of it.

Elias and Atticus raised their hands as well, and eventually Galanis and Tobias had no choice but to lift their own. They would not risk their ability to vote against us all, or test the tolerance for their lack of cooperation, on a man they did not care about.

Calix touched his hand to the top of the other arm of his chair, laying his palm on it and spreading his fingers. He winced when needles poked into each of his fingers, taking his blood as Elias followed suit. I watched as the others repeated it, glaring down at the arm of my chair before I mimicked the motion.

The pinch of pain erupted through each of my fingers almost immediately, filling the tiny fingerprint-shaped wells in the metal with blood as something glowed from the inside of the chair. The floor panels emerged from where they'd tucked beneath our seats, the wood folding on its hinges to form a staircase that started from directly in front of Calix's seat. He stood on the first platform, shrugging off his suit jacket and rolling up his sleeves as the center circle rotated down, hanging from the ceiling on a thin wire.

Eugene disappeared below the chamber level, that platform taking him down to the sands of the pit.

"Are you prepared to decide where you want to display his head, λουλούδι μου?" Calix asked, proceeding slowly down the steps to the sand below. I leaned forward in my chair as much as I dared as he disappeared from my line of sight, watching as my husband jumped off the final platform to land on the ground a few steps from where his father clambered to his feet.

Calix grabbed an axe off the wall, turning his molten stare up to me for a brief moment.

And then the fucker winked.

45

CALIX

Thalia's mouth broadened into a disbelieving grin, her head shaking from side to side oh-so-subtly. The others might not have noticed it, but I knew my wife did nothing without a reason; every movement had a purpose. I lifted the axe, pointing it up to her and touching two fingers to my lips to blow her a kiss.

Then I went to kill my father.

He cowered on the sand in front of me, scrambling backward off the circular platform to put distance between us. "Put that thing down before you hurt yourself," he sputtered.

"If you would like to die with a blade in your hand, I suggest you give me your hands so that I can free you. I've no interest in killing you while you're tied up. That is the coward's way out," I said, leaning forward until my face hovered over his. "That is what you would do, and no matter what you tried to make me into, I am *nothing* like you."

He groaned as he spun on his knees, holding his arms as far back from his body as he could manage. I placed the edge of the blade against the rope, sawing through it carefully.

The moment he was free, he scrambled to his feet and

made for the weapons hanging on the wood-planked wall behind him. He grabbed the same straight, simple long-sword he'd always favored, claiming only a barbarian killed with anything else. The sword was a weapon of class, the killing instrument that the civilized men of the ancient world favored.

Death was death, and his blood on the sand would look the same whether I severed his head from his body with a sword or an axe.

He heaved a shield into his hand, trying to hold it with the hand I'd broken. He ended up settling for feeding his wrist through the strap on the back, and it brought me great joy to watch the mangled piece of flesh dangle uselessly.

As useless as the rest of him.

"You would kill your own father for a whore?" he asked, resorting to the only weapon he thought would be of any value, but I'd long since learned to ignore anything that came from his ignorant mouth, seeing him for the weakling he was.

I'd seen real power, learned under the devil himself in Ibiza. Real strength didn't come from a man who allowed others to do his dirty work while he watched from the sidelines.

Real strength came from being willing to burn your father alive for what he'd done. It came in waiting decades for revenge, knowing that it would taste all the sweeter when you stole everything your enemy wanted and made it yours.

Real strength was exercising patience, and then reveling in the blood when the time finally came.

"I would kill *myself* for her. What are you in the face of that love?" I asked, walking slowly toward him. I swung the axe lazily, catching him in the shield intentionally.

He whimpered as the blow vibrated through the broken bones of his hand, the angle of my strike knocking his pathetic attempt to protect himself right off his wrist. He raised the sword in his other hand, swinging wildly with none of the precision he'd expected from me as a child.

I'd killed long before I should have, been the murderer to take care of those who failed the organization as a boy, because he couldn't be bothered. He'd honed me into the weapon I had become.

It only seemed fitting that I be the one to dismember his body.

I swung the axe to the side, the blade clanging against his sword. The stupid idiot let his grip on the hilt release, flinging it to the side so early it was almost disappointing. As if there'd been no point at all in allowing him to arm himself.

"You'll never be able to maintain power in this city when you let a woman sit at your side instead of forcing her to kneel at your feet. You need men in your corner who understand bloodshed, not women with delicate sensibilities," my father inserted.

A strangled laugh escaped me as I listened to Thalia laugh with her whole body from above us. She leaned forward in her chair, the angle giving her a perfect bird's eye view of the proceedings. "Who do you think demanded your head?" she called down, and I could only imagine the surprise on the faces of the men sitting around her.

"I think she understands bloodshed just fine. She wants to mount your head on a spike when I'm done with you. Where do you think she should put it? Such unique decor certainly needs the perfect spot," I asked, looking around the pit.

"Fuck you and fuck your wife. You deserve whatever fate the rest of the families give you," my father rasped. I lifted a foot, kicking him in the chest and pushing him back. He fell onto the sand, staring up at the council chamber above him as

I walked in a circle around his prone form. "You can't do it after all, can you? You always were a pussy."

"Shh. I promised my wife your head. I never promised I wouldn't play with the rest of you first. I'm trying to decide how to arrange your corpse. Let me think it over without your incessant droning," I sighed, tilting my head from side to side as I considered it.

A symbol of the life he'd lived, or a symbol of the life that could happen with him gone?

With my decision made, I swung the axe down and severed his uninjured hand from his arm. He screamed, raising his arm to clutch at the bloody stump where blood poured freely. "Fuck!" he yelled, making to get to his feet.

I swung again, taking the foot on the opposite side. His shoe stayed pointing toward the chamber above, the muscle and sinew and bone cleaved in a perfectly straight line. I hefted the axe again, turning my attention to the council. "Whoever has been caring for these weapons deserves a raise," I said, bringing the axe down on my father's other ankle.

I left his broken hand for as long as I could, watching as his body sagged far too quickly with the blood pouring free from his limbs. Only then did I move to dismember him further while he screamed, the sound a constant accompaniment to the delicate artwork. I leaned over him as I cut him at the elbow and then the shoulder of his good arm so that I had three pieces to work with. "Just end it," he whispered, his voice barely a breath as he lingered at the brink of death for a precious few seconds.

"Go to your death knowing that the pain you feel now is *nothing* compared to what I have felt all my life, knowing that I have you for a father, Eugene Regas," I said, stepping lower and slashing the axe against his legs. I cut those into three pieces as the final breath left his lungs, his eyes turning unseeing as he stared up at Thalia above. She watched in rapt fixation as I dismembered my father's other arm, and then finally lifted the axe above my shoulders to take his head.

The cut was clean at his neck, a straight line across his throat where blood flowed onto the fabric of his shirt. Without a heartbeat, it didn't pump as freely.

They were always more fun before they died.

I tossed the axe to the side, arranging his severed limbs around the stub I'd created from his torso. I saved some of the pieces to fill the place where his head waited currently, arranging his bigger pieces closest to his torso and getting smaller with points radiating out from the center.

Finally bending down, I grabbed my father's head by the hair, lifting it from the sand so that I could arrange one of the chunks of his legs and the last remaining hand into place. I finished the sun that could shine on the darkest part of Thalia's life now that the vengeance for her mother was one step closer to being finished.

Then I turned my back on the crude art piece, making my way to the stairs up to the council chamber from the pit. I had to haul myself up the first step, my father's head hanging over the edge and banging against the steps as I lifted my weight up onto the hanging structure.

The moment my weight touched the stairs, they began to retract from the top, the pieces of floor tucking themselves beneath the council members' chairs until the panels could deposit me at my own seat once more.

I took my seat, keeping my eyes on Thalia's as one-by-one the other council members removed their hands from the mechanisms in the chairs. Thalia was the last to do so, lifting her bloody fingers and placing them on the arms of her throne as she waited.

The center circle returned to its rightful position, the floor gears winding and twirling until it slid into place. Then I stood, walked across the surface, and stopped directly in front of my wife. I reached out a blood-covered hand to cup her cheek, smiling with pride when she didn't flinch away from the contact despite the gore covering me.

Then I held out my father's head, his face dangling in front of hers from where I clutched him by the hair. Thalia raised both her hands, grasping his skull just behind the ears as she lifted it out of my hand. I released my grip, letting her tilt her head to the side as she stared down at the man who'd caused her so much torment.

She pivoted, turning to face the back of her chair and the two sharply pointed tips at the center of it. Bringing his head over hers, Thalia brought it down quickly onto the spikes. His unseeing eyes looked out at the rest of the council members as his blood dripped over the metal of her chair while she settled herself back into her seat.

A trophy for a queen.

She raised her eyes to mine, a tiny smirk playing about her lips as she shifted her attention to Alexander Galanis and Tobias Hasapis for the briefest of moments. It might have seemed innocent to anyone else, but the men shifted uncomfortably with the silent threat.

If Thalia had her way, they would be next, and in this, she would always get her way.

Galanis swallowed as Thalia lifted her chin, and there was nothing in me that doubted she intended to sit atop a throne of bones and look down upon a kingdom carved from flesh and blood.

She was Persephone to my Hades, and Philadelphia was about to become the Underworld.

. . .

>> Calix & Thalia's story concludes September 30th! Pre-Order Dreams of the Wicked: https://books2read.com/dreamsofthewicked

>> Fall in love with a side character? You can find Rafe's story in the Beauty in Lies series or Ryker's in book three of the Bellandi Crime Syndicate, Grieved Loss.

GLOSSARY OF TERMS

λουλούδι μου - my flower
ο λάκκος - the pit
Νεκροταφείο - cemetery
η νύφη μου - my bride
η ψυχή μου - my soul
Θεά - goddess
Ηλίθιος- idiot

ALSO BY ADELAIDE FORREST

Adelaide Forrest writing dark romance:

Please heed the trigger warnings for each book.

Bellandi World Syndicate Universe

Bellandi Crime Syndicate Series

Bloodied Hands

Forgivable Sins

Grieved Loss

Shielded Wrongs

Scarred Regrets

Settled Scores - Coming December 2022

Massacred Dreams Series

Dreams of the Vengeful

Dreams of the Deadly

Dreams of the Wicked - Coming Sept 30, 2022

Beauty in Lies Series

Until Tomorrow Comes

Until Forever Ends

Until Retribution Burns

Until Death Do Us Part

Other Dark Romance

Black Heart Romance Presents Heaven & Hell

Wrong

Romantic Suspense Novellas

The Men of Mount Awe Series

Deliver Me from Evil

Kings of Conquest - Cowritten with Lyric Cox

Claiming His Princess

Stealing His Princess

Adelaide Forrest writing fantasy romance as

Harper L. Woods:

What Lies Beyond the Veil

What Hunts Inside the Shadows - coming August 30, 2022

Printed in Great Britain
by Amazon

84491048R00192